TWO BETWEEN WORLDS

NISSA HARLOW

NIMBLE HOPE
PUBLISHING

ISBN: 978-1-7777446-1-8

Published in Canada by Nimble Hope Publishing

Cover and book design by Nissa Harlow

To Mom,
who encouraged me to keep going,
even when I wanted to give up.
Thank you for not letting me.

CHAPTER ONE

The morning after I killed my best friend, I sit at the front window and stare across the street at his parents' house. My throat is still raw and dry. My hands and feet don't feel like they've thawed, even though Mom insisted I sit in a warm bath last night. The water eventually got cold, but I barely noticed. And when I finally crawled into bed, well after midnight, I felt as if my body were starting to turn to stone.

The plate of toast with jam sits untouched in front of me. My gaze is focused on the carpet. There's a dark patch that I've never noticed before. It's so subtle that I can only see it when I don't look directly at it. I wonder, without really caring, if my eyes have somehow been damaged. Eph's always been like the sun; maybe I just looked at him for a little too long at one point.

I can hear Mom and Grandma talking in the kitchen. They probably think I can't hear them. But Grandma's got one of those voices that carries; even when she whispers, her voice creates a disturbance in the air.

"You can't let this go on," she's saying.

"Just let her grieve. It's only been a few hours." That's Mom. Backing me up. For now.

"No, you need to nip this in the bud. You know how she is. If you let this go on, she's going to get used to being in this state, and then—"

"Mom. Enough. She watched her best friend die."

"She might not have seen it."

"So you think she just hasn't spoken a word since for fun?"

"She's wallowing."

Mom clears her throat and I hear one of the kitchen chairs scrape on the floor. "Then we're going to let her wallow. Whatever she needs to do to get through this. If we push her and she's not ready—"

"She should be on medication."

"We've tried that. There are too many side effects."

"So try another one."

"She's seventeen. I'm not going to force her to make herself sick."

"She *is* sick," Grandma says. I turn my head slowly in their direction, even though I can't see them past the piece of wall that separates the living room from the kitchen. I should feel angry at my grandmother's words, but I can't summon much emotion. My hands and feet still feel kind of numb, and the sensation seems to be spreading: up my arms and legs, past my shoulders and hips, seeping into my torso, encroaching on my heart. And, not for the first time, I will that stone-like sensation to seize that organ, to stop its frantic thud, to apply pressure until it crumbles away to dust. Or ashes.

The phantom scent of oily smoke suddenly fills my nostrils, and I cough. I cough so hard that I gag, and then even the thought of the toast sitting in front of me is too much. I kick the plate away with my foot, but the carpet offers too much friction and it doesn't go far. The breakfast sits there, mocking me.

I turn back to the window and take some deep breaths. I long for warmth and pressure on my back. Its absence feels wrong. More wrong when I realize that it's gone for good. There's no second set of breaths to synchronize with. No second heartbeat to thump against my ribs. Everything's been ripped away, painfully, all at once. I've heard some people say that losing someone they loved was like losing a limb. But it's not. It's like losing *all* of them.

I hear Skylar's socks whisper on the carpet as she creeps into the room. But I don't turn. I keep staring at the house across the street. At the two cars left in the driveway. It should be three. But one of them is ... Actually, I don't know where it is. If it survived the fire, it's probably in a scrap yard somewhere.

"I'm sorry."

The whisper makes me jump a little. But I don't look at her. My throat tightens. Even if I did feel like speaking to her, I don't think my body would allow it.

"I'm sorry," she says again. "But I couldn't have known. I just thought you were being ..."

Berlynn doesn't like the word "but" after an apology. She says it negates everything that came before. I didn't really

3

get what she meant until right now, as I imagine my sister's thoughts: *I'm sorry I wouldn't drive you home. I'm sorry you had to call Eph to come and get you. But you were just being you, and the world can't cater to your anxiety.*

It had nothing to do with anxiety. I can use that as an excuse for a lot of things, but not that. My throat feels so tight that I can't speak. I swallow, and the scratching sensation makes such an awful noise in my own head that I feel like I'm about to gag again. I manage not to, but my eyes still water like crazy. Skylar backs up a step. She probably thinks I'm crying. And so what if I am? As if I don't have a reason to cry right now.

"Do you . . . need anything?"

I needed you. Yesterday. But Eph was the only one willing to be there for me. Even though he was pissed after what I did. His love was never conditional. Unlike yours.

I don't speak. I don't even shake my head. She hovers there for a few moments longer and then bends down to pick up the plate with the toast. Her footsteps whisper toward the kitchen, going silent as she steps onto the tiles.

I lean forward until my forehead is pressed against the glass. It's the opposite of a hug. The glass is so cold. The world is still white, pristine, and perfect. At least, it looks that way. Eyes can't see the gaping wound that's been torn right through the centre of it. I let myself sink against the glass. I'll probably get an earful from Grandma about leaving smudges. I really don't care.

My forehead begins to ache from the cold after a few minutes, so I pull back and, with a last glance at the house across the street, lie down on my side facing the wall under the window. The carpet is scratchy. I hate the way it smells. Pressing my hand against it, I curl my fingertips into the pile.

The world tiptoes around me as my mind spins. Each time it does, like an old vinyl record with a scratch, it skips back to the flash of orange. The billow of black smoke. The awful knowledge that one brilliant life—a glittering star that I chose to orbit—was snuffed out in an instant.

I smack my hand on the carpet, but all it produces is a dull thump. Sitting up, I peer out the window again. Nothing's changed. The cars haven't moved. His parents are there, though. Inside. Maybe Asher's there, too. I can't imagine what's going on within those walls. Are they crying? Are they making funeral arrangements? Or are they all sitting in silence, frozen, like me?

The voices from the kitchen stop as I get up and walk back to my bedroom. Mom's probably worried I'm going to do something. Grandma almost certainly is. They don't give me enough credit. I'm not suicidal. I never have been. But some people think that if you've got one mental illness, you're some sort of unstable freak, prone to symptoms of all of them. I've never cut, but that doesn't stop Mom from keeping my razor in her bathroom and making me ask when I want to use it. (Like I could do much with a commercial safety razor.) I've never self-medicated with booze, but that doesn't stop Grandma from locking up her gin. (As if I'd want to drink that stuff.) My coping mechanisms were a lot healthier. Or so I thought. As it turns out, pretty much everyone thought I was doing something wrong.

I grab my laptop from my desk and head back to the living room, just as Skylar emerges from the kitchen.

She's chewing something, and it sounds slightly crunchy. I guess my toast didn't go to waste. She raises her eyebrows at me, and I brush past her without saying a word. As I settle myself back down in front of the window and open the laptop on the floor, I hear her footsteps retreat to her room.

"Ari?"

Ignoring Mom's voice, I bend over the keyboard.

"We're just going out to the store to pick up something for Parnell and Javier." She pauses. "Do you want to come? You know better than I do what they like."

I open up the word processor and create a new file. If I don't do this, those horrible images are going to crowd out everything else. The good stuff. I need to remember, and I need to keep those memories somewhere safe so that when they inevitably get overwritten by the repeating loop of awfulness in my head, I'll be able to access them again.

Mom sighs and I hear the jingle as she grabs her keys.

"Arianna," Grandma begins, but Mom clears her throat.

"Let's go. It's still early. We might find something at the bakery that's still warm."

Yeah, Mom. Fresh bread will make it all better. Too bad Eph's dad has celiac disease. I don't know if she's forgotten. Maybe. She'll probably remember when she's standing in line and then get a little stressed out when she realizes she'll have to get something else.

To my great relief, they leave without trying to engage with me again. I quickly save the new blank file and protect it with a password. These are *my* memories and I don't feel like sharing. Not yet. I just want to be selfish and keep the memories of Eph all to myself. Maybe that's the real reason why I'm dreading having to see his parents: I'll have to share him.

I raise my gaze and peer out the window again, wondering which memory I want to preserve first. It doesn't really matter, I guess, as long as I get the important ones. So I decide to just start at the beginning. The day we first met. When his family moved in across the street and changed my life forever.

I look down at the screen and blink away the afterimage of the bright snow until I can see what I'm doing. And then I begin to type.

Ice Pops and Thunderclouds

The summer I was seven was a hot one. The air seemed heavy and full of chaos. Mom and Grandma were in the middle of painting the house in preparation for selling it (a goal that eventually got scrapped when they couldn't find a suitable house in the area that they could afford). Their busyness meant that Skylar and I were on our own. Neither of us minded. We didn't really play together and we were fine doing our own thing. Skylar, at six, liked to set up elaborate stages for her fashion dolls where they'd put on plays for the rest of her toys. We could often hear her high voice jabbering through her open bedroom door from wherever we were in the house. I preferred more quiet pursuits. Mom would set me up at the kitchen table with a stack of paper and some markers and pencils, and I'd happily write and illustrate my own stories for hours.

The day I met Eph, though, the kitchen was the focal point of the painting, and the only other place with a table was the kitchen in Grandma's basement suite. I wasn't allowed to be alone down there, so I just wandered around the house, getting underfoot, until Mom told me to go read a book or something.

"I don't have any," I said.

"You've got plenty on your shelf."

"I've read them all."

She sighed and brushed a strand of hair away from her nose with the back of her wrist. She was still holding a paintbrush, and its bristles were covered in a sticky blue-grey. "We'll go to the library after I'm done this section."

"How long until you're done?"

"Soon."

Then it was my turn to sigh. I walked into the living room and plunked myself on the carpet in front of the big window that stretched across one wall. It was a great place for watching everything that happened on the street. When we'd had a dog, he'd liked to watch, too. But he'd gone across the Rainbow Bridge, and I was the only one left who seemed to like watching the world pass by the front of the house. I'd been the first to notice the moving truck across the street a couple of days earlier. That had been another promise of Mom's that she hadn't kept; she still hadn't taken us over to meet the kids. Apparently, there were two. I didn't know anything about them. The huge moving van had blocked a lot of the activity during moving day, and I hadn't seen any kids. Just some adults who looked kind of sweaty.

So I was staring out the front window when I saw him coming. He was dressed in nothing but a pair of orange swim trunks, yellow flip-flops, and a smile as he practically skipped across the street toward our house. I sat up a little straighter, my heart lurching into my throat at the sight. *Don't come here. Don't come here,* I thought, and the kid paused for a moment and actually stared up at the window. I leaped to my feet and ran into the kitchen, where I almost ended up with a face full of paint as Grandma turned around with the newly loaded roller.

"Out," she said, grabbing my shoulder and spinning me around. "We're almost done."

"Mom, can we go to the library now?"

"When I'm done this bit. I already told you."

I shook my head and sidled into the corner, but before I could touch the wet walls, Mom seized the shoulder of my t-shirt and yanked hard. "That's a brand-new shirt. Acrylic paint doesn't come out." She gave me a shove toward the living room, but before I could take more than a step or two, the doorbell rang. Predictably, Skylar's footsteps came racing down the hall. Mom quickly dropped her paintbrush into the tray and hurried out of the kitchen.

"Skylar!"

But my little sister wasn't listening. She reached up to undo the deadbolt, then grasped the knob and pulled the door open. After one look at what was on the other side, she turned and tried to run. Mom caught her and put her hand on her back. Skylar pressed her face against Mom's waist.

I was standing just behind them, but I still had a pretty good view of the boy who stood in the doorway. He lifted up one foot to kind of scratch it against the back of his calf and looked up at Mom with a bright smile.

"Hi," he said.

"Hello." Mom's voice made her sound like she was smiling,

and when I edged around her and looked up, I could see that she was. "And who might you be?"

"Eph." He bounced on his toes a little and switched his focus to me. "Do you want to come over and jump through the sprinkler?"

"No!" Skylar said. She shook her head against Mom, then edged around her and ran back to her room. I looked at the boy, wondering what his reaction to my sister's rudeness would be. To my surprise, he was still smiling.

"That's okay," he said before Mom could say anything. He kind of shrugged the area where his arms should've been before looking at me again. "Do *you* want to come over?"

I wasn't really sure. I couldn't stop staring at his shoulders and the long, thin lines of the scars that cut down his sides. Staring was rude, but I couldn't help it. I'd never seen anyone who looked like him.

"How did you ring the doorbell?" I asked. It probably wasn't the most pressing question, but it seemed to be the only one that had the audacity to come out of my mouth. He grinned and shrugged again.

"With my chin." He jutted his lower jaw out as if to demonstrate, then went back to his smile. "Mom said you could come over, too," he said, fixing his gaze on the person standing beside me. "She's got lemonade."

"Thank you," Mom said. "That's very kind." She turned to look down at me, her eyebrows raised. "Well? Library or sprinkler?"

That was a tough one. If I'd been thinking more than an afternoon ahead, I might've opted for the library. But I liked playing in sprinklers, too. Ours was kind of weak and not much fun, so I was curious to see what the new neighbours' was like. Eph's dark brown curls were kind of damp, which told me that their sprinkler probably squirted at least as high as our heads, something which couldn't be said of ours.

From down the hall, there came the sound of a door slamming. Mom nodded, not even having heard my answer yet, and turned back to Eph.

"We'd love to come over. Just give the girls a few minutes to get their bathing suits on. Okay?"

"Okay." Eph bounced on his toes again and then turned and hurried down the porch steps. Mom watched him go for a few moments as he scampered back across the street, then stepped forward to shut the door.

"Maybe we should go to the library," I said, suddenly unsure as I heard Skylar start to cry in her room.

"We've already accepted Eph's invitation. Besides, we can go to the library another time." She marched down the hallway and pushed open Skylar's door. "What's the matter?"

"He doesn't have arms!" my sister wailed.

"There's nothing wrong with that. His body's just different than yours." She turned back to me. "Go put on your bathing suit."

I ran and did just that while Mom tried to cajole Skylar into putting on hers. By the time I had the little pink bikini on and had sat down to put on the matching jelly sandals, the room down the hall was quiet. I hurried to the front door, just as Mom emerged from the bathroom with two beach towels from the linen closet.

Skylar acted like a cat on a leash until we were halfway down the driveway, so Mom had to pick her up and carry her. I didn't know why Mom didn't just let her stay behind with Grandma (who said she'd finish painting the kitchen while we were gone), but I didn't ask. Skylar was making enough of a fuss, and

I didn't want Mom to get all teary and tired like she did when we both acted up at the same time.

We didn't even make it to the neighbours' front door before Eph bounced out from around the side of the house.

"You can come through the gate," he said, then looked up at Skylar with a little frown. The expression made his face look so different that, for a moment, I wondered if he was even the same boy. "What's wrong?" he asked gently. "Is it 'cause of my arms?"

"I think so," Mom said, hitching Skylar up and following him as he led the way through the gate and into the backyard. "She's never seen someone who looks like you before."

He nodded thoughtfully. "Yeah. Most people haven't seen someone like me. I'm pretty different." With a starting hop, he skipped off across the lawn. "Mom! They're here!"

A woman with dark curls messily pulled back into a ponytail stepped off the low wooden deck and smiled. It wasn't the same sort of smile as Eph's, but it was still kind and welcoming. She reached out her hand as Mom put Skylar down.

"I'm Parnell Pierce," she said, her voice lit with a slight English accent. "Eph's mum."

"Rose Warne. Arianna and Skylar's mom."

"Which one are you?" Eph asked, suddenly right beside me. Curiously, I hadn't heard his flip-flops.

"Ari," I said.

"Is that short for Arianna?"

When I nodded, he grinned. "Eph's short for Ephraim." He angled his chin, as if pointing at something. "Want to jump through the sprinkler now?"

His mom laughed. "Hold your horses. They just got here." She waved her hand toward the table and chairs on the deck. "Can I get you some lemonade?"

"That would be nice," Mom said.

"How about you?" Parnell asked, turning to me. "It's the pink kind."

I shook my head and whispered a quick, "No, thank you." Eph, seeming to take that as his cue, bounded off toward the side of the house where he slipped off one flip-flop and used his agile toes to turn on the tap. The hose hissed for a moment, and then the sprinkler came to life, spinning and spraying water in flowering arcs.

"Ephraim!" his mom barked, just as he was about to launch himself into the spray. He rolled his eyes and smiled at me, as if we were sharing some sort of secret, and ran over to his mom. She pulled something from each of his ears, then gave his head a gentle shove. "Talk loudly, Ari. He can't hear very well without his hearing aids."

I nodded and turned back to the boy who was running through the sparkling droplets. He still had his flip-flops on and I could hear his feet squeaking on the rubber footbeds. When he saw that I wasn't joining in the fun, he stopped and raised his eyebrows at me. I could hear the spray of water against the backs of his legs.

A few steps forward brought me into the radius of the spray, but I didn't go any farther than that. I glanced up, and a cloud happened to catch my eye. My heart surged into my throat. I hadn't noticed it earlier. I stepped back toward the deck.

"It's not that cold," Eph said. He shook his head, and his hair sent drips flying. When he stopped, he grinned at me, wet strands dripping into his eyes.

"No, thanks."

"What?"

"No, thanks," I said a little more loudly. He frowned and walked over to me, flip-flops squeaking. Behind us on the deck, our moms were engaged in a quiet conversation. Ice clinked in glasses. Skylar was whining. And that cloud was hovering like a harbinger.

"What're you looking at?" Eph asked, then turned to peer up into the sky. What he saw there obviously didn't concern him as much as it concerned me, because he turned back with a rather perplexed expression. "It's just a cloud."

"It might be a thundercloud."

He watched my mouth carefully, and then he laughed. "It's not a thundercloud. It's just grey."

But thunderclouds are grey, I reasoned. The spray from the sprinkler suddenly felt cold and I wrapped my arms around my body in a hug. Eph shook his head, but then his attention was drawn to something over my shoulder.

"That's my brother," he said, and I turned to see a slightly older boy emerge from the house. He was wearing swim trunks, too, but his were blue and lacked the curious loops that I'd noticed hanging from Eph's waistband. He also had on a t-shirt. "His name's Asher," Eph said, "but I usually call him Ash."

The older boy didn't really look like Eph's brother at all. His hair was the same dark brown, but his wasn't curly. His skin was a few shades lighter and his build was a little heavier. He wasn't fat, but he didn't have Eph's delicate frame.

"My oldest," Parnell said, grabbing Asher around the waist as the boy reached for his mom's glass of lemonade. He took a sip and set the glass back down before wiping the condensation from his fingers onto his t-shirt.

"How old are you?" Mom asked him.

"Nine."

"Skylar's six," Mom said, trying to dislodge her from her lap.

"And Ari?" Parnell asked. She turned to me. "How old are you?"

"Seven," I whispered. Eph was suddenly at my shoulder, leaning around me.

"How old are you?" he asked.

"Seven," I repeated more loudly. The answer seemed to please him.

"We're the same age! Are you going to be in my class at school?"

I shrugged my shoulders, then looked back at the cloud. I'd almost forgotten about it. It hadn't moved. That was bad.

"Skylar," Parnell said, and my sister stopped squirming for a moment. "Why don't you and Asher play in the sprinkler?"

My sister's gaze immediately travelled over to Eph. She shook her head.

"Yeah," Eph said, scampering to the deck and bounding up the steps. "It's a really great sprinkler, Skylar. If you try really hard, you can run under the water curves and you won't get wet at all."

Skylar didn't look at him, but she seemed to be thinking about his suggestion. Asher didn't wait for her answer. He stripped off his t-shirt, handed it to his mom, and jumped over the steps to the grass. That was all it took. Skylar slipped off Mom's lap, shucked her sandals, and ran after him, careful not to get too close to Eph, who was standing off to the side, smiling.

"Are you done with the sprinkler for now?" Parnell asked, keeping her voice loud but level. When Eph nodded, she waved him over and grabbed the towel from the chair beside her. She then proceeded to roughly towel his hair and dry his ears before slipping the hearing aids back in, settling the light blue casings in place. "All good?"

"Yep." He plopped into the chair beside her and wrinkled his nose at the pink lemonade in its sweaty glass. "Can Ari and I share an Eph pop?"

Mom laughed. "What on earth is an Eph pop?"

"That's just what he calls ice lollies," Parnell said, casting an amused glance at her son.

"Because they look like me," he said. "The sticks are like legs, and they have no arms." He looked up at his mom with an expectant smile. "Well, can we?"

"If it's okay with her mum."

Eph whipped his head over to look at Mom, which made her laugh and nod. I slowly climbed the stairs to the deck and went to stand beside her. And then I went back to sneaking nervous glances at that cloud.

Parnell stepped into the house, leaving us to listen to the other two kids play in the sprinkler. Skylar was being kind of bossy, but Asher didn't seem to mind. He did what she said and without complaint. I thought Mom might ask me why I couldn't play nicely with her like that, but she didn't. Instead, she turned to Eph.

"Are you going to be in grade two?"

Eph nodded. "Yeah. I'm pretty smart."

Mom smiled. "Are you?"

"Yeah. I can do a thousand-piece puzzle all by myself."

"You've got me beat, then. That's pretty impressive."

He turned to me. "Do you want to do a puzzle?"

I shook my head and went back to looking at the sky. I heard

16

him take a breath to say something else but, at that moment, Parnell emerged from the house.

"The boys have gone through almost a full box in the last two days. All I have left are grape and orange."

"Orange!" Eph crowed.

"Why don't we see what our guests want? Ari and Skylar might both want orange."

"Skylar will want grape," Mom said.

Parnell turned to me. I saw it out of the corner of my eye, and I knew it wouldn't do to ignore her. So I looked away from that tricky cloud for a moment and said, "Orange, please."

"Perfect. Asher's a grape fan himself." She handed one packet to Mom, then braced her fingers around the other to break apart the frozen treat. Eph reached up with his foot—freed from its flip-flop—but Parnell shook her head. "Let's let Ari take hers first. Those feet don't look very clean."

Eph stuck out his lower lip and dropped his foot out of view. "I kept my flip-flops on all day."

Parnell offered me the packet, so I reached in and grabbed one of the wooden sticks. I pressed the icy treat to my tongue as I always did, waiting for the surface to melt smooth. Eph jumped up from the table and scampered over to sit on the deck steps. He slipped his foot out of its flip-flop, then reached into the packet his mom held out, grasped the stick with his toes, and pulled. He brought the ice pop to his mouth and bit off a big chunk. I watched in fascination, the frozen treat still pressed against my tongue, the cloud momentarily forgotten.

"Come sit," Eph said to me, then winced. "Ow."

"Brain freeze?" Mom asked.

"Yeah." He laughed. "*Ow.*"

"Every time," Parnell said, settling herself back in her chair. Mom called Skylar over, but since my sister wouldn't go anywhere near the boy sitting on the steps, Mom had to lean over the deck railing to offer the ice pops to our siblings.

"Ari."

I looked down to find Eph grinning up at me.

"Come sit."

With a last glance at the cloud (and another at the door to gauge how fast I could get into the house if I needed to), I went and lowered myself onto the step beside him. He stuck his ice pop back into his mouth and bit off some more, revealing the end of the stick.

"I have to eat them fast," he said. "Otherwise, they melt and get everywhere."

I sucked on my treat in silence, sneaking glances at him out of the corner of my eye. The cloud was kind of behind us, which made me nervous.

"See?" he said, his teeth crunching through the orange slush.

"See what?"

"The sky. It's just blue."

I shrugged.

"Why are you afraid of clouds?"

"I'm not."

"You keep looking at that grey one."

"It might make thunder."

"So?"

I pressed my knees together and stared at my rapidly melting ice pop.

"Are you afraid of thunder?"

I shook my head. I could tell Mom and Parnell were listening, and I didn't want to say anything. Then Mom would just talk to Parnell about it. That was what parents did.

"You know," Eph said, then took a pause to gnaw on his ice pop, his toes gripping the end of the stick. "You know thunder's not dangerous, right?"

"Lightning is."

"There's no lightning in that cloud."

"There might be."

"Nope. Real thunderclouds are different. I have a book about weather. Thunder and lightning come from cumulonimbus clouds. They're huge."

I turned to look at him. "That cloud's huge."

"No, it's not. It's small. Like a baby cloud." He pulled off the last of the melting orange ice with a bit of a slurp and set the stick aside on the step.

"Don't you dare lick your toes!" Parnell said, at which Eph turned around to laugh at her.

"I'm not!"

"Yes, well, I wouldn't put it past you. Until you wash those feet, they're not going anywhere near your mouth. Understood?"

He turned to me and rolled his eyes. "The people who used to live here had a dog. Mom's afraid I'm going to step in poop they forgot to pick up."

"You've got flip-flops on," I pointed out.

"Yeah, but my feet still get kinda dirty." He lifted his foot and curled and uncurled his toes a few times. "My toes are sticky."

"Then don't put them back in your shoes," Parnell said. "We'll wipe them first."

He shrugged and put his foot down on the step before leaning forward and peering at my jellies. "I like those."

"They're pink."

"So what?" He edged a bit closer to me and put his foot against mine. "Look! They're the same size. I bet your shoes would fit me."

I sucked on my ice pop and didn't say anything.

"Can I try them on?"

"No. Your toes are sticky. They'll make my shoes sticky."

"I can try one on the clean foot."

I wasn't sure what to say. Besides, I was kind of curious to see if my jellies would fit him. So I bent over and tried to unbuckle the left sandal with one hand. I couldn't quite manage.

"Want me to hold your Eph pop?"

I did not, but I thought it might be rude to say. So I hurriedly pulled the rest of the orange ice off the stick and chewed it up. With two hands, I was able to unbuckle the shoe and slip it off.

It was a perfect fit on Eph, even after I did it up for him. He stood and waltzed around the table—swinging his hips so hard that the loops on his trunks went flying—while our moms laughed.

"Come on, Ari!"

I stood up and was about to walk toward him, but just then a loud rumble cut through the air. My head snapped up to the grey cloud that was still hanging above us, looking so innocent. I twisted my fingers together in front of me and tried not to cry. But that cloud seemed to be taunting me.

"That wasn't thunder," Eph said, sensing the problem before either of our moms did. "That was just an airplane."

I shook my head, still staring at the cloud, and heard Mom sigh.

"Ari, it's fine. Why don't you play in the sprinkler with the others?"

"No." My voice came out so small I was surprised anyone heard it. If Eph hadn't been wearing his hearing aids, he would've missed it for sure. But he was wearing them, and he knew something was wrong. He walked unevenly over to me, one bare foot smacking on the wood, the other clapping with its plastic sole. And then he just stood there until I lowered my gaze to look into his eyes. They were green, rimmed by thick lashes. When he saw that he'd gotten my attention, he smiled.

"It's okay to be scared," he said.

I bit my lip.

"We had a bit of an incident last month," Mom said. "Lightning struck our chimney and blew it to smithereens."

"Cool!" Asher cried from the other side of the deck railing. Mom laughed and shook her head.

"Not really. It's going to be expensive to fix."

"Is that why you're afraid?" Eph asked, and I turned back to look into his eyes.

"I don't know."

"I'm afraid of stuff, too."

I regarded him skeptically. Somehow, he didn't seem like the kind of person who would be afraid of anything. "Like what?"

"Big dogs."

"Good thing you didn't move here last year," Mom said. "We had a great big dog."

"What happened to it?" Eph asked, turning around to peer at her.

"He got old and sick."

"And he died?"

Mom nodded. "He died."

Eph turned back to me. "Big dogs scare me. But Ash helps."

"How?"

"I'll show you. Then maybe you won't be scared, either."

I kind of doubted that, but I was still curious.

"Turn around."

"Why?"

"Because."

Parnell laughed. "If you want her to trust you, sweetheart, you need to be a little more specific."

"You have to turn around," Eph said to me. "That's just the way it works. I'm going to turn around, too."

I still had no idea what he had planned, but I did as he asked. A moment later, I felt the warmth of his body press up against mine. We were almost exactly the same height, so I could feel all the corresponding parts of our bodies as they pressed together: the backs of our calves, our butts, our shoulders, our heads.

"Okay. Don't move. Stay just like that."

"It's not making me not scared."

He laughed. "We're not done yet. Close your eyes."

I closed them. The warmth of his body suddenly seemed a lot stronger.

"Now breathe in when I do. Ready?"

"Yeah."

"Okay . . . now." And he took in a deep breath. I tried to do the same. More of our backs touched as the air filled our lungs. "Now breathe out," he said, his voice a bit strangled like he was trying to keep all the air in. I let my breath out in a rush, faster than he did. But with the next breath in and out, I managed to stay in sync with him. We did that a few times and, with each breath, I felt myself growing calmer. I leaned back into him and felt his body adjust to do the same.

"What are you doing?" Skylar asked. I opened my eyes to find her staring. She was soaked. Her sodden red hair hung in strings over her shoulders. But before I could answer, Asher ran past, flicking a handful of water at her. She shrieked and chased after him.

"Feel better?" Eph asked, pulling himself away and stepping around where I could see him. I nodded. Actually, I felt a lot better. My heart was no longer racing and I didn't feel like I wanted to run into the house to hide from that cloud. At least, not as much. "Just do that when you feel scared," he said. "That's what I do." He looked over at our siblings. "You could do it with your sister."

I didn't tell him that I doubted Skylar would be willing. She wouldn't understand the point.

"Mom, can I show Ari my room?"

Parnell nodded and grabbed the damp towel. She walked over and had Eph balance on one jelly-clad foot while she wiped the stickiness from his toes. Then she unbuckled my shoe and pulled it off before giving him a gentle nudge on the back. He went to his flip-flops, slipped them back on, and ran toward the door.

"Take off your shoe," he said to me as he kicked off the flip-flops just inside the house.

"Why?"

"Mom keeps the floors clean for me."

"Why?"

He laughed. "You ask a lot of questions."

I clamped my mouth shut and followed him into the dim space, leaving my shoe behind on the mat. He looked back at me with a slight frown.

"It's okay to ask questions," he said. "Sometimes people don't because they don't want to hurt my feelings." He nudged open an unlatched door with his foot and stepped into a small room. There was carpet on the floor and it looked pretty new. It smelled new, too. "I have to do all kinds of stuff with my feet," he said, bouncing onto the edge of a bed covered in a blue-and-white bedspread.

"Stuff like what?"

"Everything."

"Do you eat dinner with your feet?"

"Yeah. So they should be clean, right?"

I nodded. He wiggled back onto the bed a little. His feet were dangling.

"That's why Mom keeps the floors clean. And we don't wear shoes inside. If the floors are clean, then my feet stay clean." He reached over to a small bookcase that was right beside his bed and pulled at the corner of a book with his big toe. It slid out easily, and he laid it on the floor before hopping down to sit in front of it. "See? This is the book I was telling you about." He flipped it open with his foot and began to turn the pages until he found what he was looking for. "Cumulonimbus. See how big it is?"

I took a step closer and peered down at the book. The illustrated cloud did, in fact, look pretty massive. Not at all like the grey puffball outside.

"That's not like the cloud outside, is it?" he asked, looking up at me. I shook my head. "Do you like to read? I've got lots of other books."

"I read chapter books."

He nodded. "I do, too. But I read those on a tablet. The paper

24

ones are kind of hard to keep open." Closing the weather book, he turned to me again. "This is just my room. Ash has his own room."

"Okay."

"We used to share. We had bunk beds, but he always got to sleep on the top one."

"Why?"

"Mom was afraid I'd fall going up and down the ladder." He picked up the book with his toes and slipped it back into its place on the shelf. "I used to go up there sometimes. And I never fell." Standing up, he looked about the room as if he were searching for something else he could show me. It looked a lot like my room, except the toys were different. He had a bunch of plastic-brick sculptures sitting around. A few animal action figures. There was a stack of flat boxes in the corner, and when I saw the top of one I realized they were puzzles.

"Did you do *all* of those?"

He turned to look. "Yeah. Well, all except the one on top. I got halfway through it and then we moved, so Dad put it back in the box. I'm going to have to start again."

"Where's your dad?"

"At work. Where's yours?"

I shrugged. "I live with Mom and Grandma."

"My grandma lives in Mexico."

"What about the other one?"

He wrinkled his nose. "She died when Mom was a kid. Then Mom had to go live with Auntie Grace. That's her sister. She's *old*. And she always gives me clothes for my birthday."

"When's your birthday?"

"March thirty-first. When's yours?"

"June second."

"I'm older than you."

"We're the same size."

He laughed. "Yeah. But I'll probably be bigger than you when I'm grown up." He looked down at his feet and then turned to me, his smile still bright.

"What are those for?" I asked, pointing at the loop on one side of his swim trunks. He looked down.

"That makes it easier for me to get them on and off."

"You do that yourself?"

"Mom has to help me with some things. Sometimes my shirts end up backwards. But I can do all the other stuff myself."

"You can put socks on?"

He grinned. "Yeah. But I only wear those in the winter. Special ones with separate toes and sticky stuff on the bottoms."

"What happened to your arms?" I blurted out. For a moment, I was afraid he wouldn't answer. But his smile didn't go anywhere.

"Everybody wants to know that."

I hugged my middle. "Did it hurt?"

He shook his head. "I don't know. I don't remember. I was just a baby." Angling the side of his body toward me, he raised his eyebrows. "I had wings."

My eyes went wide. "What?"

"That's what the scars are. See?"

I did see. Even in the dimmer light of his bedroom, I could see the pinkish lines that travelled from the shoulder area all the way down to his waist. They disappeared under his swim trunks.

"When they found me, they thought I was a baby angel."

"Who found you?"

"A doctor. He was hiking with his wife and they found me."

"Where?"

"In the woods."

I frowned. "Are you adopted?"

He nodded. "I don't remember that, either." He scampered out the door, leaving me standing there in the middle of his room, feeling a little stunned. I was pretty sure that being adopted and losing your arms—or wings, if he were to be believed—were pretty big deals. But he seemed to discuss them as easily as the weather. I hurried after him, stopping only when I saw him lurking beside the open door that led onto the deck. He glanced at me and gave his head a quick shake, then turned back to listen. I could hear our moms' voices as they talked quietly. I sidled up beside him, close enough that I could feel the warmth of his body.

"Eph? Come outside, please."

He rolled his eyes and stomped lightly out the door in his flip-flops, but he didn't seem that upset at being found out.

"You know it's rude to eavesdrop."

"You were talking about me."

Parnell reached out and pulled him against her, then kissed his cheek. He tried to rub it away with his shoulder as he squirmed from her grasp.

"Mom!"

"That was hardly a hug."

"You don't like hugs?" Mom asked him as I stepped back out into the sunshine.

Eph shook his head. "Not like that. I have a special way to hug."

"You can't hug without arms," I said. He just turned to me and grinned.

"Yes, I can."

"How?"

He stepped up close and I had to force myself to keep my feet still. "Can I hug you?" he asked.

I was more curious than anything, so I nodded. He took another step forward until he was so close I couldn't focus on him, and then he leaned his forehead against mine and tilted his head until our noses touched.

Mom laughed. "Looks like a great way to pass colds around."

"It's good for their immune systems," Parnell said.

Eph pulled back with a grin. "It's sort of like how the Maori greet each other."

"Are you Maori?" Mom asked.

Parnell shook her head. "We don't know for sure. The DNA test was . . . unusual. He apparently has ancestors on every continent."

"Not Antarctica," Eph corrected her.

"I wouldn't be surprised if that shows up in the next update."

"Mom, nobody *lives* there. Except scientists. And they're not my ancestors."

"Pardon me." Parnell exchanged a look with Mom before turning to me. "So, has Eph told you his story?"

I glanced at him, then shook my head.

"I told you some of it, Ari."

"You said you had wings. That's a lie."

Parnell shook her head. "It's not quite a lie. His arms were deformed when he was born. And he had a flap of skin that stretched from the undersides of his arms all the way down his sides." She demonstrated with her hand, indicating the general area, before crooking her finger at her son. He walked over and she ran her finger over the scar so we could see. Eph shuddered.

"That tickles."

"He couldn't have used prosthetics?" Mom asked.

Parnell shook her head. "When he was found, he'd been attacked."

"My god. By what?" Mom asked, giving me a worried glance.

"Wolves. They'd already killed his mother. The couple who found him interrupted the attack. We're lucky the husband was a doctor. Otherwise . . ." She trailed off, looking disturbed.

"Tell them how the wolves ripped my arms right out of their sockets," Eph said.

I just stared at him in horror. Seeming to realize that I was not handling this information very well, he came over and stood in front of me again. I closed my eyes as his "hug" radiated its warmth through me.

"It wasn't as dramatic as all that," Parnell said. "They did dislocate both shoulders and crush the humeral head of both arms. The doctors thought they could save something, but then he contracted an infection."

"I had meningitis," Eph said, pulling back from me and turning around. I had to resist the urge to throw my arms around him to keep him there against my forehead.

"And lost a good bit of your hearing," Parnell said.

"I hear better than you with my hearing aids."

"And that's why we have the rule about eavesdropping."

He stared out into the backyard where Skylar and Asher had retreated to the far corner and appeared to be talking about something pretty funny. Skylar was sprawled on her stomach, giggling. "What's so funny?" Eph shouted.

"Mind your own beeswax!" Asher shouted back, at which Eph jumped over the deck stairs, stumbled, and ran across the yard. Parnell put her hand to her chest with a nervous laugh.

29

"That child is going to give me a heart attack."

"Why?" I asked quietly, because I didn't really see what was so scary about jumping over two little steps. Mom shook her head and waved me closer.

"What do you think would happen if he hurt his foot?" she asked me.

I opened my mouth to say that he'd have to use crutches like I'd done when I'd broken my ankle, but quickly closed it again as I understood.

Skylar suddenly came running over, looking like she'd seen a ghost. I peered at the brothers. Asher hadn't moved. Eph was standing there looking resigned.

"And I thought it was Ari I'd have to worry about," Mom said, hefting Skylar into her lap. I plucked at my lip with my finger, puzzling over her words, and walked out to meet the boys. The wet grass tickled my feet, and I realized I'd left my shoe inside.

"*Now* do you want to jump through the sprinkler?" Eph asked. When I nodded, he grinned and raced over to the tap to turn the water back on. When the droplets were arcing through the air again, Asher and I leaped into them. Eph almost joined us before Parnell called him back to take out his hearing aids. And then he was right in there with us, flip-flops squeaking as his curls loosened with the water. When I looked up into the sky a few minutes later, the grey cloud was gone.

CHAPTER TWO

When I look up, the house is quiet and I really have to pee. Mom's car is back in the driveway, but I didn't hear her or Grandma come in. I stand up, feeling stiff and kind of light-headed, and walk to the bathroom.

My chest feels bruised. I don't know how much of that is from the blast and how much is just from my broken heart. Keeping my gaze carefully away from the mirror, I head for the toilet and relieve myself. Washing my hands without looking at my reflection is a bit trickier, but I manage it.

I hurry back to the living room since I left the story on the screen, but nobody's around. Skylar's door is closed; she keeps it that way whether she's in her room or not. After standing there for a few moments, listening, I decide that it's probably safe to venture into the kitchen. My guess is that Mom's downstairs with Grandma. Either that, or they're over at the Diaz-Pierces'.

My stomach still quivers in revulsion at the thought of any sort of food, so I just get myself a glass of water, down it, and leave the glass in the sink before wandering back out to the living room and settling myself down in front of the laptop. That day of ice pops and sprinklers is one of my favourites. There are plenty more, fuelled by Eph's indomitable personality and flair for the dramatic. When we started grade two that fall, it turned out that we weren't in the same class. But that changed pretty quickly after Eph introduced himself. I later learned that he'd stood up at the front of the room and told everyone about his wings, the angel theory, and how he'd lost his arms. The school ended up fielding complaints from angry parents, half who didn't want their kids around some blasphemous liar, and the other half who claimed their kids were traumatized by his story. I remember seeing him walk into my classroom on the second day of school, looking kind of confused. But as soon as he saw me, his face lit up. When Mrs. Wood realized that we knew each other, she sat him in the empty desk beside me. And the rest was history.

Not that there weren't challenges after that. The school may have been accessible for kids with mobility issues, but it wasn't exactly equipped for Eph. The desks were too high, even if he was sitting in a chair, so he ended up doing a lot of his work on the floor. Many of us did, if we ended up in the same class as him. Despite the rough start he had on that first day, he actually turned out to be, if not popular, then pretty well liked. He didn't get picked last for teams in PE, especially if we were playing kickball or soccer, and he never ended up sitting alone at lunch or during assemblies.

I mean, he had me, and I wasn't about to stay away. After that first day, I was kind of hooked on his jubilant energy.

I check the clock in the corner of the screen. It's after noon, which means I haven't eaten anything in over eighteen hours. I still don't think I can. I don't know if I'll ever be able to. My stomach seems to be the only part of my body that's able to react to what I saw yesterday.

Even that little thought is too much. I can't let myself go there. I can't. I squeeze my eyes shut as I try desperately to think of another memory that needs to be recorded. They all do, eventually, but I need to get the most important ones down. I'm going to need them when . . .

I lift my hand and press my palm to my forehead. It's not the same as a hug, but it helps a little. It helps me remember all the other hugs. He always knew when I needed one. It was like he had this uncanny ability to just *know* when I was starting to spin out. Sometimes he even seemed to know before I did.

I wish I had that power. He was so good at reading people. Maybe, if I had been, I wouldn't have . . .

I let out a quick cough and drop my hand as I open my eyes. Positioning my fingers over the keys, I begin to type.

Chocolates and Halos

Grade eight—our first year of high school—was a big adjustment. Eph was once again at the same school as his brother, while I was, for the first time, in a different school than Skylar.

We both had our own groups of friends, with curiously little overlap. But he was my best friend, and though I didn't know if he considered me to be his at that point, he always made time for us to hang out.

At thirteen, our bodies were starting to change. Though I'd been taller than him the year before, he'd since caught up, and Mom thought that he would probably pass me any day. Eph wasn't so sure. His feet weren't that big, and he claimed that foot size was a good indicator of how tall you were going to be. Asher's feet had jumped four sizes practically overnight and, at fifteen, he was already taller than their dad.

There was a lot of buzz around the school just before Halloween, which was kind of weird, considering that most of my friends claimed they were too old for trick-or-treating. We'd gone out in a big group for the previous three years, accompanied only by older siblings. Part of me loved it. The dressing up, the candy haul, the excitement of being out in the brisk October air. But part of me hated it. Dodging fireworks tossed by the older boys was not my idea of fun, and I'd heard too many admonishments from teachers about how those things could blow off your fingers or put out an eye. The year before, I'd gone home early, leaving my friends to continue without me.

So when Georgia had told me that there weren't any plans to go trick-or-treating as a group, I breathed a slightly disappointed sigh of relief.

"Maybe I'll dress up and hand out candy," I said.

"Yeah. At least then you still get to wear a costume."

"Mom usually buys too much candy. I'll probably get to eat some, anyway."

She smiled. "Looks like you're all set."

I'd shrugged and hadn't really thought much more about it. Skylar was going trick-or-treating, which meant that just Mom and Grandma would be home. Grandma hated the whole thing and was just as glad that the door to her suite was around the back. Nobody ever rang *that* doorbell.

On the evening of the thirty-first, I had a quick snack of pizza rolls as I always did (we usually had dinner after trick-or-treating) and went to put on my costume. It was just a black, full-body leotard with a tail attached to the back, and a headband with ears. Eph had asked me to go trick-or-treating with him, but since he'd already said yes to going with his friends, I'd declined; I didn't particularly want to be the only girl in the group.

The trick-or-treating started off a little slow that night. I waited by the front window for a while, since it was more interesting than standing beside the door. Out on the street, I could see a few shadows moving around. Little kids ran to houses, then back to their parents who stood waiting at the ends of driveways.

The lights were on at the Diaz-Pierces', as they always were. I remembered Eph saying something about his brother going out with friends, so it was probably his dad handing out candy. Javier really loved doing that, not least because he could sneak mini chocolate bars all evening.

By the time the doorbell rang, I was pretty excited to see the costumes. It was always fun to see what my friends dressed up as. That year, though, I was going to get to see all the little kids in their crazy outfits. The first batch was comprised of a pirate, a princess, and something dressed in a lime-green onesie with matching makeup smeared all over their face and into their hair. I dropped a treat into each bag and closed the door to wait for the next group.

"How does it look out there?" Mom asked as she emerged from the kitchen, the slight rumble of the dishwasher following her. "Are we going to have enough treats?"

"I don't know. I've only given out three so far."

She made a little humming noise and headed for the living room, presumably to peek through the curtains which I'd pulled closed before taking up my position at the door. I leaned against the wall and looked longingly at the bowl of treats. If past years were anything to go by, there would be some left, but I didn't want to chance running out and disappointing anyone.

"What do you want for dinner?" Mom asked, startling me as she came toward the door. Just then, the doorbell rang. I pulled open the door to face a whole group of kids, half of them wearing coats over their costumes so I couldn't really see what they were. I dropped treats into bags while the kids shuffled on and off the porch. When the last one was darting out into the night, I spied another group coming, so I just left the door open. After dealing with the small horde of zombies, I closed the door and turned to where Mom had been standing.

"Are you still there?" I called.

"I'm in the kitchen." She poked her head out. "What do you want for dinner? I don't feel like cooking. There's a frozen pizza."

I wrinkled my nose. "I already had pizza rolls. Don't we have anything else?"

"I'll check. There might be a TV dinner. We can split it and supplement with a sandwich or something."

"Grandma's not coming?"

Mom shook her head. "She went out for dinner with a friend hours ago. She's probably already back and curled up in front of the TV."

I was about to make some comment about Grandma's viewing habits when the doorbell rang again. With a smile and a roll of my eyes, I reached for the doorknob. Six little kids crowded together, trying not to fall into the garden (although one of them sort of did). I loaded them up with treats and closed the door.

And so it went for about an hour and a half. The treat bowl grew empty, so I had to open another bag and dump it in. The night was getting colder, and I was starting to feel really glad I hadn't ventured out in that thin leotard.

"Mom, what time is it?" I called as I closed the door for what felt like the millionth time. There was a really long pause where I thought she might not have heard me. She was still in the kitchen, probably waiting for the action to die down so dinner could be cooked and served.

"Almost eight-fifteen," Mom said at last. "Why? Are we out of treats?"

"No. We're good. Unless we get a whole bunch of—" The doorbell interrupted my words. I reached for the knob and pulled open the door, only to find myself staring at a group of seven of my friends, Georgia standing right at the front.

"Trick-or-treat!" they sang, almost as one.

My heart sort of locked for a moment. I didn't know what to say. Behind the girls, a firework screamed and popped, causing me to flinch. But I recovered quickly and tried to plaster a smile on my face as I reached for the treats.

You told me you weren't doing this, I thought, wishing Georgia could hear me but knowing that she couldn't. *Why would you say you weren't, and then show up on my doorstep?*

As I dropped the treats into the bags, my hands shook. Some weird anger was bubbling up inside, and I started to imagine just throwing the treats out over their heads, onto the front lawn, where they could fight over them like greedy seagulls.

"Thanks, Ari," Georgia said as I dropped the treat into her bag. "See you at school."

"Yeah." I forced out a laugh. "See you."

It took all I had in me not to slam the door. I didn't even care that the street was still teeming with kids. I tore off my eared headband and ran to my room. Mom stepped out of the kitchen just in time to see me slam my door.

"What happened?" she called. I couldn't answer. I just stood there, shaking, as I twisted the headband between my hands. It wasn't long before the plastic gave up and snapped. I threw the pieces on the floor and then threw my body on my bed. "Was that Georgia? I thought you told me she wasn't going trick-or-treating this year."

I pulled my pillow over my head and started to cry as quietly as I could.

"Ari?" Her voice was suddenly a lot clearer. I unearthed my head to see her standing in the doorway. "Oh, honey."

"It's stupid. I don't care. It's just cheap crap candy."

She sighed. "That's not what you're upset about, though, is it?"

"I'm not upset," I said, turning away and pressing my cheek against the pillow.

"Do you want me to start dinner now?"

"I'm not hungry."

"You're not skipping dinner."

I flipped over and glared at her. "I'm not hungry!"

Her expression got that warning sort of look to it. "Watch your tone, young lady."

She didn't get it. Not really. I wasn't even sure if I did. All I knew was that I needed time to process what had happened. What I didn't need was to sit with my mother while she gave me judging looks and pitied the poor social pariah. Because that was apparently what I was.

Anyway, Mom didn't ask about dinner again. She just closed the door and left me to wallow. A few minutes later, I smelled something waft down the hall from the kitchen.

The doorbell rang a couple of times after that, and I could just barely make out Mom's voice each time the door opened. I still felt cold, so I peeled myself out of the leotard and left it crumpled on the floor while I put on my cozy pyjamas and the pair of crocheted slippers Grandma had made for me the previous Christmas. They were a little small, but they were stretchy, and so warm that I didn't mind that there was a lot of tension around my toes. Then I curled up under the covers and stared at the patterns of light that my blinds cast on the wall from the streetlight just outside my window.

The next time my bedroom door opened, I sat up like a shot, ready to shout at Mom even if it got me grounded. But it wasn't Mom. It was an angel. Or, at least, someone dressed like one. He dropped his bare foot from the knob and raised his eyebrows at me as he edged sideways through the door, stiff wings brushing the frame.

"Really?" I said. And, just like I knew he would, he smiled. It never seemed to matter how snarky my tone of voice was. He always knew the intent behind my words.

"What's wrong with my costume?" Having made it all the way in, he gently pushed the door closed with his foot before walking over to the side of my bed. The LED halo over his head bobbled a little on its headband as he looked down at me.

"Didn't you almost get yourself kicked out of school when we were seven for claiming you were an angel?"

"I never claimed to be anything." He bounced a little on his toes, causing the halo to bob and the feathery wings to rustle. I pulled the covers over my head. "What's wrong?" he asked.

"Who said anything's wrong?"

"Your mom."

I pulled the covers off, causing my hair to get all staticky. "What did she tell you?"

"Nothing. But something obviously is."

"It's *nothing*," I said.

"It's something."

"It's stupid."

"Maybe. But I won't know until you tell me."

I could feel my face crumpling. But I didn't want to cry. So I just turned the movement into a sour expression. "Georgia's a bitch."

"I could've told you that."

I blinked in surprise. Eph rarely had a bad word to say about anyone. At least, not out loud. Even when kids teased him or made rude comments, he never retaliated with unkind words of his own.

"Can I sit?"

I nodded and sat up, pulling my legs out from under the covers. He angled himself to the side as he lowered himself onto the edge of my bed, careful not to whack me with the stiff wings.

"Can't wait to take these off," he remarked.

"I'm not keeping you from trick-or-treating, am I?"

He shook his head. "We were pretty much done. I was about to head in when I saw your mom waving at me from the porch."

"Great." I buried my face in my hands.

"Why's Georgia a bitch? What'd she say?"

"She didn't say *anything*. That's the problem." I pulled my fingers down so I could peek at him. He was frowning.

"Why's that a problem?" His frown deepened. "Weren't you handing out candy tonight?"

I nodded and my chin wobbled. Before I could stop it, a sob burst out of me.

"Hey. Ari." He leaned his head close to mine, his forehead pressing against my temple. "It's okay," he whispered.

"No, it's not. It turns out I have *no* friends."

"I'm not your friend?"

"Other than you."

"Why? What happened?"

"They showed up."

He pulled back a little. "Here? Trick-or-treating?"

I nodded. "Georgia told me they weren't going out. But then they all did. And they didn't tell me."

"Well, she's a bitch. They're all bitches."

"Is it because I went home early last year? Because I didn't want fireworks thrown at me?"

He shrugged, causing his wings to rustle.

"I would've liked to go trick-or-treating one last time. But we'll be too old next year, and I'll never get another chance."

"Want to go now?"

In spite of the fact that I was still crying, I kind of had to laugh. "No. I'm not even wearing a costume."

"Sure you are. You're a . . . slumber-party girl."

"I'm just wearing pyjamas."

"So?"

I shook my head. "It's not even about that. It's . . ."

41

"I know," he said, letting out a long sigh and resting his head against mine again. "That was a crappy thing to do."

"What was?"

"Showing up here. Rule number one for being a sneaky ass is: 'Don't let your victim realize you're being a sneaky ass.' They could've just not come here, and you never would've known. Ringing your doorbell was a dick move."

I leaned into his warmth. "Why do *you* get it and they don't?"

"'Cause I'm familiar with dick moves."

That made me clamp my lips together. Of course he was familiar with dick moves. I turned to him and was about to apologize when he swivelled a little on the bed, making his wing tip brush against the covers.

"Don't, Ari. It's not a contest."

"How do you know what I was going to say?"

"Something about how you don't have a right to be upset because I have it worse than you. Am I right?"

"You do have it worse."

He shook his head and stood up. "My friends have never pulled a stunt like this and then rubbed my face in it. Some of them might be dicks, but this is a whole new level." He tilted his head toward the door, and the halo bobbed wildly. "Come on. I can hear your stomach growling."

"I'm not hungry."

"Not even for candy?"

"There's probably nothing left. If the trick-or-treaters didn't get it, then Mom's probably claimed the rest by now."

He rolled his eyes. "Just get up and come with me."

"I don't want to go trick-or-treating."

"We're not going trick-or-treating." He reached up with his

foot and turned the knob, unlatching the door before he swung it open and stepped into the hall. "Let's go."

"Do I need a jacket?"

"Nope. Come on."

Curious, I pulled off my slippers and followed him back to the front door. Mom popped her head out of the kitchen, but when she saw us, she didn't say anything. She just nodded and disappeared again.

Eph slipped his feet into his shoes and waited for me to do the same. Then I opened the door to a blast of frigid autumn air.

"Are you sure I don't need a jacket?" I asked, hugging my waist. He nodded and stepped close, so close that I could feel one of his big, fake wings at my back.

"We're just going to my house."

"You could've told me that." I frowned. "What's at your house?"

"You'll see."

"You know I don't like surprises."

"You'll like this one. I promise."

I let him lead me across the street to his place. When we stepped into the warm interior, I could smell something really good. It might've been grilled-cheese sandwiches. The comforting scent helped to calm me a little. I kicked off my shoes next to Eph's and followed him into the living room where I spotted his special treat bag on the coffee table. It was one his mom had made for him years earlier out of canvas. It had loops that went over his shoulders and fastened at the back, sort of like a backpack with a chest strap, only in reverse. And it was positively bulging with candy.

"Whoa," I whispered. He laughed and shook his head hard to dislodge the headband. It tumbled to the hardwood. He quickly grabbed it with his toes and placed it on the table before slipping his foot under the treat bag's strap and pulling it to the floor. Then he sat down and grabbed the bottom and upended it, spilling out a cornucopia of sugar.

"Ready?" he asked, starting to sort through some of the bigger items.

"For what?"

He looked up with a frown. "You get the chocolate. I get the candy. That's how we always do it."

"Yeah, but that's when we've *both* been out. I don't have anything to—"

"Just sit down, Ari." He turned back to his haul while I knelt down on the floor in front of the loot. "Mom doesn't want me eating all of this by myself, anyway. Do you?" he called.

"I'm going to have the audiologist turn down the sensitivity of those things if you don't stop that," Parnell said, stepping out of the hallway. She nodded at me. "Hello, Ari."

"Who's eavesdropping?" Eph asked, turning to her with a wicked grin. "You're the one lurking out there."

"Maybe I want some sweets. Do you have any red licorice?"

"Maybe." He pawed through the packets with one foot, and his toes closed around a red packet with a crinkle of plastic. With a flick of his foot, he tossed it to his mom. She just barely caught it.

"Thank you, sweetheart." She smiled, then gave me a conspiratorial wink before leaving us to divide up Eph's Halloween stash.

Half an hour later, I felt almost sick. It was definitely not a good idea to each six chocolate bars at once, even if they were mini ones. We lay on the living room floor, shoulder to shoulder as we stared up at the textured ceiling. I'd helped him take his wings off, and they were splayed across the coffee table like a dead bird.

"If you really want to go next year," he said, "we can still go. We'll only be fourteen."

I turned to look at him. In profile, he looked younger. His face still hadn't lost the cherubic contours of childhood. "I think that's kind of old for trick-or-treating. People might refuse to give us candy."

"Nah. You think they're going to refuse a kid with no arms?"

"Probably not."

He laughed a little. "I should've gone as something with arms when I had the chance."

"Angels have arms."

"Those were just sleeves. And it was kind of obvious there was nothing in them."

I shrugged. "I liked your costumes. You were usually the only kid dressed as an inanimate object."

"Not always. Don't forget the worm."

"The worm?"

He blinked and turned to me. "Maybe that was the year before we moved here."

"How do you dress up as a worm?"

"Mom made the costume." He sat up. "Mom! Where's the album?"

"Which one?"

"I want to show Ari the worm costume."

Parnell's laugh echoed from the other room. A few moments later, she appeared and headed for the low shelf unit under the TV. Behind one of the doors were a whole bunch of what appeared to be photo albums. She pulled one of them out, checked something inside the cover, and began to flip through it.

"My point still stands," I said. "You never dressed up as anything human."

"What would I dress up as?"

"Cowboy."

"Nope. Can't throw a lasso."

"Pirate. They're often missing body parts."

"Couldn't hold a sword."

"Astronaut."

He snorted. "You have to be in top physical condition to be an astronaut. They don't take deaf guys with no arms."

"It's make-believe, dear," Parnell said, stepping over a pile of empty candy wrappers to hand me the photo album. "I'm fairly certain worms don't go trick-or-treating. Or talk, for that matter." She leaned over and tapped at one of the photos with her finger. "There he is. My little earthworm."

I had to laugh at the sight of the costume. It looked like it was made out of shiny pinkish fabric. There was a hole for his face, and the costume tapered at the front down to a stuffed point that reached past his knees. His grinning face shone from under a wobbly-looking . . . well, tail.

"Which end is up?" I asked. He leaned closer to have a look.

"Who knows?"

"That was one of my favourites," Parnell said. "You got a lot of compliments."

"I got a lot of *comments*, Mom. Not the same thing." He shook his head with a bemused smile. "I look like I've got a foot-long penis."

Parnell, who had been about to step into the hallway, suddenly froze. She turned back around, her brow furrowed.

46

"What?" Eph said. "It's true. Don't you remember the way it swung when I walked?"

That mental image made me burst out laughing. I closed the album and set it aside as Parnell rolled her eyes and turned away. Eph grinned his megawatt smile and lay back down on the floor. I joined him a moment later, wiggling until my arm was pressed up tight against his side.

"Feeling any better?" he asked.

"Yeah. Seeing the worm helped."

"I bet." He turned his head to me. "I'm sorry Georgia did that to you."

"That's okay."

"No, it's not okay. It was mean." He pressed his lips together for a moment. A firework popped—loudly—right outside, and I startled a little. "I don't blame you."

"For what?"

"Being nervous. It's loud out there tonight."

"It's not thunder."

"Still." He shook his head. "Maybe you just have more common sense than those girls. I mean, boys can be pretty stupid, throwing those things around."

"You don't."

He snorted. "If I blew my toes off, I'd never hear the end of it from Mom. I kind of like being able to hold my own fork. Why do you think I quit soccer last year?"

I shrugged. "Because . . . you didn't like being on a boys-only team?"

"Yeah, right." He lifted up his feet and wiggled his toes. "Things were getting too rough. Mom and Dad were afraid I was really going to damage myself."

"What if you did?" I asked, my mind tickling toward the worst-case scenarios.

"Depends where the damage was." He let his feet fall to the floor with a smack. "Ribs, fine. Legs or feet . . . I'd be screwed. But that's not going to happen," he said quickly, his gaze boring into me. "Okay? That's why I quit. Unless there's a freak accident involving lard on the cafeteria floor or something, I'll be fine."

"That's a possibility."

He laughed. "Then I'll just have to be careful." With a grunt, he rolled onto his side. I did the same and pressed my forehead against his. "Don't worry about me, Ari," he whispered. "I'm fine."

And he was fine. Up until the moment I killed him.

CHAPTER THREE

I have to make another bathroom run. I wonder for a moment if I've got an infection or something, but then I remember that I drank that water. The afternoon sun is glancing off the snow from yesterday's blizzard. He's been gone for more than twenty-four hours now. It feels more like twenty-four years. Longer than I've been alive. Longer than he ever got to live.

My legs are stiff from sitting on the floor and my neck hurts from craning it at the laptop screen all day. But I can't stop. There are more memories I want to save. Ones I skipped over before. Like the time . . .

I hurry back to the computer, but see the battery icon flashing. So I run and get the charging cord, plug it into the outlet under the window, and stretch my arms above my head before sitting back down and moving the blinking cursor to a new line.

I'm nowhere near done yet.

Speeches and Breeches

School was usually a fairly predictable routine. The teachers were typical adults, and we kids had a pretty good idea what each of them was all about. Mr. Vanderkamp was kind of loopy, but his end-of-year parties were legendary; kids were willing to put up with his eccentricities for the final bash. Ms. Tuttle was a yeller; you could hear her pretty much anywhere in the north wing of the school, even when all the classroom doors were closed. Mrs. Bannerjee was the teacher that everyone wanted when they got to grade six; she was one of those teachers that all the kids loved. Asher had had her two years earlier, and I remembered Parnell saying that she was the kind of teacher that adults looked back on as the one who'd changed their life. I didn't know if she'd changed Asher's life, but Eph had said Asher really liked being in her class. So, of course, she was the teacher we were both hoping for.

But Mrs. Bannerjee decided to go and have a baby just as Eph and I went into grade six, and we ended up with some promoted substitute by the name of Mr. Pedersen. He was young and kind of cool, and if he'd been teaching high school he probably would've had to watch out for flirting teenage girls. On our very first day, he assigned us the worst possible thing: an oral report.

It was just supposed to be a quick presentation about ourselves. It was probably more for his benefit than anything else; after all, he didn't really know many of the students yet. At the time, though, I thought it was the worst thing ever . . . and I decided that I didn't like the guy.

On the day when I was scheduled to give my report, I slumped into the classroom feeling like I was going to the gallows. Eph, as usual, bounced ahead of me, making it to his seat before I'd barely crossed the threshold. As soon as I slid my butt onto the chair, I put my forehead down on the desk.

"What are you doing?" Eph asked. I turned my head so I could see him. He was rummaging in his desk with one foot. A moment later, he came back out with a mechanical pencil. Grasping it with his toes, he leaned back in his chair so he could lift the other foot and click out a millimetre of lead.

"Dying."

He snorted and shook his head as he set the pencil aside on the small stepstool that served as his writing surface. "You look fine to me."

"You're not even looking at me. How would you know?"

He swivelled in his seat, giving me his full attention. He'd just gotten a haircut, and his curls were so short at the sides that his hearing aids were clearly visible. The processors behind his ears were still light blue, even though I knew for a fact that he'd gotten new ones the year before. They matched the t-shirt he was wearing; despite the faded logo, it was probably brand new. "You're right," he said.

"Huh?"

"I wasn't looking. Now I am."

I closed my eyes. "I'm going to throw up."

"No, you're not."

"Yes, I am."

"It's just a quick presentation, Ari."

"In front of the whole class."

"So don't look at the whole class. Look at me."

I opened my eyes and frowned at him. "That's not going to work."

"Why not?" He leaned down for a moment to peer into his desk, then slipped his foot out of his shoe again to grab a pen. He reached across the aisle and held it out to me.

"Gross," Jared commented from the back of the room. "Don't touch that, Ari!"

I took the pen anyway, and Eph swivelled as he brought his foot to his mouth and blew Jared a kiss. A few of the other kids laughed. I gripped the pen in my fist and stared at it as I pressed my thumb down on the clicker mechanism. Once. Twice. Three times.

"Third time's a charm," Eph said, and I looked up to find him smiling at me. I tried to smile back, but my stomach was in knots and I still felt like I might scream. I gave the pen three more clicks and then set it down in the middle of my desk.

"Are you afraid?" he whispered. But that wasn't *really* what he was asking. By that time, we'd done his little back-to-back breathing trick more times than I could count. It always helped, but I had no desire to do it in the middle of our classroom with the rest of the kids staring. They wouldn't get it. Worse, they might laugh. So I shook my head. Eph continued to stare at me, and I knew the expression on his face was one of concern, even if I couldn't see it while I was glaring at the pen.

Mr. Pedersen walked into the room a few seconds later and closed the door. The class didn't get quiet right away, though. So he just stood there beside the whiteboard until it did. As the noise level in the room went down, my heart rate went up.

"We've got five more presentations today," he said. "Dylan, Ari, Kareem, Livia, and Toni. Hope you're ready!"

I wasn't. Even though I'd practised, I wasn't ready at all. I tried to run through the words I'd planned to say, but I came up blank and started to panic. *What's my name?* I thought frantically. *Why can't I remember?*

As Dylan got up to give his little speech, I sat on my hands to keep them from shaking. Out of the corner of my eye, I could see Eph's slip-on sneaker wiggling on the floor between us. He was trying to get my attention, but I felt like I was going to vomit if I so much as moved my eyeballs. My heart pounded so hard that I was sure everyone could see me jiggling in my seat.

"Ari?"

I blinked and looked up, the movement so fast that nausea lurched and I felt stomach acid rise up the back of my throat. Mr. Pedersen looked at me expectantly. Dylan was already back in his seat. I turned to Eph, who gave me a little nod.

There was nowhere to hide. I either had to get up there and start talking, or . . . well, I couldn't think of an alternative. I couldn't very well stay in my seat. Everyone was already staring, and the longer I put it off, the more they would gawk. I heard someone in the back giggle. Chin shaking, I stood up and shuffled to the front of the room.

And then I kept going. I started to run. I yanked on the door and pulled it open. Mr. Pedersen called out behind me, but I couldn't stop. I needed to scream, and I did *not* want to do it in the school hallway. I didn't want to be *that* girl. The one who lost it over an oral presentation. I was already the girl who was friends with the armless deaf boy. Somehow, that was worse than actually *being* the armless deaf boy, although I didn't understand why. In any case, I didn't want my reputation to take any more hits, so I ran down the hall, my footsteps echoing in the empty space, and headed for the exterior doors.

"Ari!" Eph shouted. A sob escaped me as I stopped and spun around in time to see him sprinting up the corridor. Mr. Pedersen appeared behind him but stayed near the classroom door.

"Five minutes," he said before disappearing again.

Eph practically barrelled into me, his soles squeaking on the floor. As he pressed his forehead against mine, I fought against the hiccupy sobs and tried to breathe.

"It's okay, Ari. It's okay."

"Now everyone thinks I'm—"

"They just think you're nervous. Everyone is."

"I'm the only one who ran, though."

He tilted his head until our noses touched. "Breathe."

"I can't."

He pulled away, quickly rounded me, and pressed himself up against my back.

"Eph—"

"Just breathe."

"It looks weird."

"So what?"

"People already think I'm weird."

He laughed. "You're not the weird one, Ari. Now, breathe." He sucked in a long, deep breath. I shook my head. But I didn't move. As he let his breath go, I adjusted my feet and leaned back against him, closing my eyes. On the next inhale, I joined him.

We did that for what felt like a really long time, but it couldn't have been more than a few minutes because Mr. Pedersen didn't come out to see what we were doing. I definitely felt like I was starting to calm down.

"Can you feel my heart?" I asked.

"Not anymore. But it was going crazy for a while." He took in

54

another deep breath and then stepped away. I immediately missed his heat. "You okay?"

I nodded. I wasn't sure if I would be once I walked back into the classroom, but at that moment I was.

The sound of a door opening made my heart surge, but when I looked, it was just some grade-seven boy coming out of the room across the hall. He headed straight for us, though, and I skittered out of the way, flattening myself against the wall. Eph walked toward me, a little more calmly, and barely paid any attention to the kid.

"I don't think I can do it," I whispered after the boy had disappeared into the bathroom.

"So tell Mr. Pedersen."

"How? Everybody will hear me."

He shook his head. "You *can* do it, Ari. Like I said, just look at me. Look *only* at me while you're talking."

"That's stupid. You already know all the stuff I'm going to say."

"Yeah, 'cause I helped you practise. Hearing it one more time isn't any more stupid, is it?"

I shrugged. From up the hall there was the sound of a toilet flushing. The boy reemerged and strolled down the hallway, veering so close to us that my heart started beating in my throat. But I wasn't the target. With a quick movement, he reached out and grabbed the loops on Eph's waistband and yanked hard.

I couldn't help sucking in a little gasp. The kid just backed up a step, smirking like he was the cleverest person in the world. Eph looked down at his pants (and the boxers that had gone down with them) puddled around his ankles, then turned to the boy with a raised eyebrow.

"If you wanted to see my dick, you could've just asked."

The boy didn't seem to know what to say to that. He just stood there, waiting to see what Eph would do. I didn't offer to help; I knew from past experience that I would be met with a refusal. He was nothing if not fiercely independent.

With a sigh, he waddled over to the wall so he could lean back against it, and then pulled his feet out of his pants and shoes. He used his toes to grab one of the loops on his boxers. By alternating his feet and tugging the underwear upward a few inches at a time, he finally got them situated at his waist. The procedure for getting his pants back on was much the same, but with a bit more struggle to get the waistband up over the boxers. When he was done, he pushed away from the wall and stepped forward. It wasn't an intimidating sort of movement, but the other kid reacted as if it were, taking a quick step back.

"Enjoy the show?"

"Freaky fag."

Eph turned to me with a frown. "Did you catch that?" he asked, angling his left ear toward me. "I think my hearing aids are acting up." He shook his head and turned to the boy. "I didn't hear you. Can you say that again?"

But the kid didn't. He just gave Eph a disgusted look and stormed back into his classroom.

"Did you really not hear what he said?" I asked when we were safely alone once more.

"Of course I heard what he said." He shook his head and walked closer to me. Close enough that I soon found myself on the receiving end of one of his hugs. "Ash taught me that trick."

"What trick?"

"When someone says something stupid like that—like a bad

joke or a mean comment or whatever—you ask them to repeat it. A lot of the time, they won't. Because they know they're being a dick."

I smiled and pulled my head back. "I've never seen you pull up your pants standing up."

He snorted. "How do you think I go to the bathroom at school? I'm not about to sit down on the floor in there."

"Ew."

"Yeah." He nudged me with his shoulder. "Come on. It'll be more embarrassing if Mr. Pedersen has to come out here and get us."

I'd almost forgotten. But as soon as I remembered, my heart started to pick up its pace once more.

"Relax, Ari. And remember to look at me. Okay?" He pulled his foot out of his shoe and reached up for the door handle. I nodded, feeling unsure and kind of shaky.

I didn't think I could do it, but I did. It probably looked pretty weird because I was staring at Eph the whole time, even when I answered one of Mr. Pedersen's questions at the end. I heard a few of the other kids snickering. But I didn't really care. All I could see was my best friend's beaming face as he showered love and encouragement on me from the third row.

Chapter Four

"Ari."

I blink and look up. The sky outside the window is dark, with only a few shreds of twilight hanging on. I turn to find Mom looking at me.

"Which do you want? Spaghetti or mac and cheese?"

I turn away in disgust. How can she think of food right now? How could I eat? Eph is lying dead somewhere. No. Not even that. There probably wasn't enough left of his body to lie anywhere. Not even on the slab in the morgue. I slam my laptop closed, unplug the charger from the wall, and stand up. The cord threatens to trip me, but I kick it out of my way as I head back to my room.

"Honey, you need to eat something."

Inside my room, I close the door with my foot and set the laptop down on my bed. Then I just stand there and stare for a moment. Not at the computer. At the bed. During one of our first sleepovers, Eph ended up in bed with me thanks to a freak fall thunderstorm. We snuggled there under my covers, listening to the rain, while Eph whispered all his knowledge about the physics of thunder and lightning (which was, actually, an impressive amount for a seven-year-old) into the room. That was only one of a couple of sleepovers we had at my house. The rest were all at Eph's, which made sense, given his challenges. My house isn't equipped the same way his is.

As I sink down onto the bed, I find myself getting sucked back into a memory that I haven't thought about in years: Eph's ninth birthday party. I open up the laptop and stare at the screen for a few moments as I try to decide how to begin.

Slingshots and Cake

I was the first one to arrive. It was an unseasonably warm day, so Parnell had moved some of the party crap out to the back deck, probably to preserve her house. When she led me out there, I noticed the table—the same one where she and Mom had sipped lemonade on the afternoon we all met—festooned with a bunch of blue balloons in various hues. I gripped the present I'd brought a little tighter as I glanced up at the cluster of rubber. Balloons, much like many other things, made me nervous. You never could tell when they were going to pop.

"We'll put the presents in the middle of the table," she said, waving her hand. I set the gift down and backed away carefully, trying not to touch the straining ribbons that kept the balloons from flying away into the clear spring sky.

"Where's Eph?" I asked.

"Still getting ready. His dad's helping." She glanced at her watch. "Which reminds me. Javier needs to go pick up the cake, or someone won't be able to blow out his candles." With a smile, she guided me back into the house. "Why don't you go see if the birthday boy is ready?"

I gave her a dubious look. She laughed.

"He's not naked, if that's what you're worried about. He should be changed by now."

I still wasn't convinced, but I padded down the hall to his door anyway and knocked.

"Who is it?" he shouted.

"Ari."

"Come in!"

"Inside voice," his dad said as I pushed open the door. Eph's face lit up when he saw me. He was standing in front of his dad; Javier sat on the edge of the bed, fiddling with the hearing aid in his hand. He glanced up with a smile. "Hi, Ari."

"Hi."

"My batteries died," Eph said, in a voice only marginally quieter than before.

"You've got a knack for timing," Javier said. He dug something small and silver out of the casing and exchanged it for a similar object that sat beside him on the bed. "Just think. You might not have been able to hear your friends sing to you."

Eph snorted. "No big deal. None of them sing that great, anyway." He grinned at me, then turned in a circle. "Like my shirt?"

I nodded. The olive-green colour of the altered garment set off his eyes nicely. But my gaze was more drawn to what he was wearing on his bottom half.

"Oh, yeah." He stuck one leg out to the side and hopped a little on the other foot. "Jeans."

"You never wear jeans."

"I'm wearing them now."

"Yeah, but you've never worn them before."

He shrugged and put his bare foot down on the carpet. "Only 'cause I can't do up the button."

"What if you need to go to the bathroom?"

He angled his head toward his dad and raised his eyebrows at me.

"I think that should do it," Javier said, not seeming to have been paying attention to our conversation. "Gimme your ear."

Eph laughed and stepped closer so his dad could put the hearing aid back in place.

"How's that?"

"Good." Battery crisis averted, he walked over to me and gave me a quick hug.

"You smell like . . ." I began, but then couldn't figure out how to finish the sentence.

"Clean?" Javier offered, at which Eph laughed.

"Dad!"

"What? Aren't you?" With a smile, he plucked the dead battery from the bedspread and stood up. "I have a cake to pick up. Don't stress out your mother while I'm gone." He plunked his hand on Eph's head and gave his curls a quick tousle. Eph ducked away with a frown.

"Don't mess up my hair!"

Javier chuckled and left the room. Eph scowled after him for a moment before turning to me.

"Is my hair okay?"

61

I shrugged. "It looks fine to me."

Seeming to trust my assessment, he started searching for something on the floor. A moment later, he pulled one of his slippers out from under the bed.

"I think we're having the party outside," I said.

"Not the sleepover part."

"Yeah, but the rest of it."

Abandoning the slipper, he pressed himself up against my side and nudged me toward the door. "What'd you get me?"

"I'm not telling. It's a surprise."

"I told you what I got you on your birthday."

"Yeah, but I don't like surprises, so that was good. You *do* like surprises."

He smiled. "Yeah. I do." He broke away to run ahead of me into the kitchen where Parnell was busy arranging some cut-up fruit on a tray around a big bowl of chocolate dip.

"Make sure they spelled his name right!" Parnell called after Javier, who was just going out the front door.

"It's too late to do anything about it if they didn't," he called back. The door closed behind him.

"Lots of people spell my name wrong," Eph said.

"You did, too," Parnell said, "when you were first learning."

"How'd he spell it?" I asked. She offered me a slice of apple, which I accepted, even though it didn't have any chocolate on it.

"E-P-H-R-I-A-M," Eph said, and it took me a moment to figure out what was wrong about that.

"Eph-ri-am?"

He laughed. "That sounds weird."

"Well, that's not your name," Parnell said. "Do you want any fruit before I set this in front of the jackals?"

"They're not *jackals*, Mom."

"That doesn't answer my question."

He shook his head. "Later."

"You wear your shoes on the deck, all right? I don't want you getting another splinter. I'm getting your dad to refinish the deck this summer, but until then . . ."

"Yeah, yeah, yeah." He smacked his bare feet against the floor as he stomped exaggeratedly around the island and back to me. "Where's everybody else?"

"I got a call from Jared's mom," Parnell said. "They'll be about half an hour late. The rest of them should be here shortly."

"Good." He bounced on his toes a little and then practically skipped over to the sliding door. He peered outside, spying the table with the sole present on it. "Is that from you?" he asked, turning to look at me.

"Yeah."

"Looks like a book."

My expression must've fallen, because he immediately shook his head.

"It's okay. I don't know *which* book."

"And you love most of them," Parnell said, wiping her hands on a tea towel just as the doorbell rang. Eph let out a squeal that made his mom laugh. "You would think you'd never had a party before."

"I haven't! Not here. We went to Mexico last year, remember?"

Parnell nodded, though her face grew a little sad. Eph frowned and walked over to her.

"Sorry, Mom."

"It's fine. Your abuelito lived a good, long life. And he was so happy to see you and Asher again." She bent down, took his face in her hands, and lightly touched her forehead to his. "Now go open the door before your guests think nobody's home."

I followed a little more slowly, eating my apple slice, as Eph bounded to the front door and used the strings that were rigged on the doorknob to unlatch it and pull the door open. (He was still a little too short to comfortably reach a doorknob with his foot.) A group of three boys practically tumbled through the opening, seeming like they'd already been eating sugary cake for hours.

"Hi, Dylan!" Eph said, his face bright, his voice even brighter. "Hi, Blaine! Hi, Dawson! Carry your shoes through the house, okay? Mom doesn't want people wearing them inside."

"Why not?" Dawson demanded. Eph just shrugged as he watched the three of them kick off their footwear.

"'Cause I have to eat with my feet. Would you want to walk on your hands all day and then have to eat with them?"

"I wouldn't care," Dawson said. He had the backs of his red sneakers hooked over his fingers. Under his other arm was a medium-sized box covered in wrapping paper.

"Can't you just wash them before you eat?" Blaine asked. Eph wrinkled his nose.

"Sometimes I have to do that anyway. Mom makes me."

"I make you do what?" Parnell asked, silently sidling up beside me. Eph smiled.

"Wash my feet."

"I know. I'm a mean mum." She shook her head. "You boys can take your shoes through the house and put them on by the back door, all right? We'll be having most of the party outside." With a frown, she looked at the three of them. "Where are your sleeping bags?"

"I can't sleep over," Dawson said quickly.

Dylan shook his head. "Me, neither."

"Yeah, 'cause you wet the bed," Blaine said.

"I do not!"

Eph was looking at his friends with a growing frown on his face. I couldn't really tell what he was thinking, and, in any case, he wiped that expression away and replaced it with a smile a moment later. "Maybe Jared will be able to. He's coming, too."

Dawson shook his head. "No, he's not."

Parnell looked concerned. "I just talked to his mum. She said they'll be over in a few minutes."

"Yeah," Eph said with a little nod of his head. He shuffled backward and turned around, giving me a quick smile as he passed us and walked toward the kitchen. I hung back as the boys followed in silence, giving each other strange looks that I couldn't really decipher.

An hour later, Jared still hadn't shown up. It didn't look like he was going to. Parnell fed us the fruit and chocolate dip, and though Eph and I both ate quite a bit of fruit, there was still an awful lot left by the time the bowl of dip was empty. Asher joined us to play kickball in the backyard, and Eph picked me first for his team. Everything was going the way a birthday party should've gone, but I could tell that Eph was a little troubled.

As the afternoon sun began its creep toward the horizon and the air started to turn uncomfortably cool, Parnell called us over to the table on the deck. We all took a seat as she brought out the freshly delivered pizza and the boys scrambled for what they thought were the biggest slices. After we'd scarfed down dinner, Parnell presented the cake, shining with nine glowing candles, and placed it in front of Eph as we sang. He glanced at me with a curious little wiggle of his eyebrows just before he leaned forward to blow out all the candles with one massive exhale.

"No girlfriends!" Dawson shouted. The other boys laughed.

"I'm too young for that," Eph said.

Dylan shook his head. "I have a girlfriend."

"You do not," Blaine said.

"I do so."

"Who?"

"Maeve."

"That doesn't count."

"Why not?"

"She just kissed you once. That's not a girlfriend."

Eph was watching the exchange with raised eyebrows. Parnell was shaking her head.

"Nine does seem a bit young for that," she said, plunking a plate with a slice of cake in front of Dawson. "What's wrong with just being friends?"

"She's a *girl*," Dylan said. Eph sat up a little straighter and seemed to bristle.

"So what?"

"I can't be friends with a girl."

"Why not? I am."

"Yeah, but you're different."

"Blaine," Parnell said, "would you like some more fruit punch?"

"Yes, please."

Her hand seemed to grip the handle of the jug more tightly than was necessary as she refreshed his glass. I could sense the tension at the table, and it was kind of making me nervous.

"Mom, when can I open presents?" Eph asked, scooting back

in the chair so he had enough room to lift up his foot and grab his fork. Dawson and Blaine nudged each other and snickered.

"When you're done with the cake. I think we'll do that inside, though. It's starting to get kind of chilly out here, isn't it?"

We all nodded in agreement and quickly ate our slices of cake. Eph ended up with a smear of icing below his lip, but he wiped it with a cartoon-character napkin before his mom could do anything embarrassing. When we all piled into the house a few minutes later, I could already feel the buzz from the sweet dessert.

Eph ignored my present and dove into the rest of the pile with gusto. We were all sitting around the living room, some of us on the floor, some on the couch. Eph sat on the floor with his back against the couch so he could lean against it while he tore at the wrapping paper with his toes. Every present was met with the same amount of enthusiasm, as if he didn't really care what the actual present was. As he tore strips of paper off a box that held a board game, his face lit up once again and he grinned.

"Thanks, Blaine! I love games."

"That one's boring. Mom bought it."

"I haven't played it before. Maybe we can play it later."

Blaine didn't say anything. Undeterred, Eph went after one of the last two presents. The one that wasn't mine. He gave it a shake, frowning at the slight rattle.

"That's from me," Dawson said.

"Cool." Eph tore off the paper and then turned the box to read the lettering on the front. "A slingshot? Wow!" He tried to open the box, but it was sealed up tight. "Mom! Can you bring the scissors?"

Parnell appeared a moment later with the requested tool.

When she saw the box, she frowned. "That definitely looks like an outside toy, Eph."

"It just shoots foam balls. Come on, Mom! I want to try it."

Looking unsure, Parnell took the box and sliced the seal with the scissors. Then she handed it back to him, and he opened it up. The other boys crowded around as he pulled out the plastic weapon and the three accompanying foam balls.

"Can I try it, Eph?" Blaine asked.

"After me," Dawson said. "I gave it to him."

I hung back and hugged my knees as I stared at the last present on the floor. The one I'd brought. Still untouched.

"Ari," Parnell said quietly. I looked up at her. She gave me a little smile and gestured to the gift. "Why don't you give Eph your present?"

I shook my head and turned back to the boys, who were trying (rather unsuccessfully) to help Eph with the slingshot. The problem was obvious. The handle was much too large for him to grasp with his toes. If he braced it on the floor, he could pull the little sling back, but the angle was all wrong and the ball just went bouncing off across the room.

"Practice makes perfect," Parnell said before heading back into the kitchen. "Try not to break anything, all right?"

Dawson laughed. "Yeah, right. He can't even do it! Let me try, Eph." Before he could get a response, he grabbed the slingshot out of Eph's foot.

"I'm going next!" Dylan cried.

"Eph didn't say so. It's his, so he gets to say."

Eph shrugged. "I don't care." He frowned as the three of them crowded close, arguing and trying to grab the toy out of each other's hands. Slingshot and balls were never held by the same person, so there was more shouting than shooting. I almost didn't notice when Eph reached out and snagged the final present with his foot and slid it over to him. But the crinkle of paper caught my attention, even if it didn't alert the three warmongers just feet away.

"Mom said you can return it if you've already read it," I said.

He looked at me for a moment, his eyes smiling, before turning back to the gift so he could rip the paper off. I'd gotten him a nice hardcover all about dragons. It was full of amazing illustrations and lots of "facts," and I just knew he was going to love it. He flipped open the cover and turned to the first page, just as Dylan noticed what he was doing.

"A book?" He snorted. "That's a stupid gift."

"No, it's not," Eph said quietly, almost absently, as he carefully turned to the next page, revealing a two-page spread with a shimmering greeny-gold dragon.

"Yeah, it is. Who gave you that? Your girlfriend?"

Eph didn't say anything. He just closed the book and slid it under the coffee table. I felt my heart sink.

"I bet I can hit the chandelier," Dawson said. He'd somehow come into possession of the slingshot and two of the balls. He stood up and fit a ball into the sling.

"Don't," Eph said.

"It's foam. It won't break anything."

Eph quickly stood up and stepped closer to Dawson. "Don't!" he whispered. "Mom'll get mad."

But Dawson wasn't listening. He lined up his shot and pulled the sling back. The ball went flying, and the next moment there was a wild tinkling as it sailed through the hanging crystals above the dining room table. The boys whooped. Well, all of them except Eph.

"Stop it!" he said, stepping in front of Dawson just as the latter readied the other ball. He soon found himself staring at the loaded slingshot.

"Shoot him!" Blaine cried. "Put him down!"

My eyes widened as the other two boys laughed. Out of the corner of my eye, I saw Parnell appear in the doorway.

"Excuse me. What did you just say?"

Dawson quickly lowered the slingshot and tossed it onto the floor with a clatter. Eph shook his head and tried to give his mom a warning glance.

"We're just playing," Blaine said, his voice small. Parnell looked at the slingshot, at the ball rolling across the floor, at the still-swaying crystals on her chandelier. She looked at me (I'd scooted into the corner by that point, afraid I was going to become a target) and then walked over to the cabinet under the TV.

"Why don't you play something else?" she asked, pulling out a set of wireless video-game controllers. "There are plenty of games to choose from."

Dawson turned to Eph in disbelief. "How do *you* play video games?"

"The same way I do everything else."

He snorted. "Gross."

"His feet are probably cleaner than your hands!" I blurted, suddenly unable to keep my mouth shut a moment longer. I felt my heart surge in panic as everyone in the room—including Parnell—turned to look at me. Everything felt hot. I swallowed hard and stood up, then hurried to the back of the house and shut myself in the bathroom.

The party continued without me. I could hear the boys shouting as they became engrossed in their game. Carefully, I lowered myself to sit on the edge of the tub and stared at the Diaz-Pierces' space-age toilet. Frankly, the thing scared me. The first time I'd used it, I hadn't been able to figure out how to flush. I'd thought Eph was joking when he yelled through the door, "Just close the lid!" I hurried to follow the instruction, only to be startled by a beeping noise and what sounded like a rather powerful rush of water.

I wanted to leave the party and go home . . . and yet I didn't. What I *really* wanted was for those boys to just go away. I didn't understand why Eph put up with them. Especially Dawson.

A light knocking on the door made me look up.

"Ari?" Eph's voice said.

"What?"

"Are you okay?"

"Yeah."

There was a long pause. "Are you sure?"

I stood up, walked to the door, and opened it a crack. "Maybe I should go home."

"Why?" His expression, usually so bright and infectious, dulled a little. "But . . . what about the sleepover? Mom's got kettle corn. And we can watch a movie. Just get your mom to bring over your sleeping bag."

I shrugged so much my shoulders came up to my ears.

He shook his head and leaned a little closer, as if to share a secret. "Nobody else is staying, Ari. So it'll just be us. Okay?"

"Really?"

"Yeah." He wrinkled his nose, then checked behind him before turning back to me. "I don't really *want* them to stay, anyway. You're a better sleepover friend."

Just like that, his words made me feel warm. In a good way,

though. Not in that hot, panicky way I'd felt when I'd shouted at Dawson. I nodded, and he leaned forward for a hug. But then he seemed to think better of it.

"They'll be going home soon. Then we can have the real party."

"Two people isn't a party."

"Ash might watch the movie with us. Is that okay?"

I nodded again. He smiled.

"Good." Tilting his head to the side, he looked at me. "Do you want to use my slingshot?"

"Not really."

He jutted out his lower lip. "Too bad. I thought maybe you could hit Dawson in the head with one of those balls while he's playing."

"You could probably do it."

"Not yet. I need more practice." He backed up a couple of steps. "Come on. They're playing *Wicked Wild Warlord*. You're so good at that, I bet you could beat Dawson. That would show him."

That sounded like a great way to make an enemy, so I didn't commit to anything. I just followed him back to the living room and sat on the couch beside him to wait for the boys' parents to pick them up.

I sit there frowning at the screen for a few minutes. Most of my memories so far have been about Eph being his usual ebullient self. Nothing ever got to him . . . except when it did. The memory of that party reminds me that his life wasn't all sunshine, even if he tried so hard to make it seem like it was. While the level of cruelty that night was about as bad as it ever got, there was other stuff that bothered him, too. He didn't tell me about it, but he didn't always have to. After a few years of being his best friend, I felt like I could read him pretty well. Almost as well as he read me from the beginning.

I don't really want to think about the not-so-great parts, but really, nothing could be as bad as the ending. And I want to keep thinking about him, remembering, and recording.

But my eyelids are heavy. My head feels like it might drop off my neck and clunk onto the keyboard. So I save the file, turn off the laptop, and set it aside. It's almost two in the morning. I won't be able to be coherent if I don't get at least a little bit of sleep. So I make a quick trip to the bathroom and then curl up in bed. I feel myself sucked into slumber almost as soon as my head hits the pillow.

CHAPTER FIVE

The house is dark and quiet when I wake up. I feel like I haven't gotten any sleep at all, but when I check the clock on my laptop, I see that it's just after four. It's a bit chilly in my room (and, I'm guessing, the whole house), so I grab a sweater out of my dresser and pull it on before taking my laptop out to the living room.

When I look out the window, I notice that the Diaz-Pierces' lights are on, which is unusual. More unusual still is the fact that only one car is in the driveway. I have no idea where any of them would've gone in the middle of the night, unless maybe someone had a heart attack or something and needed to go to the hospital. Parnell and Javier seem like they're in pretty good health, but they've just lost their son. Their hearts probably ache even more than mine, which still feels like it might stop and shatter if I think about the wrong thing for too long.

I tug my sweater around me as I settle on the floor and find the file full of memories. The ones from our childhood are great, but they're only part of the picture. I want to remember all of him, not just the sunshiny parts.

Side Effects and Teacups

When Eph and I were in grade ten, a new student joined us partway through the year. Chandra was in a lot of my classes, although I didn't really speak to her much. So I was kind of surprised when she plunked herself down next to me in the cafeteria, as if I'd been saving the spot for her all along.

"You're Ari, right?"

I nodded and pretended to busy myself with my lunch, willing Eph to hurry up. It took him a while to use the bathroom, so I usually saved him a spot on the bench beside me. At that moment, Chandra was warming it with her butt, but I wasn't too worried. There were still a few minutes before Eph would be back, and then I'd let *him* deal with it (although, he wasn't the type of person to be put off by someone messing up his routine; he would just sit somewhere else).

"I'm Chandra," she said, rather unnecessarily. My mind started to race as I tried to figure out what I was supposed to do next. Shaking hands wasn't exactly high-school etiquette. I wiped my palms on my thighs and nodded again. She had a brown bag in one hand, but she wasn't opening it up. Curious, I swivelled my eyes toward her face.

"Hi."

"Hi. So . . . um . . . I was wondering . . ."

But she didn't tell me what she was wondering about. Was I supposed to guess? I didn't know, and I wasn't about to ask. At that point, the worries that had seemed to run in the background of my life like relatively unobtrusive software had turned into full-fledged anxiety. In fact, I had an appointment with Dr. Loh that afternoon to try to adjust the dosage of my meds. I hadn't slept well in weeks, and I had a feeling that those candy-coloured pills were to blame.

Since Chandra wasn't giving me any hints, I turned to my lunch. I didn't usually start without Eph, but I felt stupid just sitting there waiting for this unfamiliar girl to say something. Suddenly, she cleared her throat, looked around, and leaned forward. Some sort of scent—shampoo, perfume, deodorant . . . I wasn't sure—wafted toward me, and I pulled back almost instinctively.

"You're friends with Ephraim, right?"

"Yeah," I said, not at all sure where the conversation was going, but fairly certain I wouldn't like it. People rarely asked me questions about Eph . . . and if they did, they were usually things they wouldn't dare to ask him. I usually told him when that happened, and each instance was met with a light shrugging-off. Those questions probably bothered me more than they bothered him.

"Can I ask you something?"

Haven't you already been doing that? I wondered, but I kept the thought to myself and just nodded.

"Is he seeing anyone?"

I blinked. From the time we'd started high school, plenty of assumptions had been made about the two of us. It seemed that the first impression we made was that of a couple, and until people found out otherwise, they usually treated us like one. Georgia had even called us Ephri for a while back in grade nine. It seemed odd that Chandra wouldn't have made the same assumption as everyone else, but it was kind of an interesting change. I shook my head.

Her cheeks suddenly got really pink. She already had kind of a ruddy complexion, and my answer had only seemed to amplify the redness. She cleared her throat and tried to look casual as she crossed her legs under the table and fiddled with the top edge of her paper bag.

"Could you, like, give him a message for me?"

"He doesn't bite," I said. "You could talk to him yourself."

Her cheeks got redder, which I didn't think was even possible. I was kind of sorry Eph wasn't there to see it. But her next words threw cold water on my little flame of amusement. "He's deaf, though, isn't he?"

"So?" I said, so loudly that a few people in the immediate vicinity turned to look at me. Chandra shrank back, frowning.

"I don't speak sign language," she said

"Neither do I. Neither does *he*." I shook my head, annoyed.

"Jeez. Sorry."

No, you're not, I thought. *You're just embarrassed. And you wouldn't need to be, if you'd just paid attention. How the heck would Eph use sign language, anyway?*

"So . . . will you talk to him for me?"

"And say what?"

"Ask him if he's interested in going out with me."

With a snort, I turned back to my lunch. "How was *that* going to work?"

"What?"

"If you thought he couldn't hear you," I said, daring to peer at her out of the corner of my eye, "how were you going to communicate with him?"

She shrugged, then narrowed her eyes a little as she looked at me. "Wow. Georgia was right. You *are* a bitch."

I was suffering from medication side effects and a lack of sleep, but she didn't know that. Nobody at school—except for Eph and our families—even knew I was seeing a psychiatrist. And a therapist. That kind of information was kryptonite in high school; I might as well have written out the details on a sandwich board, worn it all week, and kissed my social life goodbye.

"So ask someone else," I said, "if I'm so awful to deal with."

"I don't know who his other friends are. I've only seen him hanging out with you."

Please hurry up, Eph, I thought as I stabbed my cold spaghetti with my fork. My hand was shaking, and I didn't know if it was nervous energy or if my body wanted to stab Chandra without my mind really realizing it.

"Whatever," she said, getting to her feet and grabbing the crumpled top of her bag. "If I have to put up with *you*, maybe I'm not interested."

I snorted. "So you *don't* want me to pass on the message?"

She frowned, then tossed her hair as she turned to go. "Do whatever you want. I'll ask him myself later." And, with that, she flounced away. I knew there was no chance I'd ever be friends with the new girl, but I didn't really care.

"What'd I miss?" Eph asked, startling me a little. He straddled the bench beside me and settled himself down, frowning as he did so. "Why's the bench so warm?"

"Chandra."

His expression deepened into one of concern. "Are you all right?"

I let out a short laugh and stabbed at my noodles. "Yeah. Why?"

"You look awful."

"Thanks." I eyed the straps of his backpack and then reached for the chest clip. When I'd pulled the bag off and set it on the bench in front of him, he freed his foot from his shoe and tugged at the zipper.

"Not sleeping?" he asked.

"How can you tell?"

He glanced up at me for a moment, just as he got the backpack open. "Your eyelids."

"What about them?"

"They're heavy."

"Yeah, well, yours would be, too, if you'd only gotten an hour of sleep last night."

He frowned as he pulled out his lunch and set about freeing the sandwich from its container. "That's not enough."

"No kidding."

He wrinkled his nose and held up one half of his sandwich with his toes. "Seriously, Mom? Try not to get jam everywhere." With a shake of his head, he took a bite. "If she doesn't want me licking my toes, she shouldn't slather that stuff on so thick that it oozes everywhere."

"You're going to get jam in your shoes."

He laughed, still chewing. "Yeah. I don't think that's what they mean by 'toe jam,' though."

"Gross."

"Yep." He took another big bite and then let his heel rest on his backpack. "You've got practice after school?"

I nodded at the code word. "Not until four-thirty."

He smiled and licked a bit of jam from the corner of his mouth. "No problem. Want to come over first? You might as well."

With a nod, I turned back to my own lunch. I might have felt awful, but at least I had something to look forward to.

"What did Chandra want?"

I turned to find him looking at me, eyebrows raised, a curious smile playing on his face as he took another bite of his sandwich.

"Did you make a new friend?" The singsong tone of his voice was almost enough to make me smile. I snorted instead.

"Hardly. She called me a bitch."

His chewing slowed to a stop. "She what?"

"It's fine. I was. I'm crabby as hell right now. Don't tell me you didn't notice."

"I did. But I wasn't going to say anything."

"Why not?"

"Because you're crabby."

I stuck my fork into my half-eaten spaghetti with a frown. He chuckled.

"I'm just teasing you, Ari."

"I *hate* this . . . candy."

"More than the last one?"

"Definitely."

He shook his head and stuffed the last corner of sandwich into his mouth before reaching for the other triangle. "Maybe the next one'll be better."

"That's what they said three candies ago." I plunked my elbows on the table and pressed my palms against my temples.

That position kind of made me want to fall asleep, though, so I abandoned it.

Eph chewed thoughtfully for a moment. "So, what did Chandra want? I'm pretty sure she didn't come over here just to call you a bitch."

"She wanted to know if you were seeing anyone."

He didn't say anything for so long that I turned to look at him because I was afraid he was choking or something. But he was just sitting there, gripping his sandwich with his jammy toes and frowning a bit.

"What?" I asked.

"Nothing." He shook his head and went back to his lunch.

"She's kind of rude."

"Yeah. I wasn't about to go out with her, Ari."

"Why not? Not your type?"

"Doesn't matter. I don't date."

"Maybe you should."

"Nope." He quickly ate the last of his sandwich and regarded his toes. Craning his neck over toward the food-service area, he sighed. "Could you get me a napkin? If I get jam in my shoes, they're going to stink."

"More than they already do?"

He laughed and wiggled his toes in my direction. I didn't smell a thing. He seemed to be bypassing the nasty BO and various other stinky secretions that a lot of the guys were afflicted with. Probably more worrisome for him, though, was the fact that he also seemed to be bypassing things like facial hair.

I dug into my bag and pulled out a package of wet wipes. "Use this," I said, freeing one and handing it to him. "It'll work better."

"Thanks." He momentarily freed his other foot and balanced

precariously as he wiped the jam from his toes. I could feel gazes on us (it happened every time he did something unusual with his feet), but I tried to ignore it. *They're staring at him, not you,* I reminded myself, then tried to catch the dropped thread of the conversation once again.

"Why don't you date?"

He sighed and looked at me with a weary expression. "Why do you think?"

"I honestly don't know, Eph."

He finished wiping his feet and folded the little wipe before setting it on his backpack and slipping one foot back into its shoe. "Because it would never be a partnership."

I frowned. "What would it be?"

"Caregiver and caregivee."

"You don't have to *marry* Chandra."

He shook his head. "I don't even want to date her. And I'm just saying. There's no point in dating anyone, because it's never going to go anywhere. It can't."

I blinked and just stared at him. All of this was news to me. "So you're . . . What are you going to do, then? Get a bunch of cats and live alone?"

"Maybe. And hire someone to help me with the stuff I can't do." He stuck his sandwich container and used wipe into the backpack. "Stop looking so sad, Ari. It's fine."

"No, it's not fine. It's stupid."

He snorted and paused in his zipping-up of the backpack to look at me. "Stupid?"

"Yeah. You're going to pay someone to change your hearing-aid batteries and cut your sandwiches into triangles when your partner could be doing those things?"

A sad little smile crossed his lips. "There's other stuff, too."

"So? Don't you think your partner would be happy to do those things?"

"She might. But I wouldn't be happy to have her do them." Having zipped up his backpack, he slipped his jam-free foot back into his shoe and stood up. "I hate even having to ask people to do little things like this," he said, gesturing with his chin. I knew he wanted me to pick up the backpack and secure it on his shoulders, but I didn't move. "I certainly don't expect them to do the other stuff."

"But—"

"I have to talk to Mrs. Sturgess before class, Ari. Could you please . . . ?"

So I helped him put his backpack on, and we parted ways with a promise to meet up out front after school so Asher could give us a ride home. For the rest of the day, I couldn't stop thinking about what he'd said. The thought was so lonely that it made my heart ache.

Did he really want to spend the rest of his life without a partner? It didn't seem like it, but I also knew that when an idea got into Eph Diaz-Pierce's head, it didn't easily get out. For years, he'd told people about his missing wings, and I'd assumed that he was just being dramatic. I eventually realized that he wasn't, that he actually believed it. He stopped talking about it soon after we turned ten, and I still wasn't sure if it was because he'd changed his mind or if he'd just realized that the assertion sounded a little crazy to other people. (I was inclined to believe it was the latter.)

By the end of the day, I was more tired than ever and, on top of everything else, I felt like crying. I didn't even know why. There was this bubbling panic in my gut that I suspected had something to do with going to see Berlynn after my appointment with the psychiatrist, but the feeling seemed totally out of proportion to the situation. I sat slumped in the back seat, pretending to look at something on my phone. In reality, I just didn't want to talk. Eph, in the seat next to me, was staring; I could practically feel it. But I knew that if he got me talking, I'd probably burst into tears. And we weren't the only ones in the car.

When we arrived at the Diaz-Pierces' place, I pulled myself out of the car and stood there for a few moments while I debated sprinting across the street. But before I had a chance to do anything, Eph was at my side, leaning close.

"Let's go in. You look like you could use a cup of tea."

I frowned and shook my head. "Tea doesn't fix everything."

"Tell that to Mom." He smiled and angled his chin toward the door, where Asher was already disappearing with two backpacks slung over his shoulders: his and Eph's. "Hey! You going to do my homework while you're at it?" he called after his brother.

"Fat chance," came the response. "I'm going out, and I don't want to get a frantic message from you that you left your bag in my car."

Eph screwed up his nose. "Yeah, right."

"You could let me carry it," I said. But he just shook his head, as I'd known he would.

"Nope." Giving me a nudge with his side, he started toward the door. "You're my best friend, not my pack mule."

"Pack mule?"

"Whatever it's called. You get the idea."

I followed him inside through the door Asher had left ajar. We kicked off our shoes and padded into the kitchen where

Parnell was filling the kettle at the sink. She glanced at us and did a double take.

"Are you all right?" she asked.

"Gotta pee," Eph said and disappeared into the hallway, leaving me with his mom.

"I wasn't asking you, smarty-boots." She shook her head and turned back to me as Eph's chuckle echoed down the hallway. "You don't look so good."

"I'm just tired."

"Just?"

I shook my head and slid onto one of the stools at the island. "I don't feel right."

She made a sympathetic grimace and set the kettle on the stove. "The meds still aren't right?"

I shrugged. "I guess not." As I placed my hands on the cool stone surface, I noticed that they were shaking. Parnell must have noticed, too.

"Would you like a cup of tea?"

"Yes, please."

She got another cup out of the cupboard and set it on the counter. I took the opportunity to close my eyes and just take in the scents and sounds of their kitchen. For some reason, I found it a lot more relaxing than ours. Maybe it was because their fridge didn't buzz like an angry mosquito. Or maybe it was because Parnell hadn't learned to cook from someone with an obvious cabbage fetish. (Even when Grandma cooked in her own suite, it tended to stink up the whole house.)

But that day, I couldn't seem to relax, and I felt my eyes getting really wet under their lids. I quickly opened them and found Parnell watching me with concern.

"Are you sure you're all right, Ari?"

"No. Yes. It's just . . ." With a sigh, I shook my head. "I just don't feel like going to see my therapist today. Or any day. It's not that I don't like her," I said quickly, then stopped. Parnell's eyebrows rose.

"Or is it?"

"I don't know. She kind of pissed me off." I pressed my palms against my temples as I leaned my elbows on the island. "She wants me to find ways to cope. And when I do, it's not good enough for her." I sighed. "She's probably right, though."

Parnell laughed softly. "That was a whole lot of vagueness."

"Sorry."

She shook her head. "I'm not a therapist. You don't have to tell me anything if you don't want to."

But I kind of did. Even though she wasn't biologically related to Eph, she still had a calm, reassuring sort of aura about her that I would've sworn she'd passed down to her son if I hadn't known better.

The kettle started to whistle, so she went to attend to it. I rubbed my fingertips into my scalp and took a deep breath.

"My therapist thinks I rely on Eph too much."

She didn't say anything. She just poured the hot water into the teapot and set the kettle on a cool part of the stovetop.

"She said I'm using him. I didn't realize I—"

"Ari, stop." She held up her hand and shook her head. "You're not using him."

"What if I am? How is that fair?"

"All right. Let's talk about fairness. Is it fair that you're dealing with this anxiety?"

I shrugged. "I don't know."

"Well, I'll tell you, then. It's not fair." She got out the teabags and plunked a couple into the pot before placing the lid on with a clink. "Sometimes life isn't. So you have to do what you have to do."

"But it's so one-sided!"

She shook her head as she brought the cups and teapot over to the island. After taking the stool next to mine, she swivelled so she could look into my eyes. "He needs you as much as you need him, Ari."

"Not in the same way."

"Actually, it is pretty much the same way." She absently rubbed at a sparkly bit in the stone under her fingers. "Did I ever tell you about the day Javier and I first met Eph?"

"I don't think so."

She smiled as the memory seemed to pull her back in time. "He was about five months old. Or so the doctors thought. We'll probably never know for sure."

"I thought his birthday was March thirty-first."

"It is. Officially. But we have no idea if that's when he was actually born." She nodded to herself, her eyes slightly unfocused as she remembered. "We'd been wanting to adopt for a while. I couldn't have any more children of my own after Asher, so we decided we'd offer a home to a child who needed one." She smiled and looked at me. "We got more than we bargained for with Eph, that's for sure."

"What did he look like as a baby?"

"I can show you some photos if you like. But it's not really necessary. He looked pretty much the same as he does now. Those big green eyes. That special smile. And he already had a full head of curls. The nurses called him Angelo, because he reminded them of a baby angel. He was a beautiful boy." She reached for the teapot and a cup, then began to pour. "When they first put him in my arms, I wasn't sure how he would react. I was afraid I'd hurt him, and he'd already been through so much. He'd been through major surgery, lost two limbs, and survived a bout of meningitis. They suspected his hearing had been damaged at that point, but they didn't know to what extent. So when a nurse put this beautiful little creature into my arms, I didn't even want to breathe for fear I'd hurt him." She finished pouring the tea and slid one of the cups toward me. "Careful. It'll still be hot."

I nodded, eager for her to go on with her story.

"So, there I was, holding this bruised and battered little thing, and the most incredible calm feeling came over me. It was the strangest thing, almost like someone had slipped some sort of drug into me. I didn't know what it was until I looked down into those beautiful green eyes." She spun her teacup slowly on the surface in front of her. "You know that look he gives you sometimes? The one that makes you feel safe?"

I nodded. I was very familiar with it.

"There he was, this vulnerable little thing who needed my protection, and yet it felt like he was somehow protecting me. It was all over for me at that moment. Javier took a bit longer, but once Eph used that little trick on him . . ."

"What trick?"

"Maybe not so much a trick as a look. All I knew was that, when he looked into my eyes, there was an instant bond. And then he smiled." She shook her head. "That was that. I knew that if this little boy—who had just lost his mother, his arms, and his hearing—could still smile, then I wanted him in my life. I wanted to be his mum."

"Who was his biological mother?" I asked, unsure if she

really wanted to talk about that or not. But Eph never talked about his biological parents in front of me, even to speculate about them. Which made me wonder if he knew more than he was letting on.

Parnell shook her head. "We don't really know. She was killed in the wolf attack. Her arms were apparently severely deformed, just like Eph's. It must be something genetic, but his doctors have never been able to pinpoint what."

"Why were they in the woods, though?"

"The police think they were probably living there. Goodness knows how the poor woman did that, giving birth out there all by herself. They never were able to identify her."

I frowned and looked down at the steam rising off the surface of my tea. Parnell picked up her cup and took a careful sip.

"I did have a point," she said, setting her cup back down and fixing her gaze on me. "Eph's life hasn't been easy. He's made the best of it, and I'm proud of him."

"Okay . . ."

She smiled and shook her head. "It's hard to be a teenager, even when you're like everyone else. He has no choice but to be different, and it can be hard on him sometimes."

I felt my eyebrows rise in surprise, at which she laughed.

"Yes, we are talking about the same boy, Ari. Things get to him, too. He gets frustrated sometimes. He just doesn't like to show it." She leaned forward a little. "Being your friend helps. I know it does. You're good for each other. You help each other."

I shook my head and reached for the cup in front of me. "My therapist would probably say we're co-dependent."

"I don't know about that. We're all human, Ari. We lean on each other from time to time. That's not a bad thing. What would life be like if we all lived our separate lives, never relying on each other for anything? We wouldn't even have friends, would we? People need each other."

"My mom, the philosopher," Eph's voice said, and I startled so much that my cup sloshed a bit of hot liquid over my fingers. I gritted my teeth against the pain; the tea was obviously still not drinkable.

"My son, the curmudgeon," Parnell said, challenging him with a raised eyebrow.

"Curmudgeon?" He slid onto the stool on my other side and frowned at the teapot.

"I don't know. What's the opposite of a philosopher?"

He laughed, his face suddenly brightening. "I don't know. But I'm pretty sure it's not a curmudgeon." Nudging my leg with his toe, he drew my attention his way. He was about to say something else when he saw my face. "What's wrong?"

"Same thing as the last time you asked. Do I look that bad?"

"Do you want to try the breathing thing?"

I shook my head.

"Are you sure? It usually helps."

Swivelling in my seat so I could look at him, I frowned. "What happens later?"

"Later?" he echoed, looking utterly confused.

"Yeah. After we graduate. Are you going to come running every time I have a panic attack?"

He glanced at his mom. Parnell quietly took her teacup and walked out of the kitchen. "We haven't graduated yet, Ari."

"But when we do. What happens then?"

"Are you planning on going to school in Nepal or something?"

"No."

"Then why do you think we won't be close to each other?"

I shrugged. His toes played with the rung on my stool.

"Is this about earlier?"

"Huh?"

"When I told you I wasn't going to date or get married or anything."

My hands shook as I reached for my cup and carefully brought it to my lips.

"I'm not going to be caught up in a relationship," he said. "So there's no reason I wouldn't still be friends with you." His big toe tapped the rung. "Actually, I should probably be the worried one. You might get married and move away and I'd never see you except over video chats at Christm— Hey!" He slid off his stool a moment after I did and bounded after me. "Ari, wait."

"Your plan is stupid," I whispered, whirling to face him. His eyes were wide, and he stared at me in bewilderment. "Maybe I don't want to get married and only see you on holidays."

"So don't do that."

"That's what happens when people grow up. They grow apart."

"Not always."

"Why are you doing this to me? Seriously, Eph. You don't think I have enough to worry about without—" My words caught as he practically threw himself forward. Our foreheads knocked together, and he let out a grunt of pained amusement.

"Ow. Sorry."

"If you'd just let me give you a hug . . ."

He shook his head, his forehead still pressed against mine. "This way we're both hugging."

I pulled back and tried to focus on his face. "It doesn't always have to be equal. You're allowed to just receive affection, too."

His teeth nibbled on his lip for a moment. He didn't say anything. Instead, he tilted his head toward the hallway, so I knew he wanted me to follow. I went and grabbed our bags from beside the front door, then fetched my teacup before following him back to his room.

CHAPTER SIX

It's not working. As I move forward in time with my memories, the terrible final one just keeps getting stronger and stronger, dancing around the others and taunting me with its inevitability. I pull my fingers from the keyboard and work them up into my hair as I look out the window. The sun came up without me even noticing. There's still only one car in the driveway. Wherever the Diaz-Pierces went, they're still there.

It occurs to me that I haven't spoken a word in over twenty-four hours. More than that, actually. But who's counting? Who even cares? Eph was one of the only people who ever cared what I had to say. And now he's not here to hear my anguished, silent words. I rock a little against the carpet, keeping my hands on my head.

I'm sorry, Eph. I wish I could take it back. Then maybe you wouldn't have been angry with me when you died. Are you still angry? You should be. I never should've done what I did.

A toilet flushes from somewhere in the house. A few moments later, I hear someone coming down the hallway. Judging by the weight of the footsteps, it's Mom.

"How long have you been out here, honey?"

Don't, Mom. Please. I don't deserve your sympathy.

She sighs and walks into the kitchen. I hear her running water and getting the coffeemaker going. The smell's going to be overpowering in a few minutes. I've never liked it. It's a reminder of how jittery the stuff makes me. Sometimes, I feel like I'm getting a caffeine buzz just from the stink of coffee beans. It's probably all in my head, but still . . .

I turn back to the laptop, check the battery (I'm still good), and bend over the keyboard.

New Year and New Problems

The Christmas I was seventeen, Mom got me a new smartphone. My old one was acting up and crashing when all I wanted to do was send a simple text. Mom didn't point out that the only person I ever called was Eph, and I didn't really *need* a fancy phone (especially since Eph mainly used the voice feature; as agile as his toes were, they weren't designed for texting).

On New Year's Eve, we sat on the floor in his living room, curtains wide so we could see the neighbours inevitably spill onto the street at midnight. His parents were at a party, and Asher was out, catching up with friends that he hadn't seen since the summer. We'd been playing video games, but after

Eph had beaten me one too many times, I'd pulled out my phone and started fiddling with it. He didn't notice I'd stopped playing until my character died in a gory display of blood spatter. Probably because it was just standing there like a dope.

"Porn?" Eph asked, causing me to whip my head in his direction. I returned his grin with a dirty look and went back to swiping at the screen.

"Yeah, right. I'm just seeing what features it has."

He paused the game and set the controller aside, then edged closer on his knees so he could peer at the screen with me. "Nice. Wish I could use one that small."

"Wish Mom could've afforded something bigger. Not that I'm complaining," I said quickly. "This is a lot better than the old one."

Snuggling up against me so I could feel his warmth, he crossed his ankles and let out a long sigh as he leaned his head against mine. "Can you imagine if I'd ended up in some place *without* technology?"

"Like where?"

"I don't know. I'm just saying. If I'd been born a hundred years ago . . ."

"You'd probably be dead. Do you think doctors from a hundred years ago would've been able to save a baby who'd been attacked by wolves?"

"Eh. Probably not."

"Definitely not. If the surgery hadn't killed you, the infection would have."

He wiggled his toes. "Good thing I chose to be born in this time period, then."

I pulled my head back, which forced him to do the same. "Chose?"

"Why not? Who else would choose?"

"Um . . . God? I thought you guys were Catholic."

"Barely. Dad is. Well, was."

"Then what's with *that?*" I asked, pointing at the elaborate cross that had hung on the wall behind the front door for as long as I'd known the Diaz-Pierces.

"Family heirloom. Mom's big on that kind of stuff. She'll hang on to anything like that, as long as it's been passed down from somebody's great-great-grandparents."

I turned off my phone and slipped it into my pocket. "But you believe in angels, don't you?"

"Not religiously." He frowned, then shook his head. "I mean . . . not in a religious way."

"Do you still think you are one?"

He just stared at me for a moment. I wasn't sure if I'd said something wrong or maybe insulted him. But then a slow smile worked its way across his features.

"Don't laugh at me."

"I'm not," he said, though I could tell he was dangerously close to a chuckle. "I'm no angel, Ari. I'm just a guy who was born with really messed-up arms. That hardly makes me an angel."

It's more than that, though, I thought, thinking about his near-supernatural intuition and his ability to make people feel safe and loved. *But maybe that's all angels are. Special humans who are so full of love and compassion that it just sort of spills over to everyone in their vicinity.*

"What time is it?" he suddenly asked, drawing me back to the cozy living room and the warmth of his body pressed against my side.

"Check it yourself."

"Then I'd have to walk across the room. You've got your phone in your pocket." He leaned closer and rested his chin on my shoulder. "Please?" Out of the corner of my eye, I could see him batting his eyelashes. I rolled my eyes and dug my phone out.

"Eleven fifty-four."

He pulled back. "Already?"

"Yeah. We've been playing *Leavenghost* for hours. There's a great use of time."

"I taught you how to slay the elven midwife and steal her herb pouch, didn't I?"

"That's messed up."

He laughed. "I know. Ash bought the game, not me." He stood up and strode over to the window.

"Is anyone out there yet?"

He shrugged. "Not that I can see. It's cold. They probably don't want to be out there longer than necessary."

"It's not necessary, period," I said, sticking my phone back in my pocket and standing up. After sitting for so long, my butt felt a bit cramped. I walked a few steps in place, then stretched my arms above my head as I wandered over to join him at the window. He'd grown a little over the past couple of years, but he still wasn't much taller than me . . . unlike Asher, who looked like he could've taken on an entire opposing football team on his own. Neither Javier nor Parnell were particularly big, but I'd seen photos of the boys' uncle Gaspar. He was huge.

Eph suddenly turned to me. "We should go somewhere."

I laughed. "Right."

"Yeah. I guess it's a bit late for that. Next year, then."

"Where?"

"Somewhere we can see the fireworks."

I shook my head. "I hate fireworks."

"Only when you can't see them," he annoyingly pointed out. As if to prove his words, a firework screamed and popped somewhere out of view, and I flinched. "Kind of early, dumbasses," he muttered. Without a word, he stepped behind me and pressed his back against mine. I closed my eyes and took in a deep breath in time with his. I could feel my heart hammering, and my body was braced for the next pop of sound. But with Eph's warmth against my back, I felt safe.

We stood like that for what felt like forever, but was probably only a few minutes. I was afraid we might've missed midnight, but when I pulled out my phone to try to discreetly check, I saw that it was only eleven fifty-eight.

"Happy New Year?" he asked.

"Not quite."

"How long?"

"Two minutes. No," I amended, watching the clock. "One."

He pulled away and stepped back into view, just as some people out on the street started banging on pots and pans and shouting at the top of their lungs. "I think they're drunk," he said.

"Their clocks are, in any case." I watched my phone screen carefully, holding it up where we could both see it. When the numbers finally clicked over to midnight, dragging the day, month, and year with them, I looked up at Eph. He smiled and leaned forward, pressing his forehead against mine.

"Happy New Year," he said softly. "For real this time." He tilted his head slightly so that our noses touched. My heart pounded as I adjusted my stance and planted a quick kiss on his mouth. He let out a little grunt of amusement.

And then I did the stupidest thing I've ever done in my entire life. I tilted my head and went in for another kiss. A long, deep one like I'd seen in the movies. Before I could even decide whether I liked it or not, though, Eph pulled back, his eyes so wide that I wondered if my lips had actually hurt him.

"What are you doing, Ari?"

My mouth hung open, locked in an expression that felt like surprised dismay. I wanted to laugh and tell him that I hadn't meant it. But how could I?

He pressed his lips together and turned away.

"Why didn't you stop me?" I managed to get out. He looked back at me in disbelief.

"Excuse me?"

"If you didn't want me to kiss you, why didn't you—"

"So it's *my* fault? Wow, Ari. Go look up consent on that fancy phone of yours."

"No. That's not . . . That's not what I meant!"

"Then what did you mean?"

My mouth was trembling. My whole body was. Instinctively, I knew that I'd crossed a line, and there was no going back. I felt everything start to crash down around me. "I don't know."

"Then how do you know you didn't mean it?"

The sob snuck out before I could stop it. My fingers fumbled as I tried to put my phone back in my pocket, and the device clattered onto the floor. I didn't even bother to check if it was okay as I scooped it up and hurried for the front door. I grabbed my jacket from the hook, stuffed my feet into my boots, and yanked open the door, all while willing him to say something, to tell me it was okay, that he forgave me. But he didn't say anything until I was already outside, pulling the door closed after me.

"Ari?"

I paused, my vision shimmering through unfallen tears. "What?"

"You can't be in love with me, okay?"

I slammed the door and ran across the street, barely even noticing the loud pops of the fireworks less than half a block away. I turned off my phone as soon as I was in my room, just in case he tried to call, and buried myself in my bed.

It was a terrible start to the year.

And it only got worse from there, I think. I realize I'm crying. My cheeks are wet and my nose is leaking snot onto my upper lip. I wipe it with the back of my wrist and sniff hard. All I want to do is take back that kiss. But what's done is done.

And Eph is dead because of it.

CHAPTER SEVEN

I don't want to do this anymore. I don't want to remember him. I thought I did, but I don't. I ruined it all with that kiss. A decade of friendship, down the drain. Even leading up to his last moments, we were arguing about that kiss. That stupid, stupid kiss.

I slam the laptop lid closed and press my palms onto the warm surface. This is going to be the end of me. I can't handle the memories. They're just going to be there, for the rest of my life, taunting me. And maybe I deserve it. No . . . I *definitely* deserve it. Eph's gone because of me, and there's nothing I can do to change that.

Maybe, though, if I write it all down—the rest, the worst, the unthinkable—I can just shove it all into a little box, seal it up tight, and not think about it. That's probably not healthy, but neither is living in an endless loop of trauma, regret, and guilt.

I lift the lid of the laptop once more, relieved to find that my slam didn't do any damage, and start to type. For the last time.

Snowflakes and Flames

The Saturday before we were supposed to go back to school after the winter break, I lay curled on my side on my bed, watching a movie on my phone. I was tapped into the house's Wi-Fi, so I didn't have to worry about Mom getting some ridiculous bill for data charges. But my mind was wandering, and I couldn't focus on the plot. All I wanted to do was check my messages, even though I'd already done that a million times, and always with the same result. I'd see the empty inbox and my throat would get tight. My eyes would start to water. And I'd berate myself once again for the stupid action that had cost me my best friend.

I might've been pretending to be engrossed in the movie, but I was still aware of whatever else was going on in the house. Mom and Grandma were busy cleaning out the freezer, partly to make room for all the baking they'd done over the holidays. Skylar had been in the bathroom for ages, and I was pretty sure she wasn't sick, so she was probably just doing her makeup. She watched videos online of how to do these really elaborate looks, and then practised them in the mirror (usually in the bathroom, much to the chagrin of anyone who needed to pee). She usually looked great when she was done, but I couldn't justify spending that amount of time on myself. I was a lip-gloss-and-mascara kind of girl, and if I couldn't do something with my hair in five minutes, I would just pull it into a ponytail and be done with it.

During a lull in the action, I paused the movie and rolled onto my back to give my aching shoulder some relief. Past my earbuds, I heard voices. Curious, I pulled out a bud and strained to listen.

". . . have to?" Skylar was saying. "Mom, she's—"

"Keep your voice down. She can hear you."

"No, she can't. She's watching a movie."

"Still. It would be a nice gesture. She's been having a hard time since New Year's."

Skylar sighed. I was actually pretty impressed with my own ears. It wasn't always easy to hear things all the way from the kitchen. "She won't even want to come. And what am I supposed to tell people?"

"You said everybody was going," Grandma said. There was a crinkle of plastic, and then a thump.

"Yeah, but I didn't mean everybody and their mentally ill sister."

"Skylar!" Mom's voice got really loud for a moment.

"I'm serious, Mom. She's not on any meds. What if she flips out or something?"

"She's not going to flip out. She's just sad and lonely. Being around people her own age will be good."

"Yeah, right."

I didn't know what kind of look Mom gave my sister, but a moment later I heard heavy footsteps thump grudgingly down the hall. Quickly replacing the earbud, I held the phone up over my head as if I were watching the movie. Skylar appeared in the doorway. I waited, wanting it to look casual. Then I pretended to notice her and pulled out my earbuds.

"What?"

"You want to come with me?" Her voice was clipped. It was totally obvious that she didn't want to ask, which just annoyed me all to hell. I sat up and unplugged the earbuds from my phone, then set them aside on my nightstand.

"Where?"

"Tanner's. He's having an end-of-holiday party."

I wrinkled my nose and shook my head. She sighed.

"I told Mom you wouldn't want to go. But, apparently, you have to."

Raising my eyebrows, I stared at her. "I have to?"

"Apparently."

I didn't commit to anything. After turning off my phone and sliding it into my hoodie pocket, I stood up and stretched. "What kind of party is it?"

"Orgy."

"Skylar."

She threw up her hands. "It's a party, Ari. If you ever bothered to go to one, you'd know."

"If there's loud music, I'm out."

"I can't make any promises. We'll probably have a snowman-building competition or something."

"Seriously?"

She shrugged. "We did it last year. Tanner's parents have a big property. There's lots of room. It kind of turned into a battle-field, though. We had a massive snowball fight."

It actually didn't sound too bad. I didn't know many of Skylar's friends that well, but I knew *of* them, and I knew they weren't bad kids. It was a mixed group consisting of a few jocks, some drama nerds, some regular nerds, and a few kids who seemed to defy categorization. I wasn't going to stand out like a sore thumb or anything. I started to consider it.

"I'm leaving now, so if you don't make up your mind soon . . ."

"Fine," I said, and pretended not to notice her expression fall. "Don't worry. I won't embarrass you."

She snorted and turned to head into her room to grab her jacket and phone.

We barely said two words to each other for most of the drive. It took a while, because Tanner lived on the outskirts of town where all the huge properties were. Some were working farms, but others were just big pieces of land with huge swaths of lawn that would've been a bitch to mow. I checked my phone as Skylar drove, but soon tired of that since there still wasn't anything from Eph. I hadn't tried to contact him, either, but I was still disappointed that he hadn't intuited my distress and tried to reach out.

Then again, he had every right to not want to speak to me.

The road wound around sheer rock faces, the ribbon of asphalt carved into the side of a hill that fell away to a stream below. The snow was starting to melt, causing everything to look a bit dingy, but there was more in the forecast, and I could see the heavy grey clouds in the distance.

"So what happened with Eph?" Skylar asked, startling me in the silence of Mom's car. I just turned and stared at her for a moment before my brain reengaged and I figured out what to say.

"Who says anything—"

"Whatever, Ari. Lie to Mom, but don't lie to me. It's *obvious*. You haven't been over there at all in days, and he hasn't been at our house. So?"

"It's none of your business."

She clenched her jaw and tightened her fingers on the steering wheel. The ride continued in silence.

When we reached Tanner's place and turned down the long driveway, we could already see quite a few cars parked near the house. Skylar found a spot for Mom's and tucked the car in . . . which immediately made me nervous.

"Someone's going to park behind you."

"So?" she said, stuffing the keys into her pocket before checking her makeup in the rearview mirror.

"What if we need to leave in a hurry?"

She turned to me with a warning look. "Don't you *dare* bail after five minutes."

"I didn't say I was going to. I'm just saying, if there's an emergency and we need to leave fast, we won't be able to."

She made a disgusted sort of noise and got out of the car. With a last, worried glance behind us, I followed, walking in her crunching footsteps as she headed toward the side of the house, from which a worrying amount of noise was emanating.

I lasted longer than five minutes. It wasn't that bad, actually, since everyone was out in the open and I could see exactly what was going on. The large backyard was a mess of footprints, and the grass was showing through in a lot of spots. Still, there was enough snow to make some decent snowballs, especially if you scooped from the drifts. The air was full of shrieks and laughter, and I got roped into a group of marauders who were trying to ambush Skylar and a pack of her friends. Most of the kids were a year younger than me, and I didn't really know them. That was just as well; if I didn't know them, chances were that they didn't know me, either.

Tanner seemed to have a real knack for hitting my sister, and it didn't take long for me to realize that he was hitting *on* her. She tossed her red hair from beneath her hat and laughed coyly as he missed on purpose. It was kind of embarrassing to watch. *And she thought you were going to embarrass her,* I thought as she pretended to cower by the edge of the garden shed while Tanner advanced.

Everything was all fun and games until one of the girls took a snowball to the face. Then there seemed to be some silent, unanimous decision to go inside. My heart picked up its pace a little, but I followed the rest of the kids into the house, smiling and pretending like I was still having a good time. I would've preferred to stay outside, even if it had meant getting a face full of snow, but I didn't really have a choice; it wasn't like I could've stayed out there and thrown snowballs at myself. (That would've *really* given me a reputation for being weird.)

We all shucked our boots and shoes in a big pile at the back door and peeled off our jackets and coats, hats and scarves, gloves and mitts. Then everyone thumped downstairs to a massive rec room. There was a foosball table, a pool table, a huge TV with freestanding speakers that were as tall as me, and a little kitchen area with a sink and a full-size fridge. Bowls of snacks were already on the counter.

"Drinks are in the fridge," Tanner said, opening the door to prove his point. It looked like there was nothing *but* drinks in there. "Don't put them down without a coaster on any of the tables or you won't see me at school ever again."

Some of the other kids laughed, and a few headed over there to grab some cans of pop and snag handfuls of popcorn and gummy worms. I was starting to feel kind of hot, although I wasn't sure if it was just from being in a heated basement with about twenty other kids or if my body was about to betray me and flip itself into a panic attack. I hung back until the crowd around the fridge cleared a bit, and then went and grabbed myself something. Luckily, there was ginger ale, which usually helped to calm my stomach a little.

I wandered over to the foosball table with my can and watched the play as I sipped. One of the girls who'd been on my snowball team, Rina, was playing against Kurt, one of Skylar's classmates. The ball bounced and darted all over the field, bandied about by the rows of players. I frowned as my gaze stuck on them for a long moment. The little armless men reminded me just a bit too much of Eph.

A wall of windows spread across one side of the room. I drifted over and looked onto the covered patio. It was empty, which allowed me to have a pretty unobstructed view. The grey clouds on the horizon had grown darker and were a lot closer. But I wasn't worried about thunder. I knew what those clouds held, and it wasn't noise. If anything, it was the opposite.

"Snowing again," someone said, and a few of the others turned to look.

"We're supposed to get like a foot overnight," Kurt said. He spun the handle on his foosball players, and the ball hurtled down the field and into the goal. "Yes!"

"That doesn't count!" Rina cried. "You distracted me."

"You're supposed to pay attention."

"Whatever." She abandoned the game and wandered over to the couch near the TV. Another kid (whose name I didn't know) took her place.

I sipped quietly at my drink and headed back to the little

kitchen to snag some snacks. As I slipped a few kernels of popcorn into my mouth, I heard my sister's voice. I couldn't tell where she was; she wasn't visible, at any rate.

"I'm sorry," she said. "My mom made me bring her."

"No worries. She seems nice."

"She's off her meds."

The guy she was talking to—it might've been Tanner—laughed nervously. "Meds for what? She's not going to pull out a gun and murder us all, is she?"

Skylar laughed. Not nervously. The sound was harsh, like ice crystals being scraped across a driveway. "She'd be too afraid to even hold a gun. It's just anxiety."

Just anxiety? I thought. I'd always known that Skylar didn't really get it. She'd never had to deal with her brain screaming danger signals at her all day.

"That's rough," Tanner said. "My cousin's like that."

"I doubt it."

"Nice, Sky."

"I'm just tired of it, you know? Everybody's always thinking about *her*. And she won't even, like, do anything about it."

"What's she supposed to do?"

"Take her meds. She's always got some sort of excuse. They make her sleepy. They give her diarrhoea. They make her horny."

Tanner snorted. "Really?"

"Yeah, but not in a healthy way. She wants to screw Eph Diaz-Pierce."

"The armless guy?"

"He's like her best friend. Or her emotional support dog." She snickered to herself, as if the thought were just too funny. I felt my fingers tighten on the drink can. "I mean," Skylar said, lowering her voice as if she didn't want anyone else to hear what she was about to say, "what normal person wants to fuck a guy who can't wipe his own ass? Gross."

I carefully placed my can on the counter before I could throw it. Then I walked out of the room. Skylar and Tanner, who were standing just outside the doorway in the downstairs foyer, straightened up a little.

"I'm not feeling right," I said calmly, even though my heart was beating so hard my vision was jumping. "Can you drive me home?"

Skylar rolled her eyes so hard that I was surprised her fake eyelashes stayed put. "I knew this would happen."

"Yeah. You did. And you brought your messed-up sister anyway."

Tanner looked at me warily, then leaned down and murmured in her ear. "It's fine, Sky. Take her home."

"It's not fine. She's always ruining my fun."

I gaped. "When have I ever ruined your fun?"

She didn't have a good answer for that and she knew it. Her cheeks were probably turning red under her layers of makeup.

"And not that it's any of your business," I said, "but he uses a bidet. If you're that worried about shit, Skylar, maybe you should check what's coming out of your mouth."

Her eyes bugged. Tanner cleared his throat and slipped into the rec room, leaving the two of us alone.

"Give me the keys."

"You can't drive," she snapped. "You never got your licence."

"I have my learner's."

"You're not allowed to drive by yourself with that."

"So take me home."

She coughed in disbelief. "I'm not taking you home. What's the matter with you?" With a toss of her hair, she spun on her heel and stormed toward the rec room. "If you want to leave, leave. But you'll have to figure out another way to do it, because I'm not going anywhere."

My eyes prickled with tears. I blinked hard, forcing them back. I could feel my underarms getting really wet, and it wasn't just a delayed reaction from the exertion of the snowball fight. My stomach clenched. I felt a belch rise up ominously. I let it out as quietly as I could and padded to the stairs.

I had to paw through the huge pile of footwear before I found both of my boots. The rest of the house was silent. I wasn't sure where Tanner's parents were, but if they were home, they were being really quiet. I found myself tiptoeing to the front door carrying my outerwear, lest I disturb the peace. When I had everything on, I stepped outside, holding my breath as the opening door let out a soft chime. But nobody came to see who was sneaking out, and I hurried over to Mom's car (which was, in fact, boxed in). On the off chance that Skylar had forgotten to lock the doors, I pried at the handle on the passenger side. But it was locked up tight.

The light snow began to thicken as I pulled out my phone. A few flakes landed on the screen, melting almost immediately as they touched the warm surface. I went to my contacts and dialled Eph's number. And then I waited. It took him a while to answer sometimes. He usually kept his phone on his bookshelf if he was at home, so if he was anywhere else in the house, he'd need to get to his bedroom. I held my breath for a few seconds, then let it out and watched the vapour curl into the air.

"Yeah?" came his voice.

I didn't say anything. What could I say? *I went out with Skylar and now I want to go home and I'm stuck without a ride.* It was my own fault. I never should have gone, and I was paying the price for going against my better judgment.

"Ari? Are you okay?"

"Yes." My voice came out small and pathetic. "Never mind. I'll call—"

"Where are you?"

"Tanner's."

There was a long pause. "Isn't that way over on the other side of town?"

"Yeah. I came with Skylar, but she . . ."

"Are you okay?" he asked again, slowly, his voice a little louder than before. I imagined him leaning close to the phone, his curls dangling over his forehead. "Do you need me to come and get you?"

I nodded, even though he couldn't see it, and started to cry. The tears felt warm on my cool cheeks. I dashed them away with the back of my hand. "No. I can call Grandma or—"

"I'm not doing anything. I'll come." There was a thump, as if he'd momentarily lost his balance and had to put his foot down hard. "What's the address?"

I told him and then let him go. I stuffed my hands in my pockets, one of which was warm from my phone, and wandered down the driveway to wait. I wasn't expecting Eph to arrive for at least twenty minutes, but I didn't want to spend them up near the house where someone might see me and ask what I was doing (or, worse, implore me to go back inside).

I was thoroughly chilled after just a few minutes, so I walked up and down the street along the fence that bordered Tanner's parents' property. There were no other cars on the road, so at least I didn't have to worry about that.

As I paced, I tried to anticipate the conversation Eph and I were going to have to have. He hadn't sounded angry on the phone. Not that he would've shown it, even if he had been. I kicked at a frosty rock, smudging away some of the newly fallen snow, and then continued on, listening to my footsteps in the snow-blanketed silence. The clouds were still grey and heavy, but the snow was falling harder, swirling in eddies of air that seemed to mirror my mind. I pulled my hands out of my pockets for a moment to tug my hood forward over my ears. I was so cold, but going back to the house to wait seemed like admitting defeat. Besides, I knew that getting into and out of the car was a pain in the ass for Eph, and I didn't want to make him regret agreeing to come help me.

Maybe you should just apologize, I thought. *Properly. Tell him you didn't mean it. You were just . . . what? You can't say you were drunk. He knows you weren't. Would he buy that you were high on adrenaline from the fireworks?* With a snort, I turned around and walked back the other way. The road was starting to get a bit slippery. I hoped Eph's car had proper winter tires.

He's going to know you're lying, though. You realize that, right? Maybe just a straight apology is best. You can't really say you didn't mean to kiss him, because you did.

I came to a stop and stared down at the snowflakes collecting on the toes of my boots. The truth was, I didn't know if there was anything I could say to fix the rift I'd torn between us.

My legs felt like they were going to seize up by the time I heard Eph's car coming down the road. I stopped where I was and clenched my fists in my pockets, bouncing on my toes as I waited for the car to come to a stop. When it did, I yanked open the door and practically threw myself into the front seat. The interior was blessedly warm, and I let out a long groan that sounded almost sexual in nature. Eph turned to me with a raised eyebrow.

"That good, eh?"

"Just drive." I buckled my seatbelt, and then held my hands up over the vent to take advantage of the hot air that was blasting into the cabin. He frowned out the front window where the windshield wipers were doing their best to sweep the falling flakes from the glass.

"Is there somewhere to turn around on this road?"

"No idea. Better use the driveway."

Without a word, he smoothly turned the car toward Tanner's house, stopped, and put it in reverse. I noticed he was wearing his purple driving socks, the ones with separate toes and orange grippy bits along the soles. His jacket—a modified down vest—was zipped up, which meant that someone must've been home to help him. He backed the car onto the street, put it in drive, and started back the way he'd come. I watched his foot on the little knob on the steering wheel, my gaze blurring as my thoughts wandered.

"So," he said as we reached the first intersection and slowed to a stop. "You going to tell me what happened?" He used the buttons on his headrest to activate the turn signal before glancing at me.

"Nothing happened."

"Then why aren't you still back there having fun?"

"It wasn't fun. I don't like crowds."

"Then why'd you go?"

"I was forced against my will."

He snorted as he made the turn and pulled out into the flow of traffic. Actually, it wasn't so much a flow as a trickle. The snow was really coming down, and it appeared that most people had the sense not to drive in it.

"Thanks for picking me up," I said, my voice small. Out of the corner of my eye, I saw him glance at me again.

"What are friends for?"

"We're still friends?"

He sighed softly and then checked over his shoulder before signalling and changing lanes. "Always, Ari."

"You're not angry?"

"Sure I am," he said, and my heart sank. "But . . . I get it."

"Get what?"

He didn't elaborate. He didn't say anything else, either, and I didn't know what to do. I pulled out my phone and started fiddling around. It was a few minutes before he spoke again.

"Look, I know you have feelings for me. But you need to think about what you really want."

I let my phone fall to my lap as I turned to him in disbelief. "What does *that* mean?"

"It means that you need to be honest with yourself. What kind of life do you see yourself living? Does it involve marriage? Kids? Travel?"

"You don't want those things?"

He shook his head. "We're talking about what *you* want."

I slumped in my seat. "How should I know if I want all that? Even if I did, I might change my mind."

With a glance at me, he frowned. "Aren't most people pretty sure about those things?"

"Just because you are doesn't mean I am," I snapped.

He sighed. "I'm not sure, Ari. At least . . . I'm not sure about my feelings. I'm pretty sure about what I need to do, though."

"Live alone with a herd of cats?"

He chuckled. "Yeah, right. I'm sure they'd love being petted by my stinky feet."

"Why are you denying yourself a—"

"'Cause I have to. This is my life, and my body, and my challenge to deal with. I'm not going to rope some poor girl into that. She'd end up—"

"Would you love me if you had arms?"

The silence in the car was so complete that it almost hurt my ears. For a moment, I wondered if his hearing aids had suddenly malfunctioned, because he didn't seem to have heard me. But then, his expression darkened and he turned to me in disbelief. "Are you serious?"

"I didn't mean—"

"I *don't* have arms. That's not going to change."

"I know, but—"

"And it's not that I don't love you, Ari. You're my best friend. I love you more than anyone in this world." His toes gripped the knob, letting out a little squeak. Ahead of us, the road was a white blur. It was hard to see more than a few metres in front of the car. "That's *why*," he said. "I love you too much to make you give up all your dreams."

My eyes filled up and threatened to spill over. I looked down at my lap, where my phone had gone to sleep. *Maybe being with you* is *my dream*, I thought. But I didn't say it. I couldn't force my lips to form the words, and my throat felt too tight to get any air out. I curled my fingers around the warm phone and hung on tight as I tried to rein in my emotions.

Eph suddenly let out an uncharacteristic swear and I looked up, just in time to see the taillights coalesce out of the blizzard in front of us. He slammed his foot on the brake, but we were too close. The antilock brakes shuddered the car for a moment, and then we slammed into the stopped car ahead of us with a sickening crunch. The force threw my body forward against the seatbelt, and I heard my phone clatter onto the floor mat.

"Ari! Ari. Are you okay?"

I blinked hard a few times. My heart was pounding and my shoulder felt like someone had wrenched it. But I seemed to be alive and intact. I turned to Eph, who was staring at me with wide eyes.

"Are you okay?" he asked again.

"Yeah." My mouth felt dry. I swallowed and tried to move my tongue. "I think so. Are you?"

He nodded and looked out the front window. "Better see if they are." He put the car—which was still purring away—in park and plucked the keys from the ignition. He managed to get them into a pocket on his cargo pants before he twisted around and freed his other foot from its boot to get at the seat-belt button. But when he went to open his door, it wouldn't budge. "Great. Is your side working?"

I plucked at the latch and leaned against the door. For a moment, I was afraid that it was stuck, too, but then it released with a low pop. Frigid air and a few snowflakes were sucked inside immediately. I flipped up my hood again, then pushed the door wide before climbing out. Eph clambered over both seats to join me on the slippery asphalt.

"Are you sure you're okay?" he asked. "You didn't hit your head or anything?"

"No. Why? Do I look . . . ?" Trailing off, I raised my hand to my forehead. When it came back free of blood, I turned to him with a frown.

"You look white."

"I *am* white."

"Well, you're not usually *that* white," he said, and stepped forward to peer at the point of impact between the two cars. The bumpers were crushed, and red plastic from one of the tail lights was scattered on the ground. I shielded my eyes with my hands (the snow was still blowing) and looked to the front of the other car to see why it had stopped in the middle of the road. As it turned out, it hadn't stopped. It had crashed. Probably at a fairly slow speed, which was lucky; while the front of the car and the side of the pickup truck had both sustained damage, it didn't look too bad. "Sorry about that!" Eph suddenly called, and I turned to see him talking to someone on the other side of our munched bumpers. "Couldn't stop in time."

The guy squinted into the snow, then seemed to understand what he was looking at. "They let you drive like that?"

Eph raised his eyebrows. Snowflakes were catching on his dark curls, making him look kind of ethereal. I edged closer to him, glancing nervously behind the car as I realized that the weather was putting all of us in a dangerous situation. If *we* hadn't seen the fender bender until it was too late . . .

"They let *you* drive like that?" Eph asked, angling his chin toward the first accident. The guy scratched at the back of his neck in what was an obvious embarrassed gesture, then mumbled something that even Eph probably didn't catch.

My fingers were starting to freeze, so I stuck my hands in my pockets. Confrontations made me nervous at the best of times, so I wanted to stay out of it. Still sticking close to Eph's side, I turned and took stock of our surroundings. We'd just started onto the winding part of the road. I could see the rocky hill rising up on one side. The land fell away on the other, but the creek was obscured by the angle and the guardrail. I doubted I would've been able to see it anyway, thanks to all the blowing snow. As if to affirm that assessment, a gust blew up, swirling the flakes around us and sneaking into every crevice between clothes and skin. I shivered violently, but the last thing I wanted to do was get back in the car and be a sitting duck.

"You got your insurance stuff?" the guy asked.

"Yeah. In the car." Eph nodded and stepped around me to get to the door. He sat on the passenger seat and used one foot to open up the glovebox. I stood outside, stepping in place and trying to keep myself from freezing.

The guy disappeared around the far side of his car, but a moment later his head popped back up and he beckoned me with his hand. "Might want to come over here. Already been two vehicles hit from that direction."

"Nothing's going to hit us over there?"

"Unlikely. Lane's blocked, and nothing'll be coming around the corner that fast." He waved his hand over toward the rock face. "Go join them. We'll be over as soon as we get our papers."

I tried to peer over in the direction he'd indicated, though I couldn't see much more than a bit of movement. Turning back to Eph, who was pawing through the glovebox with his toes, I frowned.

"Hurry up."

"I'm trying. Do you see anything that looks like the registration?"

"No."

He shook his head and slammed the glovebox shut. "Ash probably put it under the mat or something." Squirming in the seat, he pried at the corner of the floor mat. I sighed and shivered and took a step back. Just then, I happened to glance to my left. At first, I thought it was just my eyes playing tricks. The snow was still swirling, and I could barely see more than a few feet. But I could see the lights. Two of them. Too far apart and too high to be a simple passenger vehicle. My heart surged.

"Eph."

"What?"

"Eph!" I screamed, just as my suspicion was confirmed.

Abandoning the mat, he jumped up, wearing only one boot. As he spun around to face the source of my terror, the truck emerged out of the blinding blizzard, headlight beams reaching like demonic arms. It was trying to stop, but it couldn't, and I could see the back end sliding out to one side. Eph whirled to face me.

I still don't know what happened. It was so awful that time fragmented and all the pieces of what happened next got thrown into my head at once, slicing my brain like razor-sharp shards. I remember looking into Eph's terrified eyes. I remember the force of the blast that threw me backward, up over the car, sending me tumbling onto the pavement in a pile of flailing limbs. I remember seeing the truck bearing down on him. I remember seeing the truck crash onto its side, pushing a cloud of snow ahead of it like a snowplow. I remember him disappearing from view an instant before the truck—still scraping along the road, its load on its side—slammed into the vehicles. I remember frantic figures helping pull the driver away from the cab, just as flames roared to life. I remember the heat as the fuel tanks caught and exploded, darkening the area with the choking stench of burning oil. I remember someone grabbing me under the arms and dragging me backward, away from the roaring, hellish heat.

My whole body was numb. Even my brain. I stared up at the swirling sky as I lay beside the rock face. Figures stood over me, including the driver of the other car. A plastic sleeve filled with papers was still clutched in his hand. I tried to sit up. But then all I could see was a burning mass, snowflakes silhouetted against the orange flames. I closed my eyes.

Eph? I'm sorry.

Please.

But what was I even pleading for? I had just watched my best friend get obliterated by a fireball. He couldn't come back from that.

Nobody could.

I still can't make sense of it, even as I sit in the middle of my own living room, physically safe but emotionally shredded. The memory of being thrown backward is so strong. It had to be the blast, but the sequence isn't right. Maybe the other driver pulled me—roughly—out of the way. But hadn't I been on the wrong side of the car? Or had I? Maybe I wasn't standing where I thought, and I've just blocked out the part where I went around to the other side.

Shaking my head slowly, I stare out the front window. There's still only one car in the Diaz-Pierces' driveway. Whatever his parents are doing, it's taking a long time.

"Get your jacket," Mom says, her feet pounding up the stairs from Grandma's suite. I glance at her, then turn back to the laptop. Whatever she's doing with Skylar, I don't care about it. I just want to slip back into my memories—the good ones—and be left alone. Scrolling back to the first one, I prepare myself to read. But Mom's feet stop on the carpet right beside me. I quickly lower the lid and stare up at her dully. "Let's go."

I just give her a little shake of my head. Whatever she has planned, it won't be enough to pull me out of the abyss. How could anything ever be enough for that?

"Ari, now." She frowns and looks me over, as if searching for something. "Where's your phone?"

Probably burned to a crisp, I think. I'm really not sure what happened to it. I remember hearing it fall somewhere in the car during the crash. I don't remember picking it up, though.

She sighs. "Parnell's been trying to reach you for hours."

My chin shakes as my voice finally makes its appearance. "Why?" The word comes out in a rasp.

"So you can see Eph."

My vision goes red. Then dark. For a moment, I think I might be having a stroke. But I'm too angry to care. I retch hard, and even though there's nothing in my stomach, Mom still jumps back a little.

"Honey, I think you should. You can't leave—"

"No!" I scream, and stand up so fast that my feet actually leave the floor a little. I'm so incandescently furious that it feels like I might be able to levitate. "She can ID his body herself! I'm not going! I hate her! I hate him!" My words stop as they're overtaken by sobs. I stumble forward and

Mom catches me. She's still trying to hold on to her phone, but she manages to keep us both upright as I sink against her body, clinging to her arm.

"What are you talking about?" she says softly. "Oh, honey, no. That's not what she wants. She—"

"I already saw him die. I don't need to see—"

She pushes me away so suddenly that my breath catches in a hiccup. As she holds my arm and looks me in the eye, her head shakes a little in disbelief. "He's alive, Ari."

For the second time in as many minutes, I feel like I might float away. The room starts to spin.

"Parnell's been trying to reach you for hours," she says.

I blink and look over at the window. "Where are they?" I whisper.

"The hospital."

Pressing my hands over my eyes, I start to cry again. After what I saw . . . I don't think I can go. Whatever's left of him, it can't be much. He might be technically alive, but for how long? He'll be burned, at the very least. How many more limbs has he lost? Is he conscious? Will he even remember me?

"Eph's alive?" Skylar's voice asks. I let my hands fall and see her standing just outside her bedroom.

Mom nods. "He is. Thank god."

Skylar's staring at me. I'm shaking. Hiccuping every time I try to take a deep breath. I can't seem to stop crying. And she looks disgusted.

"I don't want to go," I say, my voice coming out in a plaintive whine like a three-year-old.

"No wonder he won't date you," Skylar mutters before

starting to draw back into her room. Mom whirls on her like a striking snake.

"What did you just say?"

My sister sighs, but carefully. "Mom, it's just the same old drama. Ari's never going to have the life she wants because you let her do whatever the hell she wants when it comes to her anxiety."

Mom's eyebrows rise. "I wasn't aware you'd gotten a medical degree."

"I'm just saying. She *should* be on meds. Without them, she's a whiny little baby, and it's embarrassing. She follows Eph around like a dog and then cries about it when he won't date her. But who'd want to?"

Stunned into silence, I don't know what to say. But Mom sure does.

"She's your sister." Her voice is soft. Dangerous.

"Yeah, and I'm tired of being the only normal kid around here." She squares her jaw and lifts it a little as she looks at Mom. "Look, I'm glad Eph's alive. But I'm not glad things are just going to go back to the way they were, with Ari pining over him and trying to lick his boots. It's *weird.*"

"Why is it weird?" Mom demands.

Skylar's cheeks go a little pink. "Because. It just is."

Mom takes a step closer to her. "I know you've always been uneasy around Eph. That's my fault. I should've talked to you about him sooner. And I never should've let this go on as long as it has."

"What?"

"There's nothing wrong with him. And I'm tired of you acting like there is. How do you think that makes him feel?"

"Honestly, Mom? I don't think he cares."

Actually, Skylar's probably right. But that's not the answer Mom wants to hear.

"Well, I care. It breaks my heart when I see my own daughter treating someone with less respect because of something he has zero control over. He's a great kid. Do you know how many parents would dream of their kids' friends being like him?"

Skylar makes a disgusted noise. "Why don't you just adopt him, then? You can have *two* disabled kids and just forget about the normal one!" She turns on her heel, stomps into her room, and slams the door. The sound makes me jump. But then I bend down and swipe the laptop off the floor and hurry for my room.

"Ari—" Mom begins, but I shake my head.

"Deal with Skylar."

"One problem at a time. Eph needs you."

"He won't even know I'm there."

"Of course he will. He's been asking for you."

I stop and turn around. My heart feels like a balloon that refuses to be submerged in water. I try to cough away the odd sensation as I stare at my mother in disbelief.

"For hours, apparently," she says. "Why do you think Parnell's been trying so hard to reach you?"

My head starts shaking on its own. I turn around and walk into my room, then set the laptop on my dresser. Mom appears at the door a moment later.

"What's wrong?" she asks, her voice soft.

My voice seems to have left me again, so I can't tell her about my awful suspicion. I just get my jacket, edge past her, and head for the front door.

CHAPTER EIGHT

It's just a dream, I think, watching the greyish scenery speed past as Mom drives me to the hospital. *This part is just a dream. Maybe, if you're lucky, it'll last long enough for you to see him one last time. Even if he is burned and mangled.*

Mom's been really quiet. I don't know if she's thinking about Eph or about the accident that could've killed me or about her other kid who's apparently some sort of ableist. It's always been obvious—from the very moment Skylar met Eph—that she didn't like him. I think it was fear at first. I mean, she was only six, and it's not every day that a six-year-old sees someone without any arms. But she never outgrew her prejudice, either. And now she's turning it against me.

The hospital parking lot is crowded, even though it costs money to park there, and it takes Mom a few minutes to find a spot. By the time we walk all the way to the building, my whole body feels chilled from the cold, damp air. My nose is so numb that I don't really register the hospital smell until we're already in the elevator.

Parnell greets us in the hallway with a tired smile. She looks like she's been crying, and I can't tell if that's a good thing or a bad thing. Javier is nowhere to be seen.

"I'm so glad he's all right," Mom says, enveloping our neighbour in an embrace. I hang back, hugging myself, as I peer down the hallway. I can see nurses and orderlies walking around, but I don't know if they're coming and going from Eph's room or not.

"So am I," Parnell says as she pulls away and turns to me. "Are you all right?"

I nod, my eyes wide.

"Eph's been so worried. He didn't know what happened to you, and he's been asking me to call you every five minutes."

"I lost my phone," I say, shifting my gaze down the hallway once more. Parnell steps forward and sweeps her arm around me, guiding me toward one of the nearby doorways.

"That's what I thought might've happened. But he wouldn't let it go." She steers me into the room, which is fairly bright. There are two beds; only one of them is occupied. I feel my chin wobble and I close my eyes.

"Ari," Eph's voice says.

See? It's a dream. This can't be real. I take a deep breath. *Just go with it.*

As I open my eyes again, I take a step forward. Javier moves away from the other side of the bed to join our moms. Eph stares up at me, his green eyes bright.

"I'm glad to see you in one piece," Mom says. Eph's gaze

shifts a little, and he gives her a bit of a smile. But it's not one of his regular smiles, those special ones that make you feel like everything's going to be okay. His eyes move again, and I hear a shuffle of footsteps behind me.

"We'll take Rose down to the cafeteria to give you two a few minutes," Parnell says, somewhat loudly, considering the hospital setting. "Okay?"

Eph nods, and as soon as the footsteps fade away, he looks at me. I take a moment to make a careful examination of the scene before me, searching for any hint that this is all a dream. He's tucked up to the chest with a blue blanket, which almost matches the hospital gown that's hanging loosely from his shoulders. His hair looks strange, as if his curls have been wet down and slicked back. A small bruise darkens the left side of his chin, and there's a fine red scratch that cuts under his right eye, but I don't see any evidence of burns. Which makes no sense at all.

Suddenly, without warning, his mouth crumples. I've never seen him cry, and I have an awful feeling that I'm about to.

"God, Ari, I need a hug."

With a nod, I step forward and sit down on the edge of the bed. I'm just about to lean forward when he shakes his head.

"No. With your arms. Please."

I frown and am about to protest when I see the tears in his eyes spill over. Slipping my arms around his shoulders, I gather him close. I've never hugged him like this before, and it feels weird. Good, but weird. Not least because he's shaking. He turns his head and lets out a sob as he presses his nose against my hair.

"It's okay," I whisper. "You're all right." I release my grip

128

and start to sit back, but he shakes his head again. There's snot running down his lip, and though he tries to sniff it back up, that doesn't work. He resorts to trying to lick it away. I dig my emergency tissue—crumpled but unused—out of my jacket pocket and swipe it across his lip. He doesn't say anything about that.

"I've never been so scared in my life," he says. "Please . . . hold on."

"Hold on?"

"Hold me."

Something is really wrong. Or maybe my brain is just making this dream extra strange. I wipe his lip again, then give him another hug. He sort of melts against me, and I can still feel him shaking. I've never had my front pressed against his; it's always been our backs. I can feel his heart beating even better in this position.

When I try to pull away again, his tears resume. I swipe at his cheeks with the tissue until he fixes me with an intense stare.

"I need you to hold on to me, Ari. Please."

"I can't do that all day."

"What?" He angles one ear toward me, and I realize he's not wearing his hearing aids. "Say it again."

"I can't hold on to you all day," I say a little more loudly. He turns back to me, eyes wide.

"Please," he whispers. And the fear I can see in his expression is so intense that I feel afraid myself. So I kick off my shoes, drape my jacket over a nearby chair, and snuggle onto the narrow bed beside him, hooking him with my right arm. I keep it tight around his waist, not sure if I'm messing up some sort of medical equipment, but I figure that, if I am, someone will come and tell me.

A part of me loves lying with him like this. He's always been adamant that he didn't want to be hugged in a way that he couldn't reciprocate. But something's changed.

He turns his head toward me and, even though we're too close to really focus on each other, I can tell he's looking at me, almost as if he's trying to reassure himself that I'm still here.

"Okay?" I ask.

"What?"

I pull myself as close as I can get, making sure I keep my arm around his waist. He lets out a sigh that tickles my nose. Under my touch, I can feel his muscles start to relax.

"Stay like that, Ari. Just like that. Hold me." He takes in an unsteady breath. "Hold me here."

"Where would you go?" I ask. I know he's heard me when he starts to cry again. I slide my other arm around him and cradle his body as he continues to sob. I don't know what else I can do. I don't know exactly what he needs.

But maybe this is it.

I'm so warm and comfortable that I actually fall asleep. When I wake up, only to find myself curled around Eph's still-sleeping body, I'm somewhat surprised. If this is a dream, it's a lot longer, more elaborate, and more sequentially logical than any I've ever had. Even the accident is more jumbled, and I know that that actually happened.

The arm that's under Eph is asleep. I can't feel my fingers

at all. But I don't want to try pulling my arm out. That will probably just wake him.

"Ari?" a soft voice says. I lift my head and see Parnell sitting in a chair on the far side of the bed. It's pretty dim in here, probably to let Eph sleep. And he's really going at it. His deep, slow breaths are steady under my arm that's draped across his body.

"What time is it?" I whisper.

"Almost five. In the afternoon," she clarifies. Her voice is louder than mine and seems jarring in the silence of the room. But Eph sleeps on.

I put my head back down beside his, far enough away that I can drink in the sight of him. I can't see the bruise on his chin from this angle, but I can sort of see the scratch on his cheek. It seems unbelievable that he escaped that incident with just those two tiny blemishes. "I thought this was a dream," I whisper. "I didn't think he could've survived that."

"The kid has horseshoes in his pants." She leans forward so she can brush an errant curl off his forehead. He doesn't even stir.

"What happened?" I ask. It's the question that's been haunting me for the last two days. It's changed now, of course; I'm not asking how he could have died . . . but where the heck he's been.

"Nobody knows," Parnell says, drawing her hand away and settling back in her chair. "And he doesn't remember."

"How'd he end up here?"

"He stumbled back onto the road yesterday afternoon, completely naked. About a kilometre away from the accident scene."

I frown and lift my head, careful not to jostle him too much with the movement. "Naked?"

"Even down to his hearing aids." She pats her purse. "Remind me when he wakes up. I brought his old ones."

"Why would he take off his clothes?"

"I don't know. Neither does he. Our best guess is that he was knocked down the embankment by the truck and ended up in the stream. Maybe he took his clothes off because they were wet."

I look at the sleeping boy in my arms. It seems like there's got to be something else going on here. *That's just your anxiety talking*, I think. *He's alive. Just be grateful for that.*

"I'm so glad he's all right," I whisper. Parnell doesn't say anything. When I look over at her, she's frowning. My heart starts to beat a little harder. "Isn't he?"

She nods, then looks down toward the foot of the bed. "We'll know soon enough."

I can't help it. My body sits up as I start to panic, and Eph grunts as my movement jolts him awake. He blinks at me just as I'm pulling my deadened arm out from underneath him. I manage to bend and flex my fingers, but I still can't feel them. I wave my hand to try to speed up the process, feeling like I might scream.

"Ari?" Eph says. "What?" He looks over at his mom, who's still staring at his feet. With another grunt, he sits up a little. "Relax," he says, leaning forward to try to engage me in one of his hugs.

"What's wrong?" I cry. *I just got you back!* my mind wails. *I can't lose you again.*

"Nothing." He gives up trying to touch my forehead with

his and lets himself flop back on the bed. His eyes study me from under a concerned frown.

"It might be something," Parnell says. "We don't know yet."

Eph sighs and turns to her. "What was that?"

She quickly fishes the hearing aids—his old blue ones—out of her purse and stands up. "Javier put fresh batteries in. Can't have you—"

"What?"

She takes his chin gently and forces him to look at her. "Are you going to let me put them in, or are you going to give me a hard time?"

He sighs again and turns his head so she can put the first one in place. "These things suck. Everything sounds like it's in a tin can."

"Well, unless you can remember where your current ones are . . ." She slips the other one into place and stands back. "How's that?"

"Your voice sounds like a robot."

"At least you can hear it."

He turns to me and tilts his chin a little. "Can I have another hug?"

My arm is just starting to get the feeling back. And it's prickling like hell. But I'm scared and I can see that he still is, too. So I lie down against his side and put one arm around his body again. He lets out what sounds like a breath of relief.

"What does it mean?" I ask, my voice tiny.

"What does what mean?"

"'It might be something.'"

Parnell shakes her head. "We'll deal with that if it happens."

"If what happens?"

"If I lose my toes," Eph says. His voice sounds almost conversational, but I can feel the tension in his words.

"Why would you lose your toes?"

"He was walking in the snow," Parnell says before Eph can say anything. "We don't know for how long. There's frostbite, but the doctors aren't sure how much damage there is yet."

I pull back a little and look at Eph. He gives me a tiny smile that looks anything but happy. That brave face is just for show.

Nobody needs to say anything else. I already understand the implications. If he loses his toes, he loses his independence. All the things that most of us take for granted, that he found workarounds for, could be gone: getting dressed, playing video games, typing, driving, even eating. And for someone who values his ability to do things for himself, a blow like that would be devastating. I study his face carefully, wondering what's going on behind those green eyes. His expression is guarded, but not from me. I have a feeling he wants to say something . . . just not when his mom's in the room.

"Where's my mom?" I ask, looking over at Parnell. She glances toward the door.

"She'll be back. After you fell asleep, she didn't want to wake you. She said you haven't slept since the accident."

"I slept a little. Not very well, though."

"I don't think any of us have. Except maybe this one." She smiles at her son, then shakes her head. "Rose also said that you haven't eaten, Ari. Do you want anything from the cafeteria? I should go see if I can find Javier."

"How'd you manage to lose Dad?" Eph asks.

Parnell shrugs as she stands and picks up her purse. "You know your father and hospital jelly."

Eph glances at me. "You want anything?"

My stomach still feels like it's doing somersaults, so I just shrug. He turns back to his mom.

"Pudding?"

"I'll see what they have." With a smile, she leaves us alone in the room. I turn back to Eph, but before I can say anything, his expression falls and his eyes well up. Without even thinking, I pull him closer and hold him tight.

"Thank you," he whispers.

"When you get tired of it, let me know."

"Never." He shakes his head and leans it against mine. "I need you to hold me here, Ari."

"Where? The hospital?"

"No. Just . . . here."

I close my eyes as I tighten my grip. "You're scaring me." My voice comes out in a whimper.

"I'm sorry."

"No, I'm sorry. This is all my fault. I shouldn't have kissed you like that."

"I forgive you."

"But you almost died because of it!"

He sniffs hard. I have a feeling his nose is running again. "No, I didn't."

"Yes, you did! If I hadn't kissed you, we probably would've been hanging out together, and I wouldn't have gone to that stupid party, and you wouldn't have had to come and get me at—"

"Stop. That's not what I meant."

I frown and loosen my grip a little. "What did you mean?"

"I mean . . . It wasn't your fault. And I didn't almost die. At least, I don't think I did. I *thought* I did, but . . ." He breaks off and lets out a sound that's half sigh and half sob. "I was so scared," he whispers. "I thought . . ."

"What?"

He shakes his head slowly. "Ari, I lied."

"About what?"

"Not remembering."

Keeping my arm across him, I lift my head so I can see his face. "What? Why?"

"Because the doctors will think I'm crazy if I tell them. And then they'll send a psychiatrist in here." He lifts his head and then lets it fall back heavily so he can stare at the ceiling. "Maybe they should. Maybe I am crazy."

"No crazier than me."

"You're not crazy, Ari," he says, so quickly that it seems like a reflex.

"Skylar would beg to differ."

"Yeah, well, Skylar doesn't get it. Anxious isn't crazy. If anything, it's the opposite."

I shake my head and pull myself against him. "You know *that's* a crazy thing to say, right?"

He's silent for a few moments. I just listen to him breathe, feeling the warmth of his body so close. We've never been shy about getting right up next to each other, but this is more physical contact than we've ever had. "Ari," he says at last, "if I tell you what really happened, do you promise not to tell anyone else?"

"What am I supposed to tell them, then?"

"That I don't remember. That's the official story, okay? And . . . it might be true."

"You're not making a lot of sense right now. You know that, right?"

He sighs. "Yeah. I know. But . . . I need you to promise."

I nod and lean my head against his. "Of course."

It's quiet as we lie here. As quiet as a hospital gets, anyway. The door is open, but I doubt anyone would be able to hear us, especially with our voices as low as they are.

"Are you all right?" he suddenly whispers. My fingers tighten a little on his hospital gown.

"Physically? Yeah."

"Mentally?"

"We'll see."

He sighs. "I keep seeing your face, right before the truck hit. All I could think about was how helpless I felt. I just wanted to grab you and throw you out of the way." After a deep breath, he goes on in a whisper. "For a moment, I actually felt them."

"What?"

"My arms."

I frown. "You've never felt them before?"

"Not that I remember. Mom says I used to complain about my arms prickling when I was little. Must've been some sort of phantom-limb thing. But I obviously haven't felt that in years, because this sensation was totally new. And weird." He shakes his head slowly on the pillow. "It wasn't like I had hands or anything, either. It was just like . . . I don't know. There was *something* where my arms should've been. And there was this urge to reach out with it and get you out of the way."

I blink and chew on my lip for a moment, remembering the sensation of flying over the damaged vehicles into the empty lane on the other side of the road. But before I can puzzle over any of that, he takes another deep breath.

"Then I was surrounded by white, and I couldn't see you anymore. I couldn't see anything. And then I was just falling. Everything was gone, and—"

"Gone?"

"Yeah. The snow was gone, and I was stumbling down the side of the hill. I lost my balance about halfway down and kind of rolled the rest of the way. I landed in the creek."

"Is that why you took your clothes off?"

He shakes his head. "I didn't take *anything* off. Everything I was wearing was just gone. I realized that as soon as I stood up and I could barely hear. I couldn't hear anything from the road, but when I looked back up the hill, I couldn't see anything, either. There wasn't anything to see."

"You didn't see the fire?"

"What fire?"

"From the truck. When it exploded."

"It *exploded?*"

"Kind of."

He lets out a reverent breath and shakes his head. "And you thought I was caught in it, didn't you?"

I don't answer with words. I simply snuggle closer.

"I'm sorry," he whispers.

"Don't be sorry. It wasn't your fault."

He sighs. "I don't know if it's anyone's fault. Something *weird* happened."

"Weird like what?"

"Like . . . I wasn't here anymore. In our world."

My heart's pounding a little faster than is comfortable. Despite the fact that a lot of Eph's story doesn't make a ton of sense, I feel like there's some sort of truth to it. At least . . . it's what he believes is the truth. "Then where were you?"

"I don't know. At first, I thought I must've been dead. That place where I was . . . It was like our world, but not quite. It was a bit warmer. There was no snow on the ground. There was no road cut into the side of the hill. It's like I was out in the middle of nowhere." He turns his head toward me and rests his forehead against mine for a moment, as if to give himself more strength to continue. "But I was naked, covered in scratches from that roll down the hill, and I still didn't have arms. I always thought that, when I died, I would get them back. Even if they were deformed. But . . . I wasn't any different. I was cold and scared and I just wanted you to be there, but I thought you must've been dead, too, and you'd ended up . . . somewhere else."

"Somewhere else?"

"Heaven." His voice hitches on the second syllable.

"You thought you were in hell?" I whisper. His chest shudders and I know he's trying so hard not to cry again. "You're the last person who'd ever end up in hell, Eph."

"I didn't know," he says miserably. "And I'd just broken your heart, so I thought . . ."

My throat tightens. I wish I could tell him he's wrong. But he's not. He did sort of break it.

"I screamed," he goes on. "I just wanted you to answer me. But there was no answer."

"So what did you do?"

"Started walking. The hill's so steep there that I knew I wouldn't be able to climb it. So I wanted to get down to the little bridge. You know the one just before the parkway?"

I nod, so he goes on.

"Seemed to take forever, and I was freaking out the whole time because I couldn't hear anything."

"You didn't have your hearing aids."

"I know. But I still would've heard car horns or big trucks or something. But there was nothing." He takes in a shuddering breath. "And when I got to the bridge . . . there was no bridge."

"How do you know you were in the right place?"

"The bend in the creek is the same. There should've been a bridge. There should've been a road and a visitor centre. But . . . there was nothing." He shakes his head slowly, looking up at the ceiling. "It was almost dark by that point. By then, I was shivering so bad I thought I was going to pull all the muscles in my body. I figured that was just one of the torments of hell. It wasn't like I could *die* from it, so I tried to ignore the pain."

"And then what?"

"I kept walking. Following the creek. It got so dark. I mean . . . dark like you've never seen. Our sky always gets the glow from the lights on the ground, but wherever I was, it was like there was no electricity." He sighs, the sound almost wistful. "You should've seen the stars, Ari. I've seen pictures of that kind of thing, but never in person. It was so beautiful."

"Are you sure it was hell, then?"

"It was, in a way. You weren't there. And I was terrified, wondering if you were okay or not." His body shivers, as if it's remembering the . . . I don't even know if I can call it an experience. He's obviously had some sort of really lucid dream.

"What happened next?" I ask, hoping he'll continue with his story. I'm kind of curious as to how it's going to end.

"I walked until it felt like my feet were bleeding. Then I found a dead log and kind of wedged myself in there to wait for morning."

"Weren't you cold?"

"Freezing. All I could think about was that poncho you gave me as a joke for my birthday last year."

"You still have that?"

"It's warm, it doesn't have sleeves, and I can get it on and off by myself. Why would I get rid of it?" The smile I can hear in his voice makes my muscles relax the tiniest bit. "I just imagined that around me. It helped a little. But . . . imagining you helped even more."

"You imagined me?"

"Yeah. You walked out of the woods carrying that poncho, wrapped me up in it, and then held me until the sun came up." He takes a deep breath and lets it out in a sigh. "I know you weren't there. That's what's so weird. Whenever I think I might've just dreamed the whole thing, I remember imagining you there. Can you even do that in a dream?"

"I don't know. You're the one who's interested in that sort of thing."

"Well, I don't remember reading about anything like that. So that really freaked me out, because I was obviously *somewhere* real. Or so I thought . . ." He trails off and doesn't say anything else for so long that I think he's not going to continue.

"You can't just leave it like that," I say.

"What?"

"That's not how you end a story. 'Or so I thought . . .' *Dun, dun, dun!*"

He chuckles softly and turns his head toward mine. "I wish you could've been there with me."

"You wish I'd been with you in hell?"

"No! I just wish you'd been with me. Especially when . . ." He trails off again and I sigh.

"Stop that."

"Sorry. I'm just not sure what to say. I don't want . . . I don't want to scare you."

He doesn't want to scare me, but his words do just that. "Why? What would scare me?"

"I've never been so scared in my life, Ari. I . . ." His body shudders like it's been overtaken by a sudden chill. "When the sun came up, I thought I'd better try to find something to eat. I couldn't, but there was the creek, so I drank and then started back the way I'd come. I figured I needed to at least try to climb that hill. I didn't know what else to do, but going back to where I started was as good a plan as any. So I walked along the edge of the creek. My body was starting to really hurt. My feet, my sides—from shivering—everything. I didn't think I was going to be able to climb there, so I turned around again and headed back to the bend in the creek, thinking I'd try to go along the side of the hill, but . . ."

"But what?" I ask, pulling back a little so I can focus on his face. The look in his eyes is so wrong that I immediately start to shake. "What?"

"I saw them." He blinks slowly and his mouth crumples.

"Don't tell anyone about this, Ari. I was probably hallucinating, but . . ."

"Tell me," I whisper. "Tell me what you saw."

He takes a deep breath and licks at his lip. I notice that there's some snot glistening there. I don't have the tissue anymore, so I grab at the edge of his blanket and use that to wipe the shimmering trails away. "They were flying," he says.

"What were? Birds?"

He shakes his head. "No. I thought so, at first. They were huge, and I thought maybe they were eagles or something. So I stood there, watching them. But then . . ." He swallows hard. "They started to come closer. And then I could see them. I could see what they were."

"What were they?"

"People." His voice cracks. "I know that doesn't make any sense. But they were people. I could see their legs. And their wings. They started flying toward me. So I turned and ran." His body shakes with the effort of trying not to cry.

I hug him a little tighter and lean my chin against his shoulder. "Eph, it was just a dream. Obviously. You spent years telling people about your wings, so maybe your brain—"

"No." He grinds his head into the pillow. "This was too real. It hurt too much to be a dream. I think . . . I don't know." He takes in a long breath and lets it out slowly, shakily. "I ran," he whispers. "Down the creek. *In* the creek. And they followed me."

"How do you know?"

"I just did. I could hear them in my head, telling me to stop. I *know* that sounds ridiculous," he says before I can say a word. "I know, Ari. But that's how it happened. They just kept telling me to stop, and I couldn't. I was too scared to even turn around and look, but I knew they were getting closer and closer. I just kept running until I tripped and went down. I felt this rush of air on my back and I screamed. But . . . nothing happened."

I blink and wait for him to go on.

"I heard something," he says. "I stood up and . . . I was alone. But everything was different. There was snow on the banks. Everything was so cold. I looked up, and I could see the guardrail on the road. I knew it hadn't been there before. I'd looked up that hill so many times, and it had just been empty. But now the guardrail was there and so was the snow. So I climbed the hill."

"The snow. That's what happened to your feet?"

"I wasn't about to stay down there a moment longer. It was already . . . I don't even know what time it was. But I'd been walking for hours. So I climbed the hill. It hurt at first, but then I didn't really feel anything. I got to the top and climbed over the guardrail, and then there weren't even any cars. So I just started down the road, trying to go home. I don't think I made it very far, though. I remember my legs kind of crumpling and then I was just kneeling there on the side of the road. Mom says when I was found, I was curled up in the fetal position. I don't even remember getting brought to the hospital. When I woke up, Mom was all over me and Dad was crying, and it was dark outside." He takes another breath and lets it out quickly, like a punctuation mark for the end of his story.

I don't know what to say.

"It's okay, Ari. I know I've probably lost my marbles. Maybe a chunk of my brain got frozen or something. You don't have to believe—"

"You don't think it was just a dream?"

He chews on his lip for a moment, still staring up at the ceiling. "I don't know. Maybe. I guess the truck could've knocked me down the hill and I just lay there for a full day before climbing back up and passing out on the road. But that brings up a lot of questions."

"Like?"

"Why didn't somebody see me? Why didn't I die from exposure? Why did I take my clothes off? Where did my clothes *go*? I can't deal with my hearing aids at the best of times, so how would I have managed to get them out under those circumstances?" He shakes his head.

I wish I could give him answers. But I know even less about what happened than he does, and I think this is one of those situations where information is really important. So instead of trying to make something up (he'd see right through that, anyway), I readjust my head next to his and hold him close.

"It feels like you're holding me here," he whispers. "Keeping me safe."

"Where would you go?"

"I don't know. Back there. Wherever that was."

My fingers knead into his shoulder as I mull over his words. He takes another shaky breath and then squirms, as if he's trying to sit up a bit. I glance up to see Parnell step through the door, a couple of pudding cups and some plastic spoons clutched in her fingers.

"All they had was vanilla," she says, holding out one of the little plastic cups. I sit up so I can take it. Eph lets out a desperate grunt.

"I'm not going anywhere," I say, taking the offered spoon.

He looks over at his mom with a sigh. "Guess you have to feed me."

"For now." She peels off the plastic top while I get more comfortable sitting on the side of the bed. "Positive thoughts, sweetheart. Don't write off those toes before . . ."

"They're hatched?"

"Dispatched," I say, then freeze as I realize the word actually came out of my mouth. I look at Eph, but his expression is one of sad amusement. "Sorry."

"It's not a sure thing," Parnell says, licking the excess pudding from the lid before dropping it on the rolling table nearby. She settles herself on Eph's other side, perched on the edge of the bed, and takes his chin in her hand. "And even if we're dealing with a worst-case scenario, you're going to be all right. You just might have to let people help you."

He screws up his nose and gives me a suffering sort of look. I turn my attention to my own pudding cup. Now that it's in my hand—and I know Eph is safe—my stomach is really starting to make its desperation known. I busy myself taking off the lid, pretending not to notice as Parnell starts to spoon vanilla pudding into her son's mouth.

CHAPTER NINE

Life goes on, I guess, even when stuff happens and shakes your foundations.

I go back to school, feeling lonelier than ever without my lunch buddy . . . and ride. I have to start waiting around for Skylar, which sucks, because she has a drama club meeting after school twice a week. So I spend a lot of time alone in the library, getting through as much of my homework as possible so I can help Eph with his when I visit him every afternoon. He's still at the hospital, but Javier's going to take a couple weeks off work so he can be at home and help. And Eph's going to need it. The doctors don't want him walking yet.

"If I don't get out of this bed soon," Eph says on a Tuesday afternoon about a week after the incident, "I'm going to scream."

"You never scream," I say, tapping away at his laptop keyboard. Then I pause. "Or was that part of your essay?"

He sighs and throws his head back against the pillow. Despite the fact that his hair hasn't been washed in over a week, it doesn't look much different than it did when he got here. I have to admit, I'm a bit jealous. "Forget the essay. It's not due for another week." He lifts his head so he can look down at his toes. He's been running a fever and complaining he's hot, so the first thing I do as soon as I arrive every day is pull the blanket off his body. "I could *probably* get away with everything but the baby toes," he says, scrunching up his nose as he appraises the ten still-intact digits. They look pretty normal to me, but when I looked up frostbite, I read about all kinds of lovely stuff like nerve damage. Quickly closing the laptop, I shake my head.

"Don't you need them?"

He snorts. "I barely use them. It's not like I play the piano or anything." Squirming a bit, he tries to sit up a little straighter. After a few moments, he gives in and uses his heels for leverage.

"Are you supposed to do that?"

"No. But my ass is asleep. If they have to amputate *that*, I'm screwed."

"That's not even a thing."

"I'd have to get a prosthetic butt."

My mouth twitches at his stupid joke. When I look at him, he's smiling. But it's not the same smile that I remember. Ever since the incident, it's been . . . duller. Like someone used a dimmer switch and dialled it way down.

"Can you go get us some snacks or something?" he asks. I glance over at the rolling table where a couple of empty pudding cups are sitting.

"Are you hungry?"

"You are." He angles his chin toward me. "I can hear your stomach."

"It's just gas."

"Yeah, right. If you're hungry, go eat. I don't mind."

I shake my head. "I don't like eating in front of you."

"So we'll eat together."

Raising my eyebrows, I give him a dubious look. "Really?"

"I think there's popcorn in the vending machine. You could just throw it into my mouth."

With a snort, I stand up and set the laptop on the table, pick up the empty cups, and shake my head. "You'd starve if you were dependent on my aim."

"Good thing I'm not that hungry."

"Are you sure you want popcorn?"

He nods, looking not quite sure at all, but I head out into the hall anyway. After dumping the cups into a recycling bin, I find the vending machine. There might've been popcorn at one point, but I don't see any now; it was probably in that empty spot in the upper right corner. I get a couple of bags of chips instead. Then I make my way back to Eph's room. Before I even make it through the doorway, though, I hear voices. Parnell and Javier usually come after dinner, so I know it's not them. Asher should be at university. It's definitely a male voice I'm hearing. I figure it must be medical staff of some sort, so I hang back for a moment. The voices stop.

"Ari?" Eph says.

"Yeah?"

"You can come in."

As I step into the room, I notice the older man standing

beside the bed. He's not much taller than me, with a slight build like Eph's. His hair is grey, the curls cut fairly short. I don't think he's a doctor, based on the way he's dressed; under his black wool coat, he's wearing a sweater. His gaze follows me with cool indifference as I make my way over to the far side of the bed. The crinkling packages in my hand sound overly loud in the crowded space.

"This really is a private matter," the man says. His voice is soft, and not all that deep, but it commands obedience. I drop the packages on the table as my heart starts to pound.

"No!" Eph says, his voice sounding desperate as he sits up and leans toward me. I realize I've started to edge back toward the door. My feet shuffle to a stop. "Ari stays."

"Ari is not privy to this information." The guy has a really strange accent. I can't place it.

"Ari's privy to *everything*," Eph says, his eyes seeming to flare in defiance. But I can feel his unease, too.

"Do you know him?" I whisper. He gives his head a little shake.

"No," the man says. "We've only just met." He holds his hand out to me. It's covered with a black leather glove, and when I hesitantly take it, I notice the cool temperature, as if he's just come in from outside. "I'm Hezekiah."

"Arianna Warne," I say. "And that's—"

"Ephraim Diaz-Pierce. Yes. I am aware." He pulls his hand away and his gaze slips back and forth between us. "You may not know who I am, Ephraim, but we are well aware of you."

Eph wrinkles his nose. "Who's aware of me?"

The man gives his shoulders a little shrug. "That's a question that requires a long answer. Will we be undisturbed for a few minutes?"

Eph nods, his eyes wide. "Dinner's not for half an hour or so."

"That should be sufficient." Hezekiah walks over to the door—which is almost always open—and closes it softly. Suddenly, I feel like crying. I edge toward the bed, and Eph quickly scoots over to give me room, as if he's just had the exact same thought as me. I'd love to be able to hold his hand, but I have to settle for snuggling up close. Hezekiah's gaze lingers on us for a moment before he turns away and grabs the chair, pulling it closer to the bed. As he sits, he tugs the bottom of his coat out from under him. "How much do you know about your origins?"

I feel Eph flinch against my side. We turn to look at each other, and I can tell he wasn't expecting *that* question.

"Are you him?" he asks. Hezekiah frowns.

"Who?"

"The one who found me. The doctor who saved me from the wolves."

"Ah. No." He leans back in the chair and places his hands on the armrests. "We're aware of the doctor. And you were very lucky that he and his wife were there to find you. But that's not what I meant."

Eph takes a deep breath. "My origins. You mean . . . my mother?"

Hezekiah nods.

"I know she was like me. I mean . . . she had deformed arms like me."

"Deformed." Hezekiah's face twists into a grimace of disgust. "That's a matter of perspective."

"What perspective?"

Hezekiah lifts his chin and stares at Eph, and I notice that his eyes are a soft golden colour. Not the dark brown that I would've expected, given the rest of his complexion. "What if I told you that your limbs were perfectly normal?"

"Then I'd say you have no clue what you're talking about. My parents showed me the original x-rays."

"They did?" I whisper. He nods.

"Yeah. When I was six, I got mad when Ash beat me at some video game and I had a massive meltdown about hating the doctors because they stole my arms. Mom thought it would help if I saw what they'd actually looked like."

"And did it?" Hezekiah asks.

"Only because she told me it looked like I had wings. So I figured I must've been an angel."

Hezekiah's eyebrows rise. "Interesting."

"Yeah. Interesting." Eph sighs. "So are you here to tell me that I *am* an angel, and my mother was, too?"

Hezekiah smiles, but he doesn't say anything. I suck in a little noise that sounds like a hiccup. Eph starts to laugh.

"Great. Someone escaped from the psych ward."

"You're not an angel," Hezekiah says, shaking his head. That little smile is still on his lips, hinting at secrets yet to be revealed. "You're human."

"With deformed arms."

"No."

"Look, I don't know who you are or what—" He suddenly breaks off, staring past Hezekiah's shoulder. I follow his gaze, only to see the two chip packets I just bought hovering inches above the table. "Ari?"

"Yeah," I manage to get out. "I'm seeing it."

"Good. I thought I was having a stroke or something."

The chips fall back to the table with a rustle. I turn and curl myself against Eph, closing my eyes as I grab him around the waist. *I need to leave. I need to get out of here. But Eph needs me. I can't just—*

"We've been watching," Hezekiah says. "From a distance. We were always going to reveal ourselves to you, but the timing had to be right. We hadn't seen any indications that you had discovered your inherent abilities, so we waited."

"Inherent abilities?" Eph asks. His voice is a little shaky. "Meaning what?"

"You watched the snacks rise just now, didn't you?"

"I did that?"

Hezekiah sighs. "No, I did that. You merely tossed your friend across two lanes of traffic in front of multiple witnesses."

My eyes snap open. Still keeping my hand tight on Eph's waist, I crane my neck to stare at Hezekiah. "What?"

"Did that not seem odd to you?"

"I . . . The explosion . . ."

"It wasn't the explosion. It was Ephraim."

Eph grunts. "How do you even know about that?"

"There's a traffic camera in the vicinity. And there are, shall we say, agreements in place when such footage turns up."

"Meaning?"

"Very few people have seen the footage. And those who have are . . . friends."

"What is this?" I ask, carefully rolling onto my back so I

can more easily look at Hezekiah. "You make it sound like there's some sort of worldwide angel network that—"

"Not worldwide. And not angels. We've already covered that."

"Throwing things through the air isn't exactly a human trait," Eph says.

"And yet"—Hezekiah holds up his gloved hands—"here we are."

Eph's quiet for a moment. And then he takes a deep breath. "Are you saying you're like me?"

"Yes."

"Are you my father?"

Hezekiah smiles. "No."

"Do you know who my father is?"

"I'm afraid the only person with that information is dead. We weren't even aware that your mother was pregnant when she was sentenced. That would have been discovered during her surgeries, of course."

"What the fuck?" Eph says in an uncharacteristic burst of crudeness. "Are you going to elaborate?"

"Of course. But, like I said, your question has a long answer."

"So start answering."

Hezekiah looks a little miffed, but I can't really blame Eph for being rude. There've been a lot of hints dropped in the last few minutes. The man lifts his hands from the arm-rests and starts to pluck at the fingertips of his gloves. As soon as they're off, I see why he's wearing them.

"Whoa," Eph whispers. I know he's staring at the obviously artificial hands, just like I am. "How are—"

154

"My limbs were the same as yours," Hezekiah says. "They were removed within days of my arrival." He holds one hand up just above his elbow, indicating, perhaps, where the limbs were cut off.

Eph's shaking his head. "So you've got some fancy android arms?"

"No. These arms—these hands—are as basic as they come. On someone without our abilities they would be merely cosmetic." He slowly wiggles his fingers. "It takes practice, but most learn, if they have the capability."

"Most?" Eph repeats. "How many of you are there?"

"Nine resisters, seventeen liaisons, and fifty-two convicts."

"*Convicts?* Are you kidding me? What is this? Am *I* a convict?" He shakes his head. "What crime did I commit?"

"You," Hezekiah says, "didn't do anything. Your mother, on the other hand, was sentenced to removal."

"For what? And what the hell is 'removal'?"

Hezekiah slips his gloves on and leans back in the chair once more, gripping the armrests. "What does it sound like? How do you think she ended up here?"

I turn my head to look at Eph. He's quiet as he processes everything, and I can practically see the wheels turning. Suddenly, his eyes widen.

"Don't do that!" he shouts. Hezekiah flinches.

"Keep your voice down."

"Then keep your voice out of my head."

"Very well. I see we'll have to do this . . . their way."

"Who's they?"

Hezekiah waves one hand in my direction. Eph tenses.

"Their way is my way," he says fiercely. "I'm one of them."

Hezekiah's eyebrows rise.

"I am. Whatever I was before . . . My parents raised me, so . . ." He throws his head back on the pillow and lets out a frustrated grunt. "Are you telling me that I'm an alien?"

"Perhaps that word comes the closest. You're not from this world. Or perhaps I should say you're not from this version of this world." His fingers drum slowly on the armrests. I watch in amazement. Given what he's just told us, that casual gesture has to be taking a lot of concentration. "As far as we can tell, the two versions were once one. At some point, there was an evolutionary split. Our human origins are the same. But the end results of millennia of natural—or unnatural—selection have diverged into two very different paths. In one, humans have the ability to fly, communicate primarily telepathically, and manipulate matter with their thoughts. In the other, humans are earthbound, communicate primarily orally, and manipulate matter with their hands."

"So you're saying I'm from the flying mind-readers group."

Hezekiah's lips twitch in a smile. "That would be a fair assessment."

"And you are, too."

"Yes."

"And my mother . . ."

"Her name was Aleq'a." The harsh consonant pop sounds like it's coming from the back of his throat. It's definitely not a sound used in the English language. "To some, she was a hero."

"So what was she convicted of?"

156

"You must understand," Hezekiah says, grasping the armrests and pulling himself forward so he can stare intently at us. "Our world—our original home—is different. It's more . . . utilitarian."

"Oh, my god," Eph says. "Are you a bunch of winged Nazis?"

"Nazis? Ah . . . Yes, that may be an apt comparison in this instance. I won't try to justify our laws, Ephraim. I don't agree with all of them."

"Obviously," I mutter, then shrink back when his golden eyes turn toward me. "You must've done something, too, if you're here."

He nods, his expression looking a little surprised . . . and impressed. "Yes, Ari. I'm not considered a model citizen in our home world."

"What did you do?" Eph asks. "And what did my mother do? And how do you even get here from . . . wherever it is?"

"One question at a time," Hezekiah says. He glances at the packets of chips. They're just out of his reach on the table. But only for a moment. The next thing I know, he's got one in his hands and is pulling the plastic open. "My crime is irrelevant," he goes on, examining a potato chip that looks a bit like a hippopotamus. "It has no bearing on your story. Your mother's crime, on the other hand, does." He bites into the chip, sending crumbs onto his lap. He dusts them away with the back of his hand. "She was trafficking resisters."

"What were they resisting?"

Hezekiah shakes his head and pops the rest of the chip into his mouth before holding the bag out to me. When I shrink back, he shrugs and reaches for another chip. "They weren't resisting anything. The word is simply an English approximation of a concept. A resistor is someone through whom our abilities don't run."

"They can't fly?"

"That's the one thing they *can* do. No, I'm talking about the other abilities. Manipulating matter with their minds. Speaking telepathically. A small percentage of the population never develops these abilities."

"Develops?" I say.

"Yes. Nobody is born with these traits. It's a wise design. Can you imagine the havoc that would be created if infants could lift objects with their minds?"

Eph snorts. "Chaos."

"Yes, it would be. The ability to communicate develops early enough, at roughly the same time as our oral abilities. Yes," he says before either of us can ask for clarification, "we have those, too. I wouldn't be able to talk to you, otherwise." He eats another chip and chews thoughtfully. "Now, the telekinesis—as this world calls it—develops later, at around the time of puberty."

"Which is?" Eph asks.

"Roughly the same as it is here. Perhaps a little later." Seeming to have lost interest in the chips, he sets them aside and brushes his gloves together. "Resistors can be identified from a fairly early age, due to their mind silence. From that point on, they're monitored and tracked so that, when they've reached full maturity, they can choose their sentence."

I wasn't sure I wanted to know what the choices were. But I also knew Eph was going to ask anyway.

"And the choices are . . ."

"Euthanasia or removal."

Eph swears. I just stare at Hezekiah.

"As I said, I don't agree with all of our laws. But they play an important role, as I'm sure you can understand, Ephraim."

"I don't even know what they are. How would I understand?"

Hezekiah shakes his head slowly. "You're stuck in that bed right now, aren't you?"

"My toes had frostbite."

"Yes. And you depend on your toes, because you think they're your only means of manipulating matter."

"They are."

"Yes. We'll come back to that." He laces his fingers together and leans forward. "Our people have wings, Ephraim. Not hands. What happens if one of us *can't* use our minds to manipulate matter?"

"You use your feet?"

Hezekiah smiles. "Not quite. Yes, our children sometimes use their feet, but only until their abilities manifest. For adults, though, those abilities are extremely important. How else would we hold our young, build our dwellings, make our clothing, feed ourselves and our children, bathe—"

"Okay, I get it."

"Do you? Our world is different, Ephraim. We're more connected to each other. We must be. There is no stigma when a parent feeds an older child, as there would be here. There is no embarrassment when they bathe them. These are considered sacred duties, and parents treasure those moments. But when a resistor grows up and can't manifest their abilities, they become a drain on our society. They take valuable resources away from others."

"So you kill them?" Eph asks in disbelief. "I have news for you, but here we don't just kill people who can't contribute to society in some arbitrarily agreed-upon way."

Hezekiah's expression darkens a little. "I didn't say I agreed with these ideas, did I? Your mother didn't, either. She wasn't a resistor, but her younger brother was. After he chose euthanasia, she started to get involved in one of the resistor networks. She was caught trying to help a resistor reach a sanctuary in the north. The choices for someone convicted of such a crime are the same as those for resistors."

"Execution or banishment," Eph says darkly.

"Euthanasia or removal," Hezekiah counters. "And the choice is entirely theirs."

"Why did my uncle choose to die?"

"Most resistors do. Without the ability to manipulate matter with their minds, they would be severely disabled by a removal sentence."

"Because 'removal' refers to your limbs, too, doesn't it?"

"Yes."

Eph swears under his breath. "I'm descended from lunatics."

"Tell me, Ephraim. What choice would you have made?"

"I don't know. But I know I would never force anyone to make a choice between dying and having their arms cut off."

"Wings, technically."

"My point stands." Eph shakes his head. "How do you even get here?"

"How does one move between worlds? The same way you did when the truck was about to hit you."

Eph blinks in disbelief. "I . . . don't even know what I did."

Hezekiah nods. "The ability to move between the two worlds at will is rare. Which is why removal is such an effective sentence. Few can come back."

"What happens if they do?"

"They're immediately euthanized. And they know this," Hezekiah goes on, "so don't tell me that it isn't fair."

"What if they do it by accident like I did?"

"Like I said, the ability is rare. Those that have it are often recruited as liaisons. They move between the two worlds, helping to facilitate communication."

Eph laughs. "I think winged people would be a little conspicuous in our world."

"Their wings are, of course, removed," Hezekiah says, which brings Eph's amusement to an abrupt halt. "It's nonnegotiable, and one of the reasons why so many choose euthanasia. When a resistor, liaison, or convict chooses to come here, they're agreeing to the removal of their wings and sterilization."

"*What?*"

"Our genetics are compatible for breeding. Unfortunately, wings seem to be a dominant trait, and all offspring of such unions will have what doctors here consider gross malformations of the arms. To keep our existence hidden, the sterilization policy was introduced."

"But why is it such a secret?" Eph asks. "It's not like people from this world can invade that world and mess it up." He frowns, as if a thought has just occurred to him. "Can they?"

"No." Hezekiah shakes his head. "Aside from liaisons,

everyone else requires a particular stimulant drug to facilitate the process."

"So how did *I* do it?"

"Perhaps you could be a liaison."

"Maybe I don't want any part of this."

Hezekiah smiles. "I'm afraid, Ephraim, that you're already part of this. This is your heritage."

Eph sighs. "I *still* don't have the full picture, do I? What happened to my mother? How did I end up out in the woods to get eaten by wolves?"

"You were hardly eaten by wolves. As for your mother, she escaped custody. All new arrivals are transported directly into a secure facility where they await their surgeries. But your mother, somehow, evaded the guards."

Eph doesn't say anything. When I turn to him, I see the little smile on his lips.

"Yes," Hezekiah says. "I agree. Good for her. But she obviously didn't anticipate the difficulties of living in an unfamiliar environment. She lasted only a year before she was killed by the local fauna, leaving you defenceless and at the mercy of those creatures." He peers at Eph, his golden eyes intense. "By the time we heard about you, you'd already been taken to the hospital. We tried to intervene, but it was too late. The doctors had already completely removed your wings. It was an unnecessary act."

Eph jerks against my side. "What?" he whispers.

"Your childhood anger wasn't misplaced. The bone structure and composition of our wings is somewhat different than, say, Ari's arms. With some tendon repair, your upper limbs most likely could have been saved, and you could have learned to use prosthetics, just like a child amputee from this world might do."

"Yeah, right. If you know so much about me, you'll know I had an infection. Why do you think I lost my hearing?"

Hezekiah raises an eyebrow. "Perhaps you didn't."

"Okay, now I know you're—" He breaks off as Hezekiah angles his head toward us. I'm not sure what I'm supposed to see for a moment, but then I notice the tiny device nestled in the man's ear canal, just as Eph sucks in an astonished breath.

"Your hearing," Hezekiah says, "was perfectly normal. *Is* perfectly normal."

"So why are we both wearing hearing aids?"

"We're living in this world. We have to interact with the . . . indigenous people." He glances at me with a small smile. "Effective communication without telepathy requires two things: a voice and the ability to hear."

"What about sign language?" I ask, then quickly shake my head before Hezekiah can say anything. "Never mind."

"As I'm sure you just realized, Ari, such a method of communication would be next to impossible for resistors." He turns back to Eph. "If I can give you nothing else today, let it be the knowledge that there is nothing wrong with you. In fact, you appear to be an extremely typical example of a teenage boy from our world. Your limbs—"

"Stop," Eph says. His voice sounds so tired. And devastated. When I turn to look at him, he's got his head back and is staring at the ceiling. His eyes are just about to overflow.

"It's—" I start to say, but then I stop. *It's not okay,* I think. *None of this is okay. None of this is right. How much of this is even real? Hezekiah could just be some weirdo from the psych ward, for all we know.*

But then . . . he *did* float those chips, and I've never heard of prosthetic arms that can do what his appear to be able to do.

"I assure you, Ari, that I'm telling the truth. If there's one thing I pride myself on, it's my honesty."

My gaze moves to him and just sort of sticks there. He raises his eyebrows and gives me a small smile.

"Are you reading my mind?" I whisper.

"No. I'm sensing your skepticism. You aren't telepathic. At least, not enough for me to communicate effectively with you. All humans have these abilities. They're simply developed to varying degrees and, in your world, those degrees are very small."

I raise my eyebrows at him. "So I could've thrown myself across the road?"

"It's unlikely. Next to impossible, in fact. Your kind didn't need to be able to manipulate matter with your minds, and so the ability . . . atrophied."

I turn back to Eph. He's still staring at the ceiling. Trying hard not to cry, from the look of it. I can see the tears glistening as they're suspended against his lower eyelids. He takes a deep breath, holds it for a moment, and then opens his mouth.

"So what do you want? Are you here to sterilize me? Take me back to wherever I came from?" He lifts his head. The movement causes the tears to detach and roll down his cheeks. "Do I have to finish paying for my mother's crimes?"

Hezekiah looks taken aback. "Of course not. Even our

system of justice, no matter how cruel it might seem, wouldn't punish an innocent child for his mother's crime." He reaches into his coat pocket and removes a small white card, which he holds out to me. I take it, noticing the simple black text that includes a name and a phone number. "You've fallen through a fairly large loophole, Ephraim. There's nothing I nor any of the rest of us can do. The choices are entirely yours."

"And what choices would those be?"

"You have some decisions to make." He plucks his thumb with the forefinger of the other hand, as if he's counting. "First, what you're going to do about your current situation."

"You mean, if I lose my toes?"

"You're not going to lose your toes. Our bodies are better adapted to the cold. Your doctors' threat of amputation was likely based on an erroneous assumption about your healing capabilities."

Eph sucks in a breath. "What?"

"The choice I was referring to was that of how you manipulate the world around you. As it stands, you have three choices. You can continue with the methods you've been using for your whole life. You can augment that with your telekinetic abilities. Or we can have you fitted for prosthetic arms and you can learn to use them as many of us have."

Eph shakes his head. "Wouldn't it be pretty conspicuous if I suddenly had functioning arms?"

"It would. Which is why that option would require relocation and a total break from your current life."

A snort is all the answer Hezekiah gets.

"There is also the matter of sterilization," Hezekiah goes on. "Normally, that would be done upon arrival. But in your case—"

"You're going to force me?"

"No. There's nothing we can do. At this point, all we can do is strongly recommend it."

"What's so bad about having a kid with unusual arms?" I ask. Hezekiah's gaze slips to me once more. I press the little white card tightly between my thumb and forefinger.

"Nothing. It isn't so much the physical traits of this hypothetical child that concern us now. It's the potential for them to end up in a dangerous situation should they accidentally slip back to their ancestral world, as Ephraim did." He turns to Eph and fixes him with an intense gaze. "Had you been caught, you would have been assumed to be a convict in violation of your sentence, given your lack of documentation. Euthanasia would have followed."

I turn to Eph, only to find he's looking at me, his eyes wide.

"Guess that's a pretty good reason not to have kids," he says, his voice thick with some sort of emotion I can't place.

"There's no need to go that far. You'd be a perfectly capable parent. But it's perhaps best if you don't father your own genetic offspring."

"I wasn't going to, anyway." He digs his heels into the bed and tries to sit up a little straighter. "I don't know what you're seeing when you look at me, but saying I'd be a perfectly capable parent is pretty messed up."

"Is it?"

"Do I look like I can hold a baby?"

"How do you think your mother held you?"

Eph opens his mouth, then closes it again.

"If you wish to develop your abilities, call me. I can put you in touch with someone who'll be able to teach you what you need to know." Grasping the armrests, he stands up. "And I believe it goes without saying that this conversation is to remain between the three of us."

"I can't even tell my parents?"

"Would they believe you?"

Eph wrinkles his nose. "Maybe."

"I'm afraid 'maybe' isn't a good enough answer to take that risk."

"How am I supposed to explain it when I start floating my cutlery into my mouth?"

"I would suggest you don't. If you choose to use your abilities, you must be discreet." He nods his head in a sort of bow and then strides to the door. Eph watches him go in astonishment. I almost wonder if Hezekiah is going to turn back and say something dramatic, because leaving a conversation like that is kind of anticlimactic. But we hear the door open and his footsteps recede, and then it's just me and Eph sitting here in his bed.

"Great," he mutters. I frown and turn to look at him.

"Isn't it?"

"What part of it is great? The fact that I'm some sort of alien freak? Or the part where I can't even use my superpowers unless I lie to everyone and go into some weird-ass witness protection program for angels?"

"He said you're human."

He snorts. "Right."

"You are. Just because you're not from around here—"

"I'm probably from right around here, though, aren't I? Just some other universe that's layered on top of this one. Or something." He sighs and looks down at his toes, then gives them a slow wiggle.

"You *could* learn how to use your abilities."

"At the expense of my friends and family?" He shakes his head.

"You already said you weren't going to date or get married. Who's going to see you throwing meatballs around the kitchen?"

He leans back and turns his head away. "If my mother hadn't screwed up so badly, I . . ."

"What?"

"Maybe I'd be flying around happily."

"In that other world."

"It's my home."

"So go back." I sit up and slide off the bed. Realizing the card is still in my hand, I flick at the edge with my thumb for a moment before setting it down on the table beside the half-eaten bag of chips.

"I can't. You heard what he said. And don't leave that there."

"Why not? You're not interested in his help?"

He sighs. "I don't know what I want."

"Really?"

He shakes his head slowly on the pillow. "I can't have what I really want."

Join the club, I think. But what I say is, "And what's that?"

"The body I was born with."

"Well, that's not possible. So what's plan B?"

His lips are clamped together so tightly they're almost white. I step back toward the bed.

"You want the arms, don't you?"

He closes his eyes. "I can't. I know I can't. That would mean leaving you and Mom and Dad and Ash . . ."

My throat feels tight. "But it's your life, Eph." *Stop!* my mind screams. *Don't make him want that. Don't give him any reason to leave.*

"My life's intertwined with a whole bunch of others. I can't just—"

"Is that what you want?"

"I don't know." His voice is barely a whisper. "I don't know, Ari."

I frown down at him. "I think you do."

He doesn't say anything else. The tightness in my throat surges and I swallow hard, afraid I'm not going to be able to breathe.

"I should go," I say, grabbing my bag and slipping the strap over my shoulder. His eyes pop open.

"But . . . Mom's not here yet."

"She will be soon."

He stares at me for a moment and then sighs. "Yeah. You're right. You don't want to have to watch me get fed like an infant, anyway."

"I've seen you eat."

His shoulders make a tiny shrug. "I'll see you tomorrow?"

"I've got . . . practice."

"Since when?" he asks with a frown.

"Since I told Mom I would." I slip my thumb under my

bag's strap and step toward the door. "We'll work on your essay on Thursday."

"Okay." He doesn't say anything else, so I walk to the open door. "Ari?"

"What?" My boots squeak to a stop, but I don't turn around. I still hear him take a deep breath, though.

"Are you angry?"

I didn't realize I was until he asked. But I shake my head and continue out into the antiseptic-scented hallway.

CHAPTER TEN

I can't very well tell Berlynn about Hezekiah and his visit, so I can't talk about what's really bothering me. As I sit in her tiny office—which is way too hot, thanks to the space heater that's purring in the corner—I pluck at a loose thread on the hem of my sweatshirt and try not to make eye contact. It probably drives her nuts, but the quiet waiting thing she does drives *me* nuts. It's probably some trick that she thinks will get me to talk, but it's not working.

"How's Eph?" she asks at last, after what feels like about ten minutes of silence. I glance up at her momentarily before returning my gaze to the thread.

"Fine."

"Is he still in the hospital?"

I nod.

"Have you been visiting him?"

She knows I have, so I don't know why she's even asking.

I roll the thread into a little ball between my thumb and forefinger, then abandon it and lean back in the chair. She doesn't have a stereotypical couch; instead, it's this uncomfortable puffy chair that makes me feel like I have the worst posture ever.

"Are you glad he's alive?"

I give her a dirty look, and she holds up her hands with a smile.

"I'm just making sure you're paying attention," she says. Flipping through the notes on the clipboard in her lap, she frowns a little. "The last time we talked, you were upset because he didn't want to date."

"When was that?"

"A couple of years ago. Has anything changed?"

Everything's changed, I think. *Except for that.* "Not really. He's still planning on being a cat lady."

"And how does that make you feel?"

"Sad," I say, because I know that's what she wants to hear. I just want to get out of here, go curl up with a cup of tea, and work out my feelings. But I can't seem to catch a break. If it's not school, it's homework. If it's not that, it's sitting in a therapist's office and pretending I'm actually trying.

She flips through the papers again. "What medication are you taking at the moment?"

"Nothing."

"Nothing?" Her overplucked eyebrows rise.

I shake my head. "Too many side effects."

"I understand. But there are plenty of other medications to try. Have you discussed those with your doctor?"

"I've tried eight different ones," I say, and my voice comes out sounding kind of peeved. "Is nine the magic number?"

She lets the papers flutter back down and just stares at me. Again. I dig my fingertips into my thighs and imagine letting out the words that are on the tip of my tongue. *Maybe what I'm feeling right now has nothing to do with what's going on in my brain and everything to do with the fact that I just found out that my best friend is from another dimension. Oh, and that he might have been able to fly had some overzealous doctors not cut off his wings when he was a baby. I can't even be there for him emotionally because I can't relate, and all I'm able to think about is how I'm going to lose him to this other world that I'll never be a part of. But, please, tell me how more side effects are going to help the current situation.*

"Do you think I'm co-dependent?" I ask. The question seems to surprise her. Her eyebrows rise up so high they disappear under her bangs. For a moment, I feel a twinge of triumph. She's probably not supposed to let her clients know when they've startled her with a question.

"Co-dependent? Do you think you are?"

"I don't know. That's why I'm asking you."

She nods sagely and rests both hands on her clipboard. "I could give you the standard definition, and you could work it out for yourself."

"I already have an opinion. I want to know what you think. You're the expert."

Her mouth twitches. "Flattering as that is, Ari, I think it's more important if you answer that question for yourself."

"Fine. We're co-dependent. So how do I . . . fix that?"

"What makes you think you're co-dependent?"

I shrug and look down at my lap. "We need each other."

"You know that's not the actual definition."

"We rely on each other," I say. "To the exclusion of everyone else."

She nods slowly. "I'm not sure if that really applies in this case, Ari. Eph has unique challenges. It's not co-dependency when someone with a disability has to rely on assistance from others."

"Yeah, but *I'm* not disabled."

"Not the way he is, no. But your anxiety impairs you in other ways." Her eyes seem to pierce me, and I wonder if she's somehow found out about everything that I've never told her. Including the ill-fated trip to the party at Tanner's house. "Doesn't it?"

"I don't know." It's getting too hot in here. My sweatshirt is starting to live up to its name. The walls feel like they're closing in, and all I want is the pressure of Eph's body against my back. I take a deep breath and close my eyes as I try to imagine it, but all I can hear is the heater, and all I can smell is my deodorant, and my mouth is so dry that I'm afraid I'll never be able to swallow again.

"What's wrong?"

I shake my head and try to draw my awareness back to the feelings that I so desperately need. Calm. Warmth. Safety.

"All right. I want you to breathe in for the count of four and then out for the count of eight."

My swallow sounds like a clunk in the quiet room. I open my eyes and spring up from the chair. Given the angle at which it's been holding my body, I'm sure the movement looks more like a flail than anything else. "I . . . need some air."

"I can open the window, if you like."

"No. I just . . . need . . ." I snatch my jacket from the hook and pull the door open. The air in the hallway feels positively icy in comparison. I hurry out to the reception area, tugging my jacket on as I go. Berlynn's behind me; I can sense her presence even before she says anything.

"Okay, Ari. I'd like to see you next week, if—"

"Yeah. Okay." I nod and glance at the receptionist. "I'll make an appointment later. I . . ."

"It's fine," Berlynn says. "Go get some air. Try the breathing exercise."

I nod again and exit the blessedly empty reception area. The door chime sounds like a chiding scream. But as soon as I'm standing outside with the cold, damp air nipping at my cheeks, I feel a little better. My heart starts to calm down a bit. I flatten myself against the brick wall beside the door, trying to look casual as I search for that familiar pressure on my back that always seems to help me relax.

A wall isn't Eph, though, and it takes a while before I feel like the panic has passed. I stand there, watching my breath curl in white clouds with each deep exhale, and scan the parking lot for any sign of Mom's car. It's too early for her to show up, so I figure I might as well take the bus home. But then I see the hospital just a couple of blocks away, and I change my mind.

When I get up to Eph's room, I stop in the doorway and gape. He gives me a little smile as he peers past his mom. She's just finishing tugging a grey toque down over his curls.

"What's going on?" I ask. Parnell turns to me with a smile.

"He's coming home."

"Finally," Eph adds. He's sitting on the edge of the bed, feet swinging. They're wrapped up and encased in a couple of very ugly medical-looking booties.

"What happened to your toes?" I squeak. He quickly shakes his head.

"Nothing. They just don't want me damaging them. They're fine, remember?"

Parnell's busy tucking a few things into a bag. There's a wheelchair sitting beside the bed, presumably to help Eph get out of here, but he's not in it yet.

"Dad's bringing the car," he says, then tilts his head at me. "What are you doing here? I thought you had practice today."

"It got called off early."

"Weather?"

"Something like that."

He chuckles and slides forward until his feet are touching the floor. Parnell quickly dumps the bag on the bed when she sees what he's doing and grabs the back of the wheelchair to keep it from going anywhere.

"Do you need my help?" she asks.

He shakes his head as he leans forward to try to stand. I can see his legs already shaking.

"Ari, make sure he doesn't fall."

I rush over to him, just as he shakes his head.

"Mom, I'm not going to fall."

"Humour me. I want to get out of this hospital today . . . not have you stuck here when you give yourself a concussion or break your ribs."

176

He sighs, but he lets me steady him with my hands as he carefully shuffles—keeping his weight on his heels, I notice—into position in front of the wheelchair. He sits heavily with a bit of a grunt.

"Are you all right?" Parnell asks.

"I'm fine."

"Are you sure? I don't want to have to come back here tonight because you busted something and didn't tell me."

He rolls his eyes and looks up at me. "Will *you* drive me home?"

"I can't. Let your dad do it."

His nose wrinkles. "The only driving my parents are doing is driving me crazy."

Parnell gives his hat such a tug that it ends up down over his eyes. "Watch it, mister." She grabs the bag from the bed and rummages through it. "Have we got everything?"

"How should I know?" Eph says, tilting his head up in my general direction. "I can't see a thing."

As I reach out to pull the brim of his toque back into place, he grins at me. I find myself smiling back, but only a little. My appointment with Berlynn is still hanging on me like a bad smell, and I can't seem to shake the feeling. Nothing particularly bad happened, either. Well, other than the panic attack. But it's not like I haven't had one of those before.

Parnell takes the bag and strides ahead of us out the door. Eph watches her go, then turns to me with a confused expression.

"Did she forget me?"

"Maybe she thinks I'm going to push you."

He sighs and carefully settles his feet on the footrests. "Wish I could push myself."

"How? With your feet?"

He chuckles as he leans over to peer at one of the wheels. "I probably could, if they hadn't mummified them."

"I think that defeats the purpose of the wheelchair."

"Probably." He looks up at me with a little tilt of his head. "Are you okay?" His voice is suddenly a lot softer. My heart flutters with gratitude.

"I am now."

"Want to talk?"

"Not here." I sink down onto the edge of the bed. "I didn't know you were going home today."

"I didn't, either. But somebody decided that my toes probably weren't going to fall off, so I can go."

"When are you allowed to try walking?"

He shrugs, causing his old winter vest to rustle. "Maybe next week? I don't know. My toes feel fine. A little numb, but I can move them and they don't hurt." He wiggles his butt in the wheelchair as he tries to get situated more comfortably. "If I don't start doing stuff soon, though, I'm going to lose some flexibility. And I don't want to end up dependent on Mom to feed me for the rest of my life."

I frown. "Where's the card?"

"Garbage." He juts his chin toward the small trash can in the corner of the room. I hurry over there. It's getting full and looks like it's about due to be emptied. "Ari, don't."

I rifle through the refuse, which is mostly just pudding-cup lids and used tissues, and find the card tucked against the side. I pull it out, give it a quick examination, and stick it in my pocket. When I turn back to Eph, his eyebrows are high.

"I memorized the number yesterday," he says. Slowly, his face blossoms into a smile. "You didn't *have* to paw through all that."

"It's mostly tissues. I'm not afraid of a little snot."

"You sure that's all that's on them?"

I just stare at him for a moment. He bursts out laughing. The sound is like a balm to my still-vibrating nerves. "You're disgusting, you know that?"

He shakes his head. "Come here, Ari."

I walk over, unsure what he wants. He just stares up at me, his green eyes bright.

"Closer."

I shuffle as close as I can get.

"Hug?"

"Which kind?"

"Well, since you're the one who needs it, whichever kind you want."

It feels a bit like a trap. Or a test. He waits, and I know he's wondering which kind of hug I'll pick. To be honest, I'm wondering the same thing myself. My instinct is to reach down and pull him against me with my arms. But . . . I don't. Instead, I brace my hands on the wheelchair's armrests and lean down until my forehead touches his.

"Is that really what you wanted?" he whispers.

"We don't always get what we want."

He tilts his head until his nose brushes against mine. "I know."

Those two little words feel like a harbinger somehow. It's

as if we both know the truth of them . . . but we don't yet know how that truth is going to play out. I press my lips together as I straighten up. He smiles sadly and leans back in the wheelchair. I unlock the wheels and carefully push him out the door, keeping my gaze fixed on the top of his toque as we head out into an uncertain future.

CHAPTER ELEVEN

Skylar doesn't say a word to me as she marches from the car up to our front door after school. I'm used to it. She's barely said a word to me since the day we found out that Eph was still alive. I take stock of my bladder, and when I decide it's probably fine for a few more hours, I head across the street.

The house is quiet when I push open the door. Slipping off my shoes, I listen for sounds of habitation.

"Eph?"

"In my room," he says. After taking off my jacket, I hoist my bag over my shoulder and hurry down the hallway. His door is open, and when I step inside, I find him sitting on the floor in front of a half-finished jigsaw puzzle. His bare feet are planted on either side of what he's already finished. When I step closer and stand over him, he looks up. "Want to help?"

I shake my head as I set my bag down on the floor. "Looks like you're doing okay on your own."

He expels a frustrated breath and leans back against the side of his bed. In his hoodie and sweatpants, he looks like he's ready to do some serious relaxing. But the expression on his face is anything but relaxed. "I think I'm missing some pieces."

"How do you know? You're not even a quarter done."

"Still. There should be four corners. I can only find three." He pushes a piece across the carpet with his big toe until it's sitting next to a pile of others that are approximately the same colour. "I think this thing is out to get me."

"Get you?"

"Drive me insane."

I peer at the lid of the box that he's got propped up against his bookcase. "Baby otters are going to drive you insane?"

"Yeah. They're cute, but evil." He abandons the puzzle (at least, it looks like he does, since he stretches his legs out on either side of his workspace) and looks up at me. "Can you help me finish that essay?"

"I thought you had plenty of time."

"I do. But I'm tired of worrying about it. I just want to get it done."

"Where's your laptop?"

He shrugs. "In the kitchen, I think."

"How'd it get in there?"

"Dad needed to borrow it. His crapped out." He leans back against the bed, using it as leverage as he carefully gets to his feet. I notice that he's still keeping his weight off his toes.

"Do you want to work in there?"

He raises his eyebrows at me as he flops onto his bed and lies back. "What's wrong with my room?"

"Aren't you tired of it?"

"Extremely. But I promised Mom that I wouldn't leave it except to pee. She's still worried about my toes."

"Are you?"

He shrugs. "Not particularly. You heard what Hezekiah said. And I think he's right." With a wiggle of the ten digits in question, he jerks his chin at the doorway. "Laptop?"

I walk out to the kitchen. Sure enough, a laptop is sitting on the island. I grab it and am just stepping back into Eph's room when the doorbell rings. Ignoring it, I swat gently at his feet with one hand.

"Move 'em so I can sit."

"Can you get the door?"

"Why? It's probably just somebody selling something."

He shakes his head as he sits up and looks down at his hoodie. With a grunt, he twists his shoulders until the shirt is sitting a little more straight. "Please, Ari?"

"Do you have any cash?" I ask as I set his laptop down on the bed.

"For what?"

"Cookies. Or whatever it is they want us to buy."

"It's not cookie season."

"Eph."

"Ari." He raises his eyebrows at me. Figuring the sooner I get rid of whoever it is, the sooner we can get working on his essay, I thump down the hallway. But when I pull open the door, the person I find on the other side is definitely not selling cookies.

"Hi," she says, looking a bit confused. "Do I have the right house?"

"I don't know. Do you?"

"I'm looking for Ephraim," she says, and her accent suddenly twigs. My gaze immediately goes to her hands, which are at this moment clutching the straps of a backpack.

"Who is it?" Eph shouts.

"I don't know!" I yell back. The woman smiles.

"I'm Rebecca," she says. "I'm here to—"

"Let her in, Ari!"

I turn and frown at the hallway. "How do you even know who it is?"

"I've been expecting her. Just let her in."

Still a bit unsure about this whole situation, I stand back to let the woman step forward. She doesn't look like she's that much older than me and Eph. She's a few inches shorter than me, though, with the same slight build that Eph and Hezekiah both have. Her dark hair is pulled back into a cascading ponytail of shiny curls that allows me a good view of her hearing aids. When she's standing inside on the doormat, I look down.

"Take off your shoes," I say, eyeing the rather fancy-looking sneakers.

She bends over and does as I ask, her agile fingers tugging on the laces. When she stands back up, she raises her eyebrows.

"Where's Ephraim?"

I don't say anything, but just lead her back to Eph's room. He's sitting stiffly on the edge of the bed, and I notice that he's put on his slippers. When he sees Rebecca, his eyes widen a little. His gaze goes immediately to where mine did.

"You're kidding," he says. "Those are artificial?"

She glances at me for a moment before turning back to Eph. "What are?"

"Your hands."

She shakes her head, sending her ponytail swinging.

"It's fine," Eph says, jutting his chin over in my direction. "Ari knows all about it. She was there when Hezekiah explained everything."

The woman visibly relaxes. Her hands are still clutching those straps, though. Eph scoots forward a little on the bed.

"That's insane," he whispers, then looks up into her eyes. "How much of your arms do you have left?"

"Just the parts above my elbows." She hooks her thumbs into the straps and pulls off the backpack in a smooth movement so she can set it down beside the door. As she walks over to stand in front of Eph, I see him sit up a little straighter. I would laugh ... but there's this pang of jealousy tweaking my innards that's not so funny.

"Hezekiah wasn't exaggerating," she says. "How have you managed for as long as you have?"

Eph shrugs. There's a weird expression on his face that I've never seen before. "Mostly with my feet."

"You won't have to resort to that anymore. Unless ..." She folds her arms carefully across her chest and gives him an appraising look. "Do your parents know?"

"About the whole telekinesis thing?" He shakes his head.

"So you're not getting prosthetics."

He glances over at me, then looks up at Rebecca. "I haven't

decided yet. Shouldn't we see if I can actually move anything with my mind before I make any big decisions like that?"

"What's to decide?"

She doesn't see my mouth drop open. Eph doesn't either. He's too busy staring at this beautiful girl in front of him. *What would you know?* I think. *You don't even have a family here.* Suddenly, her eyelids flutter and she turns to me with a frown. I shrink back from the look. It's almost like the one Mom used to give me and Skylar when we were misbehaving.

"Maybe I should go," I say, taking a step back toward the doorway. Eph's head snaps around so quickly, I'm surprised he doesn't hurt himself.

"No, Ari. Stay."

"Are you sure?"

He nods and stands up, seeming to forget his toes for a moment. He looks down, then sinks back onto the bed.

"I guess it doesn't really matter," Rebecca says. "She's not going to interfere with anything."

"I can't," I say. She nods and unfolds her arms.

"That's true. Could you hand me my bag?"

It's sitting right next to my left foot, so I really have no excuse not to. As I heft the backpack by one strap, I'm struck by the weight of it. But she takes it easily from my outstretched hand, artificial fingers working in perfect harmony to close around the strap. As she crouches down and unzips the small pocket on the outside, she glances up at Eph.

"Can you sit on the floor? It might be easier."

He bites his lip for a moment before sliding one foot out of his slipper to kick away the partly finished puzzle. Then he settles himself down on the floor, folding his legs. I'm not part of this, so I just perch on the edge of the bed where I can see over his shoulder.

Rebecca pulls a variety of objects out of the pocket and sets them on the floor. I don't know if there's any significance to them, or if they're just representative of different weights and shapes. There's a hot-pink feather that looks like it was plucked from a tacky flamingo; a cat's-eye marble; a pencil that needs sharpening; a folded tissue; a smooth, bluish stone about the size of a baby's fist; one of those tiny travel tubes of toothpaste; and a small brown teddy bear that, for some reason, looks like it's been chewed. I can tell Eph's checking out the objects in front of him. When they're all laid out to Rebecca's satisfaction, she pushes the backpack to the side and sits down.

"Hezekiah said you're pretty much a beginner."

"He claims I threw Ari across the road. That sounds pretty advanced to me."

She smirks. "You may have strength, but you don't have any control. Not yet." Reaching out, she points to the feather. "Let's start small. See if you can lift it."

He grunts in amusement. "With my mind?"

"That's why I'm here, isn't it?"

Sighing, he leans forward. I can see the feather past his shoulder. It doesn't appear to be doing anything.

"Maybe I'm a dud after all," he says after a full minute of absolutely nothing happening.

Rebecca shakes her head. "Obviously, we'll have to start even earlier."

"Earlier than the beginning?" I ask. She ignores me and

leans forward so she can take Eph's face in her hands. My skin immediately starts to prickle. If I were a dog, my hackles would be up.

"What were you thinking when you threw your friend?" she asks.

"Uh . . ." The uncertain noise sounds so weird coming out of his mouth that I feel like laughing. I nudge him gently in the back with my toe. He sits up a little straighter. "I just wanted to get her out of the way."

"And how were you feeling?"

"Scared shitless."

She raises her eyebrows and lets go of his face.

"It means really, really scared," I say. Her gaze flicks to me, and I can see her annoyance.

"I know what it means. I've been here for four years."

"What did you do?"

Eph cranes his neck around to look at me in disbelief. I'm almost tempted to do the same, because there's got to be some other version of me sitting back here, asking that question. I don't know why I'm being so bold. And I don't know why this person—who's here to help my best friend— bothers me so much.

"My older sister is a resistor. I chose to join her in removal."

"You can do that?" Eph asks, turning back to face her. She lifts her chin and gives a little nod.

"In a way. I chose to commit a crime to ensure my removal."

"So what did you do?"

"We made a halfhearted attempt to escape to one of the

188

sanctuaries. It was never our intent to make it. We planned to get caught."

"Why?" he asks, and I can hear the anguish in his voice. "You could've been whole."

She shakes her head. "Life in the sanctuaries is precarious. They have to relocate frequently to avoid raids. My sister didn't want such a life. Neither did I."

"So you chose to come here and lose your wings?"

With a quick, darting glance in my direction, she shrugs. "This life is better than death. We're both happy with our decision."

"But if your sister can't use her mind . . ." Eph begins. He can't seem to finish the thought.

"I help her. And she has rudimentary prosthetic limbs to assist with certain tasks. She's able to dress and feed herself." Her gaze slips to Eph's shoulders.

"I can do that, too," he says.

"With your feet."

"So what?"

"It's inconvenient, isn't it? And you can't carry anything while you're walking."

She has a point. I look down and notice that Eph's posture has gone kind of rigid. Without really thinking about it, I slip off the bed and sit beside him on the floor. He gives me a grateful smile.

"Try again," Rebecca says. "This time, try to feel some urgency."

He snorts. "Lift the feather or else?"

"It's up to you whether you learn to manifest your abilities. I'm simply here to help. But I can't do it for you."

With a sigh, he looks down at the feather. Once more, it just sits there. He lets out a grunt and shakes his head. "I can't."

"Imagine it rising."

"I *am*. It's not working."

"Try harder."

His eyes narrow a little bit as he looks at the feather again. This time, though, it starts to rock. And then, as if it's been lifted by a draft, it skitters a few inches across the carpet. He sits up straight.

"Good," Rebecca says.

"Did I do that?"

"You must have. It wasn't me."

A slow smile is spreading across his face. He turns to me, and his expression is brighter than I've seen it since before the incident. I try to smile back. He must know I'm not feeling it, but he's distracted. He turns away, and the movement seems to tug at my heart.

After about ten minutes of him lifting the lighter objects, I stand up. I'm not even sure he notices.

"I have homework," I say. That gets his attention. The tissue floats to the carpet as he turns to me.

"But you were going to help me with my essay."

"It's getting late, Eph."

His eyebrows twitch in a little frown and he glances at Rebecca. Her expression doesn't reveal anything. She just seems to be waiting for him to respond.

"I'll help you tomorrow," I say.

"But I really wanted—"

He stops talking as I turn and walk from the room. Under normal circumstances, he would jump up and come after me. With the state of his feet, I know that's not possible. Still, when he doesn't call out to me, I feel my chest tighten. I hurry to the front door, slip on my shoes and jacket, and head for home, wishing I were brave enough to do what I'm fantasizing about: telling Rebecca to get lost because Eph's fine just the way he is.

But . . . he needs this. Or he thinks he does. And so I try to shift my thoughts to the mundane homework tasks I've got in front of me so I don't have to imagine what might be going on in his bedroom.

Chapter Twelve

I don't go over to Eph's house after school on Friday, or any other time over the weekend. I'm not even sure why. There's a part of me that wants to punish him, but for what, I couldn't say. Reconnecting with his heritage? Learning a new skill? It's not even about Rebecca. At least . . . I don't think it is.

The weekend ends up being really boring. Skylar is out for pretty much all of it, which leaves me at home with Mom and Grandma. I spend Sunday afternoon downstairs in the cabbage-scented suite, trying to get Grandma's new router set up so she can video-chat with her friends. My new phone, tucked in my back pocket, is silent the whole time. Not that I'm surprised; nobody has the new number yet. And, to be honest, I'm kind of relieved. A few times, I entertain the thought of not giving that number out to anybody. But that kind of defeats the purpose of having a phone in the first place.

Eph's still not back at school and, by the end of the day on Wednesday, I'm really starting to miss him. I have an appointment with Berlynn, though, so I don't want to go over to his house and start something. It's not like I think he's going to start yelling at me for not being there. He'd never do that. This whole situation is just weird, though, and I'm not sure what to expect anymore.

But after sitting with my homework for half an hour and barely touching my laptop, I give up. After a quick sprint across the street, I find myself turning the knob on the Diaz-Pierces' front door. It's locked.

For a moment, I debate going home. If the door is locked, there's probably nobody there. I don't know where Eph would be (a doctor's appointment, maybe?) and I don't know his number offhand to call him and ask. Just out of curiosity, I ring the doorbell.

"Just a sec!" Eph's voice shouts from somewhere deeper in the house. I lean closer to the door.

"Why is it locked?"

There's a long pause, and then I hear the deadbolt thunk. "Okay. Come in."

I turn the knob and push open the door. Eph's standing near the kitchen, about fifteen feet away. When I look down, I notice his feet.

"Oh, my god," I whisper. "What—"

"No!" he says quickly, as if he's already figured out what I'm thinking. He stares down at his feet, which are encased in what looks like a pair of regular socks over a ton of bandages. "We were trying to keep me from using my toes."

"We?"

"Yeah. Rebecca. She left about an hour ago." He pads closer, walking gingerly. "I've got four pairs of socks on. Feels like my feet are stuffed in giant marshmallows."

I frown. "Why can't you just *not* use your feet?"

"Habit." He steps forward, and I can tell he's aiming for a hug. I draw back and turn my head to the side, pretending to examine the cross on the wall. When I see him stop out of the corner of my eye, my heart twangs in regret.

"Did you finish your essay?" I ask.

"Yeah. Mom helped me a little, but I finished typing it up myself." He steps closer, but not in a pre-hug sort of way. I dare to look up at him. He gives me a sad little smile. "What's wrong?"

"Nothing."

He snorts. "Ari, we've been best friends for a decade. I think I know when something's bothering you."

"It's nothing new. Just . . . the usual."

He shuffles even closer, his feet silent on the floor. "You've been quiet since the accident."

"So've you."

"I've got a lot to process." He gives his shoulders a bit of a shrug. "So do you. It's not every day someone finds out that their BFF is an angel."

"You're not."

"Close enough. I was born with *wings*, Ari. It's not like I'm completely normal."

"Normal's subjective."

He grunts and shakes his head. "Want to see something *really* abnormal?"

"I don't know."

"Don't worry. It's nothing scary." He steps forward and nudges me with his side. "Turn around. Watch."

"Watch what?"

"Just watch," he says, and falls silent. When I look at him, I see that he's staring at the front door, an expression of intense concentration on his face. Suddenly, there's another thunk as the deadbolt slides back into place. I jump, even though I know what the sound is. And I know what he's just done.

But I don't say anything. I just stare at the little lever, which is solidly in the horizontal position. Just moments ago, it was standing vertically. And I *know* he didn't touch it. Even if he had reached up with his foot, those four pairs of socks would've prevented him from doing anything to the lock.

"Ari?"

"What?" I ask, my tongue finally freeing itself from its paralysis.

"You do realize I just locked the door with my mind, right?"

"Yeah."

He doesn't say anything. His expression is unreadable as he stares at me.

"What happens with your parents?" I ask.

"What about them?"

"You can't exactly do *that* when they're around."

"So I won't. I'll just practise when I'm alone."

"For what? What's the point, Eph? A party trick? You can't use your powers where anyone can see them. And if you stop using your feet to do everything, won't you lose the ability to use them?"

"First of all," he says, "they're not *powers*. That makes me sound like a superhero. And I'm not."

"You saved me from certain death."

He shakes his head. "If my kind all have these abilities, then they're just abilities."

"Maybe to you."

"When I watch people using their hands, *that* seems like a superpower. But it's not, is it? Not to you, anyway." He turns and walks carefully down the hall toward his bedroom. "I'm not going to stop using my feet, Ari. Not yet."

My eyes widen at his words. I kick off my shoes and hurry after him. When I reach his room, he's settling himself down on the floor in front of his laptop.

"Are you getting as much homework as I am?" he asks. "It seems excessive. Aren't we supposed to be doing exam review or—"

"'Not yet'?"

He looks up at me in confusion. "Huh?"

"You said you're not going to stop using your feet yet. Are you going to at some point?"

"I might."

"You're going to get arms?"

"Maybe. Rebecca and I have been talking about it. I'd really have to make a clean break and start over somewhere else where nobody knew me. And I'd have to keep my arms hidden all the time. So the Caribbean would be out."

"Why?"

"Because I don't even have proper shoulders. Rebecca

can get away with it. If someone figures out her arms are artificial, she can excuse her dexterity by saying she's got really advanced prosthetics. But in my case . . . I couldn't."

"So you'd have to hide under long sleeves for the rest of your life."

"Yeah."

"And nobody could ever see you naked."

He snorts and raises his eyebrow at me. "Who would see me naked?"

"Right. No girlfriends." I hug my waist and shake my head slowly. "You realize that if you learn how to use your mind to move stuff, you can't use the 'I'd be a burden' excuse anymore, right?"

"I'd have to hide my abilities, so—"

"Not if she already knew about them."

He lets out a sigh so long and so heavy that I regret bringing up the topic in the first place. "I miss us, Ari," he says.

"Us?"

"Yeah. Before you decided you were in love with me."

"I didn't *decide* that, Eph. Jeez. You're the one who decided he was never going to allow himself to have a relationship."

"For good reasons."

"Maybe to you." I shake my head and turn to leave. "Never mind. I'll let you get back to your—"

"No! Stay."

"Why? I can't help you practise flinging things through the air with your mind, Eph."

"I've done enough of that for today," he says, leaning back

so he can bring his feet together. I have a feeling he's trying to get his socks off, but he isn't having much luck. With a dramatic flop onto his side, he lets out a groan. "A little help?"

"I thought you hate it when people help you."

"I do. But if I don't get these off, I don't know how I'm going to explain to Mom why they're on there. Or how they got on there in the first place." He cranes his neck to look up at me. "Please?"

"How'd you do it the other times?"

"There haven't been other times. Rebecca just got fed up with me forgetting and trying to use my feet today." He struggles to sit up and then holds one foot out toward me. "They're not even my socks. They're Ash's. So Mom's going to have a lot of questions if she catches me like this."

I frown at him for a moment before crouching down and reaching for the cuff of the outermost sock. After peeling it off, I turn it right side out again and reach for the one underneath.

"Thank you," he says.

"I'm not even done yet."

"No, I mean . . . thank you. For sticking with me through all of this crazy stuff."

Pulling off the final sock, I peer at his toes as he wiggles them.

"Hezekiah was right. They feel more normal every day. Mom said she'd think about letting me go back to school next week if I'm up to it."

"Are you?"

"If I don't bother with the bathroom all day, I should be able to manage it."

I reach for his other foot and start to peel the sock layers off. "Can you hold it that long?"

"I," he says, a wicked grin forming on his lips, "am an expert at holding it." He leans closer, as if he's about to share a secret. "I promised Ash I'd never tell anyone, but—"

"Maybe you shouldn't, then."

"But it proves my point! A few years ago, we had a contest to see who could hold it the longest."

"And you won?"

"Of course. I drank a litre of pop and held it in for over six hours."

"How long did Asher hold it?"

"Six hours." He raises his eyebrows. "And he didn't make it to the toilet."

I snort and look down at the pile of socks in front of me. "Guys are weird. What's with all the pissing contests?"

"It's just the nature of the beast."

"How do you know your kind doesn't have some sort of super bladder?"

He shakes his head and uses one foot to gather up the socks and separate them into matching pairs. "If anything, wouldn't it be the opposite? If you're flying, you'd want less weight, not more. Having to haul around a bladder full of liquid wouldn't be very efficient." He looks up with a smile. "I think Ash just has really weak peeing muscles."

I don't even know what kind of response I'm supposed to have to that, so I don't say anything. Eph finishes stacking the socks in neat pairs and turns to me.

"Want to play *Leavenghost?*"

"You can do that?"

He shrugs. "No idea. I haven't tried yet. But I probably should." Very carefully, he gets to his feet. His slippers are sitting near the foot of his bed, so he slides them on. "You might get lucky and beat me today if—"

"I can't. Practice."

"Again?"

"Yes, again," I snap. "It's a permanent condition. You should understand that better than anyone."

His eyes widen and, for a moment, he almost looks like I've slapped him. My heart squeezes as the instant guilt crashes over me in a wave.

"I should go," I say. "Mom will be wondering where—"

"Skip it," he says. I stare at him in disbelief.

"What makes you think I can just skip it?"

"It's not helping, is it?" He looks down at he adjusts his left foot in its slipper. "Why bother if it isn't helping?"

"How would you know if it isn't helping?"

He shakes his head and steps toward me, head lowered as he comes in for a hug. I don't even realize why until I feel the tears trickling down my cheeks. But I don't let him get close enough. My hands rise and catch him in the chest.

"I really have to go," I say, my voice choked.

"Call me later."

"I have homework."

He doesn't say anything, and when I dare to look up, I see that he's biting his lip. His eyes are studying me, but in a sort of unfocused way that makes it look like he's listening for something rather than looking. I take a step back.

Just let me go, Eph. It's what you want, isn't it? Even though you're afraid to say it.

His frown deepens. I turn and hurry out of his room.

erlynn's office is too hot (as usual) but I'm feeling weirdly chilled and wishing I'd kept my jacket on. We've sat here talking about basically nothing for almost forty minutes, and I'm getting frustrated. *Maybe Eph was right,* I think. *This isn't really helping. Maybe I should just—*

"How's Eph?" Berlynn asks, and the suddenness of the question makes me jerk a little in the slouchy chair.

"What?"

"I was just wondering how Eph was doing. You haven't mentioned him at all today."

"Haven't I?"

She smiles and shakes her head. "Is something going on between you two that you'd like to talk about?"

"Nothing's going on," I say a little too forcefully. I'm embarrassed to see a fleck of spit arc through the air into the space between us. "He doesn't even want to be my friend anymore, so . . . yeah. Nothing's going on. And nothing *will* be going on."

Her eyebrows rise a little. "Did he say he didn't want to be your friend anymore?"

"He didn't have to." I slump in the chair. It's not very dramatic, given the fact that I'm already curled up like a prawn. "I've been replaced."

"By who?"

"Some girl." I practically throw my arms around myself.

"And that bothers you?"

I glare at her. *Yes, it bothers me. Stop with the stupid psychobabble BS and help me. Isn't that what Mom's paying you to do?*

"Do you still have romantic feelings for Eph?"

"Wouldn't matter if I did," I say, staring down at my knees. There's a tiny imperfection in the denim, and I keep my focus on that so I can concentrate on my thoughts. "He says he's going to be alone forever."

"Did you tell him that's a baseless assumption?"

I shake my head. "No. He's *choosing* to be alone. He says he won't date. Won't get married. He wants to be a crazy cat . . . guy."

Berlynn nods. "Then why are you worried about this girl?"

"Because she's . . . like him."

"An amputee?"

I nod, not sure how much more I should say. I don't want to get Rebecca in trouble, even if she has stolen my best friend out from under my nose.

"Sometimes," Berlynn says, "it helps to be able to talk to someone who understands exactly what we're going through." She absently taps her pen against the clipboard. "Have you given any more thought to one of the group sessions?"

I shake my head. "No."

"You haven't thought about it, or you don't want to do it?"

"I don't want to do it."

"Why?"

"Because it makes it worse," I say. "It's not the same as missing a body part. That's not *catching*." When Berlynn

202

raises her eyebrows, I go on. "Being around other people with anxiety makes me . . ."

"Anxious?"

I nod. "I can't even read books with anxious characters. I relate too much. And then I start to feel it." Absently scratching at my ribs through my sweater, I go back to studying the spot on my knee. "I need to be around people who aren't anxious. It . . . grounds me."

"That's very insightful."

"Yay."

She laughs softly and sets her pen down on her clipboard. "Do you feel like Eph grounds you?"

I nod, but I say nothing. Eph's always grounded me. Ever since that first day when he helped me forget about that stupid grey cloud with his little breathing trick, he's been keeping me tethered to the earth, unable to spin off into wild flights of panic. "But we're growing up," I say. "He's not always going to be there. We want different things."

"Is this just since the accident?"

"No."

"Okay. I was just asking. That sort of dramatic event can cause people to change their worldview. It wouldn't be surprising, given what's happened to him, that he might . . ."

I close my eyes and draw into myself as my blood begins to rush through my ears, drowning out the rest of her words. *What about me?* my mind wails. *I was there, too. I had to watch what I thought was my best friend's death. Just because he's still alive, nobody seems to care that I'm still traumatized. He's fine. He always was. He's got way more people on his side than I'll ever have, and—*

"Ari?"

I open my eyes and blink, which causes a torrent of tears to cascade down my cheeks. I quickly brush them away with the cuffs of my sweater.

"Care to share?"

I shake my head. I don't want to share. I just want to go home. No, I just want a time machine, so I can get into it and go back to the day of that stupid party. I'd refuse Skylar's grudging invitation and just stay home. Eph wouldn't come get me. He wouldn't be dragged into a world of flying humans and telekinetic abilities. He wouldn't meet Rebecca.

Having a front-row seat to Eph's life for ten years has made me hyper-aware of his challenges. But, just for an instant, I find myself wishing that I was like him. Like Rebecca. Because maybe then there would be a chance—no matter how small—that I wouldn't end up losing my best friend.

CHAPTER THIRTEEN

It turns out to be pretty easy to ghost someone. Especially when they're still stuck at home because of their frostbitten feet. Eph doesn't come back to school that Monday, but he does come back the week after that, and by then, I've got it all worked out. He doesn't have my new number, so there's no chance of him calling me. I start eating lunch out front, perched on one of the low log fences that surround the parking lot . . . even though it's still only January and kind of freezing. When I go back inside to class, I always keep my jacket on so I don't shiver too much and look like a weirdo.

I know what Berlynn would say about all of this, too. It's not Eph's fault. It's me who's done the abandoning. She wouldn't understand that it's already over. I'm just speeding things up. Making a break while I can, on my own terms. If Eph wants to be alone, that's fine. But he can't expect me to forgo my own life while I hover in his orbit.

And maybe he doesn't expect that. He certainly doesn't seem to care. I quickly gain a reputation as a loner for eating outside in the cold, and I'm sure it must get back to him. But he never approaches me about it. In fact, the only contact we have is short glances in the hallway, where his eyebrows twist into a little frown and he looks like he's about to walk over and say something. He never does, though.

Until one day near the end of March, that is. The weather is getting a lot nicer, and even though there's still some residual crusty snow in the shady spots, the day is actually pretty bright and bordering on warm. I'm just pulling my sandwich out of its container when a shadow falls over me. I ignore it at first, but when it doesn't move, I look up to see who's blocked the sunlight (and meagre heat). Eph stands there, his curls aglow from the light behind him.

"Mind if I sit?"

"You can if you want."

He settles himself down on the log beside me. His backpack is clipped at his chest, and he's not exactly dressed for the weather; all he's got on are a t-shirt and track pants.

"Have you eaten?" I ask.

"Not yet."

"Want some help?"

He shakes his head. "I'm not really hungry." He leans a little closer, in a familiar way that nevertheless makes me feel awkward. "Actually," he says, "I don't *need* help with that. I could unclip this thing myself if I wanted to now."

"Yeah?"

"Gotta keep up the act."

I take a big bite of my sandwich and start to chew, but my mouth is so dry that the bread feels like a big lump of dry dough. "Have you progressed to throwing people?"

He grunts with laughter. "Not yet. I need small humans to practise on, and I don't have any of those around here. All my suitable cousins are in Mexico."

"Want to throw Skylar?"

He frowns. "Why? What's she said now?"

"Never mind." Abandoning the sandwich, I put the rest back in the container and close the plastic latch. The first bite feels like it's stuck halfway down, pressing against my heart.

"Ari. Talk to me."

Why should I? You've found your people. You don't need me. I toss the sandwich container in my bag and zip it up before standing. He leaps to his feet almost as fast, causing me to startle.

"I might not need your physical help anymore, Ari, but I still need you. You're my best friend."

I shake my head. "Friendships don't always last."

"Why can't they?"

"Because. We want different things. Our lives are going to go in different directions. Maybe literally."

He sighs. "I still haven't decided about that."

"Why not?"

"Because it's a huge decision. I either continue as Eph Diaz-Pierce, or I start over completely as someone else. Either way . . . it'll be permanent."

My body shudders involuntarily. "You wouldn't come back?"

"I couldn't come back. If someone were to connect the two identities, I'd be in a ton of trouble."

"Why? People reinvent themselves all the time."

He snorts. "Do people cross some sort of barrier between the universes and start using their abilities to manipulate matter with their minds all the time?"

"In comic books."

"Yeah, well, we're not in a comic book. This is *weird*, Ari. I'll be the first to admit it. Sometimes I feel like I'm not even living in reality anymore."

"Maybe you aren't. Maybe you did die and this is . . ."

"Hell?" He chuckles and shakes his head. "Believe me, the thought has crossed my mind. But I don't think hell has Dad's tamales."

I frown at him, wondering how he can joke about it so easily now. When he first got back from that other world, he was so scared. The sensation of his whole body trembling in my arms is one I don't think I'll ever forget.

"I've given myself until the end of the school year to figure things out," he says. "It'll be easier to make a clean break then, if that's what I decide to do."

"But you've already applied to universities as Eph, right?"

"So I won't go to those ones. It's not like psychology programs are hard to find."

I stare at him for a long moment. Finally, he just raises his eyebrows.

"What?" he asks.

"You're going to suck as a therapist."

"Why?"

"Because you get people."

He laughs. "Wouldn't that be a *good* thing?"

"You'd think. But in my experience, therapists have to stare at their clients until they're really uncomfortable and then make some ignorant observation that's *way* off."

With a scowl, he braces his feet shoulder width apart and leans down a little so he can fix me with an intense gaze. I raise an eyebrow.

"What are you doing?"

"Are you uncomfortable yet?"

"Not really."

He sighs dramatically and straightens back up. "Guess I'll just have to talk to my clients, then."

"I wish I could be your client."

"That's probably frowned upon. We're too close."

Are we? We've barely spoken in months, Eph. You've been busy with Rebecca and—

"Did I tell you I met Rebecca's sister?"

I blink in surprise. "The . . . resistor?"

He nods. "She's not what I expected at all."

"What did you expect?"

"I don't know. Someone nicer. She's like . . . vinegar and chilli powder rubbed into a paper cut."

"Nice."

"No, definitely not." He shakes his head. "But . . . I get it. She's frustrated. She's not great with her feet or her prosthetic arms. And she's angry."

"Wouldn't you be if you were forced to choose between death or dismemberment?"

"Hell, yeah. Like I said, I get it. But that doesn't mean I want to spend time around her. I feel sorry for Rebecca."

She's kind of rude, too, I think. Not that you would've noticed. You were probably too busy checking out her boobs.

He suddenly snorts and glances back at the school. "What time is it?"

"I don't know. Why?"

"Want to get out of here?"

I frown. *You haven't spoken to me in months, and now you want to play hooky?*

"It's okay if you don't," he says. "If you've got a class you can't miss or . . ."

"It's not that."

He sighs. "I miss you, Ari."

"Why?"

With a jerk, he straightens up like a soldier coming to attention. "*Why?*" he repeats. "Are you really asking?"

I pull my bag over my shoulder and start to walk back toward the school; he jogs after me, the loops on his pants swaying as he moves. "Berlynn says maybe we're too close," I mumble.

"Really."

My throat is tight as I swallow. It's like the lie has burned me from the inside out. "She's probably right. You're going away no matter what, right?"

"I applied to two of the local unis."

"And how many others?"

He sighs. "Six."

"And you'll probably get into all of them."

"I don't have to go to any of them."

I stop and whirl to face him. He keeps walking for a moment, looking baffled. When he stops, I shake my head. "Are you kidding me?"

"What?"

"You're just going to stay here and . . . what? Try to work your way back into my good graces?"

He lets out a frustrated breath. "I wasn't aware I was out of them."

"It's . . . complicated."

"I'll say. I don't even know what's going on right now."

"I thought you knew everything," I snap.

With a roll of his eyes, he tilts his head back. I have a feeling he'd throw up his hands if he had any. "Jesus. I can't win with you right now."

"Why do you need to win? I thought it wasn't a competition!"

He lowers his head to look at me. "Huh?"

"Nobody cares what I need. Nobody cares what I want. And nobody will leave me the fuck alone!"

"Is that really what you want?"

"Yes!" *No. I just want . . . I can't have what I want.*

"I'm on your side, Ari. I always have been." He bites his lip for a moment and fixes his gaze on me. "If you really want this friendship to be over, if that's what you need . . ."

"It is." *What am I doing? No! It's not what I want. It's not. Eph, please . . . If there were ever a time for you to read my mind, it's now!*

"Okay." He steps closer for a moment, as if for a hug, then seems to think better of it, stepping smoothly away again like he's just executed a dance step. "I guess I'll see you around, then."

I nod.

"No hard feelings."

I shake my head. I don't trust myself to speak. My chest hitches. I hope he can't see it.

With a tired smile, he turns and heads back toward the school. I stay where I am as a spring breeze skitters over the parking lot and causes me to shiver. He presses the accessible door button with his knee and waits for it to open . . . and I wait for him to disappear into the school before I let out my breath in a sob. Thankfully, there's no one around to hear it.

CHAPTER FOURTEEN

I don't have the patience for Berlynn's staring routine. As soon as I've crumpled into her posture-wrecking chair, I take a deep breath.

"It's over."

"What is?" she asks, a little distracted as she sits down in her own (probably more comfortable) chair and reaches for her clipboard.

"Me and Eph."

She turns to me with her eyebrows raised.

"Yeah," I say.

"Whose idea was this?"

"Mine. But it's what he wants, too. Obviously. He hasn't reached out in the last week at all."

"Did you want him to?"

"I don't know." I try to cross my legs, but I'm so scrunched up that it's too uncomfortable. I settle for folding my arms across my chest instead. "No. Not really. That'll just . . . drag things out."

She tilts her head a little. "You don't want to be his friend?"

"It doesn't matter," I say. The words come out through gritted teeth. "It never has. I don't get to have what I want."

"What do you want?"

I shake my head and look over at the ugly painting on the wall beside me. It looks like a mass-produced thing, with gaudy daubs of paint that look more like shiny plastic than anything else. Berlynn doesn't say anything. I wiggle my toes inside my shoes, adjust my butt in the chair, and try to avoid eye contact for as long as I can. The last thing I want to do is bring up what I really want, because I know I'll just start crying. I can't have it.

"Do you think it was fair to break off a longtime friendship just because he didn't reciprocate your feelings?"

"That's not what happened."

"Then tell me what happened."

I press my lips together hard. Already, the heat in here is getting to me. I can feel a trickle of sweat running down my side from my left armpit.

"Did something happen with this other girl he met?"

A shrug is all I can manage. Truth be told, I don't really know what's been going on with Rebecca . . . other than the fact that she can relate to Eph in a way that I can't. And if Eph ever does change his mind about dating, who is he going to pick for that? My eyes fill with tears, and it makes me furious.

"Relationships are complicated," Berlynn says at last. "I'd

have to get a second job slinging burgers if we didn't have them. Their problems account for a lot of my practice."

"It's not a relationship, though," I say. "Not anymore. He doesn't want it to be."

"Is that true? Or are you projecting because he's not giving you what you want?"

I stare at her in disbelief. "Are you taking his side?"

"I don't take sides. I'm just trying to get you to think about the situation. Put yourself in his shoes for a moment and try to think about how he's seeing this."

I can't, I think. *That's the problem. I can imagine it all I like, but I'll never really know what it's like for him. I'm not missing my arms. I can't throw adults across the road or speak telepathically. I'm not like him at all.*

"A lot of relationship problems can benefit from communication," Berlynn goes on. "Have you talked to Eph about your feelings? Have you told him how you're feeling?"

"I don't usually have to. He just . . . knows."

"He's human, Ari. And as intuitive as some of us are, we can't read minds. He might be just as confused by this whole situation as you are."

"I'm not confused."

She smiles a little, her eyebrows high.

"I'm not," I insist. "The confusing part was being his friend."

"Why was that?"

"Because we were too close. I never really got to become my own person or learn how to take care of my own needs."

"Needs?"

"Emotionally. I just coasted along in his shadow, and now

I'm almost eighteen and I don't know how to deal with life without Eph and his little calming tricks. *That* is messed up."

"That's friendship, though. Isn't it?"

I frown. "That doesn't sound very healthy."

"It's not, if you rely on it completely. But I don't think you're giving yourself enough credit, Ari. The fact that you made the choice to push away from Eph—and how healthy that decision will turn out to be remains to be seen—tells me that you're trying to become more independent. That's a good thing."

"It doesn't feel good."

"Lots of things that are good for us don't always feel great at first. But sometimes we need to push through a little bit of discomfort before we make a breakthrough."

With a sigh, I sink back in the chair. The tail end of the exhale sounds a little squeaky. I squirm around until my diaphragm isn't crushed.

"I'd like you to do something," she says.

"What?" My voice comes out sounding so suspicious that she smiles.

"It's nothing awful. In fact, you've already done it countless times." She drums her fingertips on the side of the clipboard as she takes a dramatic pause. "I want you to talk to Eph."

"Why?"

"So you're both on the same page. If you talk things through and come to the decision that the friendship is best left in the past, that's fine. But life-changing decisions like that—especially when they involve more than one person—should be mutual ones. Don't you think?"

"No," I say, even though I know she's right. She smiles, nods, and makes a note on her clipboard.

"I think it'll be good for both of you."

Easy for you to say, I think as I glare at the tip of her pen scritching across the paper. *You're not the one who has to do it.*

As soon as Mom pulls into the driveway, I'm out the car door.

"Don't do that!" she calls after me, almost getting drowned out by the sound of the parking brake and the door slamming. I jump up the steps and into the house, then head straight for my room. Berlynn didn't specify *how* I was supposed to talk to Eph. I figure that if I don't have to see his face—and those green eyes that seem to know how to bore holes into me to access all my secrets—then I might be able to get through this conversation.

But even though I give him a ton of time to answer his phone, he doesn't, and I realize he probably doesn't recognize my new number and thinks I'm just some random butt-dial. Shaking my head, I set the phone down on the dresser and walk over to the window. If I peek through the blinds, I can sort of see the corner of the Diaz-Pierces' house. That doesn't really help, though.

As I wander toward the living room, Mom gives me a dirty look as she comes in the front door, loaded down with paper bags full of groceries.

"Thanks for the help."

"Is there any more in the car?"

"No, this is the last of it." She walks to the kitchen and sets the bags down on the floor. "And I'd appreciate it if you didn't jump out of the car while it's still moving. You nearly gave me a heart attack."

"It wasn't still moving," I say absently as I wander over to the window in the living room. The streetlights are already on, even though it's not that dark yet. The light on the Diaz-Pierces' porch is also on, making their front door look like a friendly portal.

"Whatever. Just don't do that again, please." There's a thump from somewhere in the house, and then the sound of something heavy—most likely Skylar's desk chair—rolling across the floor. "Skylar! Are you home?"

"What?" my sister's peeved-sounding voice says from the other side of her bedroom door. A moment later, the door opens. She raises her eyebrows at me and asks again, the word clipped and sharp: "What?"

"It wasn't me," I say.

She rolls her eyes and storms toward the kitchen. She's obviously in the middle of following some makeup tutorial, because she looks kind of unbalanced; the eyeliner swooping past the corner of her left eye looks lonely all by itself. (Although, maybe that's what she was going for. I honestly can't keep up with all the trends.)

When she and Mom start arguing about who was supposed to prepare the toppings for our homemade pizza, I turn back to the window. Javier's and Parnell's cars aren't in the driveway, so they aren't home yet. But if the lights are on, someone is. The last thing I want is for his parents to overhear what might end up being a messy argument, so maybe now's as good a time as any.

"How long until dinner?" I ask. There's a pause, and then Skylar starts to whine.

"How come *she* doesn't have to—"

"I *do*," I snap. "I start dinner twice a week."

"Taking leftovers out of the freezer isn't starting dinner."

"Neither is chopping a green pepper. Grow up."

"Enough," Mom says, sounding so weary that I'm glad I can't see her face. "Dinner's in about an hour, Ari. Skylar, get busy."

Heavy heels pound on the floor. And they're not Mom's.

"I need to go over to Eph's for a minute," I say.

Mom pops her head out of the kitchen. "Dinner's going to be even later if you don't help."

I chew on my lip and glance back toward the window. Mom sighs.

"Fine. Don't be long, though."

"I won't."

She nods and moves out of view again, just as water starts running in the sink. I hurry for the front door.

As I cross the street in the twilight, I feel a chill slip over me. Eph's house gets closer and closer, and yet it somehow feels farther away at the same time. For the first time in a decade, I feel like I'm walking up to a complete stranger's house, and I don't know what I'm going to find on the other side of the door.

I pause on the porch, listening. If Eph's playing video games, he's got the sound turned way down and . . . Scratch that. He's not playing video games, then. I don't know what he's doing.

My finger pauses, hovering just in front of the doorbell. *What if he's got Rebecca in there? What if they're . . . ?* I usually just walk right in, and maybe that's what I should do now.

Catch him in the act. But . . . we're not friends anymore, so that would be kind of weird. Trespassy.

Screw it, I think, and press the button. Then I take a step back so that whoever's on the other side can see me through the peephole. A few moments later, I hear the door unlock and the knob turn. As the door swings open, Eph jumps back a little on one foot, dropping the other one from the knob.

"Hey," he says, like we haven't broken off our ten-year friendship. He smiles and angles his head toward the kitchen. "I was just making some tea. Want any?"

"Since when do you make tea?"

"It's good practice."

I blink. "It's telekinetic tea?"

He laughs and stands back to let me step into the space. I do, noticing the smell inside the house.

"Is something burning?"

He takes in a quick sniff and then darts away, leaving me to close the door and kick my shoes off. When I make it into the kitchen, there's a flaming teabag hovering over the sink; he grunts, and it falls harmlessly into a water-filled bowl with a sizzle. "Good thing Mom didn't do all the dishes yet."

"How are you going to explain a scorched teabag?"

"I'll just say I used my feet."

"You can barely reach the counter. They'll never buy that."

He rolls his eyes. "You've never seen me cook, Ari."

"You don't cook."

"Yes, I do. Just not in front of people."

"Why not?"

"Because people get squeamish when they see someone

220

sitting their butt on the counter and stirring stuff with their toes."

"You should probably use a whisk, not your toes."

He grunts with laughter and turns back to the stove. A moment later, I hear a click as the burner shuts off.

"Do you want some help with the kettle?" I ask.

He shakes his head, still staring at it. Slowly, it starts to rise. It hovers for a moment before sweeping silently to the side, and tilts as it pauses over the glass mug that's sitting on the counter. I watch for a few seconds, not really getting how weird the whole sight is until it sort of hits me all at once. He's floating a kettle with his *mind*. I mean, that's not something you see every day.

"Don't tell Mom I made tea like a non-Brit. She might ground me for a month." The kettle wobbles and sinks a bit, and he lets out another grunt. As it slowly rises again, he pushes it back over the stove.

"You only made one cup," I say.

"I wasn't going to drink it, anyway. I was just practising."

"That's a waste of tea. What if I hadn't shown up?"

"Mom'll be home any minute. She'll drink anything that smells even remotely like tea leaves." He finally turns around with a triumphant look on his face. "Sugar?"

"That's okay."

"Really? It's kind of gross like that."

"Like what? Hot water?"

He swivels around on his heel to stare at the mug and then laughs. "Right. Forgot the bag."

"Never mind," I say. "If your mom's coming home soon . . ."

He turns back to face me. "What?"

We need to talk, I think. *And I don't want to have to do it in front of anyone else.* I look down at the floor and run my toe over one of the seams between the boards.

"My room? Just in case."

I nod and follow him as he pads down the hallway in his bare feet. When he gets to his room, he quickly tugs the covers up on his bed with his foot in a rather hasty making. He's wearing cargo pants today, and I can see the bulge of his phone in one pocket.

"You didn't answer," I say.

He turns to me with his eyebrows high. "That was you?"

"Yeah."

"Sorry. I was in the middle of trying to fill the kettle. By the time I got my phone out, you'd hung up."

"Oh."

"I wasn't ignoring you or anything."

My stomach clenches. "What's that supposed to mean?"

He sighs and sinks down onto the edge of his bed. "Come sit."

"That's okay."

"What did you want to talk about?"

I shrug. Now that I'm here, I'm not sure I want to do this after all.

"Come sit, Ari."

I sit down on the floor in the middle of his room and glance over at the items on the shelf that's at eye level. Feather, marble, pencil. There were more objects before, but that's all that's there now. The pink feather is somewhat curled, and it rocks gently in the subtle air currents of the room. For a moment, I find myself wondering what it would be like to lift it. How does Eph do it? Just think about it? Imagine it lifting into the air? The feather rocks once, and suddenly lifts up about an inch. I sit up straight, as if someone's jolted me with a cattle prod. When I look over at Eph, he's smiling.

"What happened to the toothpaste?" I ask.

"I've been using it."

"With your mind?"

He chuckles. "With my feet, mostly. But being able to get the cap off without my toes is actually kind of cool." Wiggling those toes at me, he grins. I look away. "Have you gotten your dress yet?"

"For what?"

"Grad."

I turn back to him with a frown.

"You're going, aren't you?" he asks.

"I have a ticket. But only because Mom made me buy one."

He nods sagely. "Might be a good idea. We only graduate once."

"*You're* not going."

"I'm going to the dry grad after." He scoots forward on the bed and stands up. For a moment, I think he's going to sit down beside me. *Please don't*, I think. "Are you?" he asks, still hovering on his feet.

"Am I what?"

"Going to the dry grad."

"Maybe." That's another ticket that Mom made me buy. Just in case, she said. *Just in case I feel like hanging out with a bunch of sleep-deprived teenagers all night?*

He grunts, amused, before sitting down right where he is

and leaning back against the bed. As he frees his phone from the large pocket on his left leg, he frowns. "Force of habit," he mutters.

"What?"

"I shouldn't be using my feet. It's still easier, though." He places the phone on the shelf beside the feather before turning back to me. "Ash said his grad banquet was awesome. You should go."

"Why?"

"So I'll have someone to tell me all about it."

I shake my head. "Why don't you go yourself?"

"Lots of reasons. Chief among them, I want people to remember the event, not the kid eating hors d'oeuvres with his toes."

"It's not like that would be a surprise to anyone."

"Still." He smiles and tilts his head at me. And that easygoing expression irks me all to hell.

"I'm not going by myself," I say. "That's just sad."

"So go with your friends."

"I don't have any."

He twists his mouth in a wry grimace. "I'm sure you could come up with at least one. What about Georgia?"

"I haven't really talked to her in the last year."

He drums his toes on the carpet. I peer at the nicely pedicured nails, and he tilts one foot up on his heel as if he's examining the toenails himself. "Dad still trims them. I don't trust my abilities enough yet to go using scissors that close to my skin." Dropping his foot, he looks at me, his expression alight. "Remember when you painted my toenails to match my hearing aids?"

"They didn't match."

"They were blue. Close enough. And they matched *your* toenails."

I smile a little at the memory. I can't help it.

"Ash teased me about it for days. I told him he was just jealous." He leans back against the bed with a sigh and looks at me. "So . . . are we friends again?"

The suddenness of the question alarms me for some reason, and I find myself breaking out in a cold sweat. I rub my clammy palms on my jeans and look down at my lap.

"Guess that's a 'no,'" he says.

"Isn't that what you want?" I ask, my voice small. When he doesn't say anything for a long time, I dare to look at him. His expression is a mixture of confusion, hurt, and disbelief.

"Where did you get that?"

"You've got Rebecca now. And her sister. Hezekiah. Your own kind."

He snorts so hard that he seems to choke a little. "Are you kidding me, Ari?"

"What?"

"They're not my kind. I mean . . . physically, yeah. But they're not like me. At all. They were raised in this twisted system of utilitarian eugenics where they killed their undesirables or dumped them in a parallel universe." He sits forward and gets up onto his knees so he can edge closer to me. I don't move away. My head tells me to, but my heart won't let it happen. As he gets close, snuggling up against my side in a familiar way that fills me with a deep, longing ache, I bow my head and turn it away. "I'm sorry," he says. "I never meant to hurt you. And I did, didn't I?"

I shake my head. "You're allowed to feel the way you feel."

He sighs and I feel him rest his chin on my shoulder. "Finding out what I am messed me up a little. You're the only one I can even talk to about it."

"What about Rebecca? Or—"

"Rebecca's great with her abilities. But I really don't enjoy spending time with her."

I sniff. My nose is running thanks to all my unshed tears. "Could've fooled me, the way you were staring at her."

"Huh?"

"She's pretty."

"She's pretty. So what?"

"So . . . you could be with someone like that. You wouldn't have to hide anything from her. And once you get full control of your abilities—"

"Ari, Rebecca and her sister come as a package. By necessity. And I'm *not* about to get involved with that. Nobody in their right mind would. Not if they value their self-esteem." He pulls his head away with a grunt. "That sister's got a tongue on her."

"But—"

"You don't need to be jealous. I'm not hooking up with anyone. And I'm not going to date anyone, okay? Nothing has changed there."

I know. You're stubborn when you decide to be.

"Nobody could compare to you, anyway," he goes on.

Don't say that! Why do you have to make it worse?

He nudges me with his side. I turn to face him. His eyes study mine for a moment, registering the tears that haven't yet fallen. "What do you want?" he whispers.

"You already know that."

"No, I mean . . . this friendship. Or whatever it is. Because if you want to walk away, I'll let you go. If that's what you really want."

No, Eph.

He blinks his thick eyelashes slowly. "Is it?"

The sob catches me off guard. I look down at my lap again, letting the tears drip onto my jeans. "I just don't know if I can do it."

"Do what?"

"Not be . . . everything to you."

He sighs. "Ari, you *are* everything to me."

"Not everything."

"Yes, everything. And that's . . . *why*. When I thought I died, my life suddenly came into focus. And I had all these regrets. Things that I didn't get to do. The disappointment almost crushed me."

I sniff and watch another tear fall onto the denim, spreading out in a dark little circle.

"I don't want to stop *you* from getting to do any of the things you might want to do."

"That's such a bullshit excuse. You can do anything you want. You're not going to hold me back."

"I can't play volleyball. Or the violin. I'll never be an astronaut or a trapeze artist."

Dashing away the tears on my cheeks with one hand, I turn to glare at him. "You don't want to do those things, anyway."

"I can't braid my own hair. I can't jerk off. I can't use chopsticks."

227

"Are you trying to use the stupidest examples possible?"

"I'm trying to make you understand. Life with me as a partner would be limited. What if you want kids?"

"Sperm donor. Or adoption."

"Do you really believe anyone would think I'm a suitable adoptive father? I couldn't even hold a baby."

"Yes, you could. With help." I jerk my chin at his lap. "You could hold a baby and feed it and be its dad, and they'd think you were the coolest guy in the whole world."

He gives me a sad little smile. "Only because their mom thought so, too."

The little laugh escapes before I can stop it. "You're not *that* cool."

"Aw." He sticks out his lower lip. But the expression transforms back into a soft smile a moment later. "I want you to live your life as you, Ari. Not as the partner of that guy with no arms."

"I'd still be me."

He shakes his head slowly. "Mom and Dad are the parents of 'that kid.' Ash is the brother of 'that kid.' It sucks, but that's just the way things are. And the last person I want to be reduced to an accessory is you. You deserve a great big life full of everything you've always dreamed of."

But what if that dream includes you? I think. Despair is curled up in the middle of my gut like an innocent-seeming cat. But I can feel that, given the chance, it could spring up and kill the little bird of hope that's fluttering in my heart. I look into Eph's eyes and feel my face crumple again.

"Go to grad," he says gently. "Ask someone."

"Yeah, right."

"What? It's the twenty-first century. You're allowed to ask someone out if you want to."

"If I can do it without barfing on them."

"Don't make it a date, then. Just go as friends."

I frown and shake my head. "These are teenage guys we're talking about here."

"So make sure they don't get the wrong idea. Just friends. Ash went to grad with a whole bunch of his." He sits up on his knees and walks on them over to the bookshelf. Then he sits down and reaches up to grab his phone. "Damn." He drops his foot and frowns at the device. It slowly rises. One corner falls, tapping against the shelf, before the whole thing swoops toward him and lands with a soft thud on the carpet. He taps at the screen with his big toe. "Dawson and Jared are going, at least. They don't have dates, so they're just going as a group. Maybe some of the other guys as well."

"So?"

"So, ask one of them."

"I don't want to be the only girl!"

"You won't be. Knowing them, they'll probably end up with dates before the big day. Some of them, anyway." He reads something on his phone. "Want Brad's number?"

"I don't want anyone's number."

With a glance at me, he raises his eyebrows. "Then how are you going to ask them?"

He's got a point. The only other way would be in person, and I'm not sure if I can do that without puking. Actually, I'm not sure if I can do it, period.

"Maybe I'll just stay home."

He shakes his head and shoves the phone aside with his

foot. "At least come to the dry grad. We can stay up all night together slugging pop and eating pizza."

"We could do that at home."

"It wouldn't be the same."

"Right. It would be better. Quieter. With fewer people."

"What if you regret not going?"

I let out a huge sigh. "I wish we could age the other way. I'd rather be seven again."

"Why seven?"

Because when I was seven, I think, *I didn't yet know that the most awesome person I'd ever met would one day break my heart.* But what I actually say is, "Because things weren't complicated yet."

He frowns. "Are we still friends, Ari?"

My nod comes almost automatically, before my brain can even register what my body is doing.

Getting up on his knees again, he edges toward me and leans forward. I let out a gentle breath as I feel his forehead rest against my own. "If you need space," he whispers, "I'm okay with that, too. Whatever you need." He tilts his head until our noses touch. And I keep as still as I possibly can so he doesn't feel the sobs that are churning just under the surface, desperate to break free.

CHAPTER FIFTEEN

It takes me more than a week to work up the courage. I didn't really want to do it at all, but I made the mistake of telling Berlynn about Eph's suggestion that I go to grad, and she thought it might be a good idea. Of course she did.

So now I'm standing just inside the cafeteria, waiting for a particular group of boys to show up at their regular table. Eph won't be with them yet, which is just as well; I don't think I could do what I need to do with him smiling at me.

When I see them, they're in a tight clump, laughing and shoving each other as they make their way over to their usual spot. Dylan and Brad obviously haven't brought anything from home, because almost as soon as they sit down, they're back up again and heading for the lunch line. But that's fine, because I wasn't going to ask either of them, anyway.

I grasp the strap on my bag, take a deep breath, and walk over to the table, trying to make it look like I'm just casually strolling past. Of course, I know it looks nothing like that, and when I get close enough and slow down a little, Dawson looks up with a confused frown.

"D-P's not here yet," he says, turning back to his ragged-looking peanut butter and jelly sandwich.

My lungs lock, and I start to panic. Quickly, I imagine Eph's warmth at my back. The latch in my chest melts a little and then breaks free, and I'm able to draw in a shaky breath.

"I . . . uh . . . I wanted to talk to . . . Jared."

The guy in question blinks and looks up at me, almost doing a double take. I might be amused by his reaction if I didn't feel like I were about to puke all over his ham and cheese.

"'Bout what?" Blaine asks, opening up his insulated bottle. He's the only guy—heck, the only *person*—that I know of who brings soup to school. I watch the pale red drips of what looks like cream of tomato fall back into the bottle. My mouth, rather paradoxically, goes dry.

"Uh . . ." *Suck it up, Ari. It's just Jared. You've known him longer than you've known Eph.* "Grad!" I say, the word exploding out of my mouth with such force that all three guys turn to look at me. I might as well have hacked up a hairball in the middle of the table.

"What about it?" Jared asks. "You going with D-P?"

"He's not going," Blaine says.

Dawson snorts. "Fine by me. I don't need him spilling anything on my tux."

"Since when has he spilled anything on you?" I ask, a little more harshly than I intended. Swallowing hard, I turn back to Jared. "Eph said you were going."

"Yeah. A bunch of us are."

"Okay. So . . ." My voice trails off as I notice Dawson elbow Blaine in the ribs. The movement causes the latter's spoonful of soup to go splashing onto the table.

"Thanks a lot, asshole."

I take a step back. This isn't going the way I expected. Well . . . I did expect to be nervous and flustered, but I didn't account for soup spills and distractions.

Jared looks up at me and sets his sandwich down. "Does Georgia want to go with me?" he asks.

I blink, taken aback. "What? N-no. I mean . . . I don't know. That's not why—"

"Ari's asking you out, moron," Dawson says. Jared flinches a little, and his cheeks darken. I quickly shake my head.

"Never mind. It's okay. I'll—"

"Yeah," he says, cutting me off. I frown, not sure I've heard him right.

"Yeah?"

"Yeah. I don't want to be the only one without a date."

"I don't have a date yet," Blaine says.

"But you will. Even if you have to rope your cousin into it." Jared raises his eyebrows at his friend, then turns back to me. "Sure. It's a date."

"I . . . thought we could just go as friends," I say, only to startle a moment later as Dawson bursts out laughing.

"Ouch, man!"

"Shut up," Blaine says. "I'm with Ari. I wouldn't want to fuck Jared, either."

Half of Jared's sandwich goes flying. It catches the top edge of the soup bottle, and I know what's going to happen before it even does. As cream of tomato splashes onto the table, Blaine stands up like a shot.

"Fuck you!"

"I thought you weren't interested."

I back away, my eyes wide, as I feel the collective stares of the whole cafeteria on me. Or maybe they're on the commotion. Still, I'm within the blast radius, and I need to get out of here. Without waiting to see if Jared is going to say anything else, I quickly make my way to the exit, only to almost run smack into Eph.

"Whoa," he says, taking one look at my face (which must be bright red) and a second glance into the room. "What happened?"

"Kill me now," I say, leaning close so I can rest my forehead on his shoulder. I don't even care who sees.

"Did you ask Blaine to grad?"

I pull back with a frown. "Why would I ask the gay guy?"

"Because you're going as friends." He frowns into the cafeteria. When I turn to look, I see that Dylan and Brad have returned . . . with lots of napkins.

"I knew I'd mess it up," I moan.

"Why? Did you spill Blaine's soup?"

I shake my head. "Jared did. After I asked him to—"

"You asked Jared?" he says, aghast. The look on his face makes my heart beat a little faster.

"Should I not have?"

He lets out a little sigh and shakes his head. "He's kind of had a crush on you since grade nine."

When I go to swallow, it feels like there's a petrified mini muffin stuck in my throat. "You could've told me that!"

"I didn't know you were going to ask *him*."

"Who did you think I was going to ask?"

"Since you just wanted to go as friends, Blaine. Or maybe Dylan."

"Ew."

He chuckles. "He's not that bad."

"He farts when he thinks nobody's listening."

"Okay, that's true." Wrinkling his nose, he stares at the guys. Then he turns back to me. "I'll talk to Jared, if you want me to."

"Why?"

"To make sure he knows this is a hands-off situation."

"Hands-off?"

He shoots me a cheeky grin. "I'm kind of an expert with those," he says as he strolls into the cafeteria toward his friends. By the time he's straddled the bench and Brad's helped him get his backpack off, the atmosphere seems to have calmed down. I debate just finding a seat somewhere on the other side of the room, but decide I don't want to be close enough to hear the inevitable laughter when the subject turns to my awkward proposal. By this time, I'm used to eating lunch by myself, and besides, the weather's nice today. So I head for the exterior door and push my way out into the sunshine.

It doesn't really hit me what I've gotten myself into until I'm biting into my sandwich. Not only did I have to humiliate myself to ask Jared out, but I still have more tortures in store. Including getting a dress. I don't even know what's in style . . . which means I'm going to have to enlist some help.

I should get some sort of therapy points, I think as I chew on my sandwich and try to figure out how I'm going to bring the subject up without getting an eye roll or a sarcastic comment. *Berlynn better be happy after all this.*

"You're joking," Skylar says. She shakes her head, keeping her eyes on the road. "You asked Jared?"

"What's wrong with Jared?"

"He's had a crush on you since—"

"Yeah. I know. Apparently, so does everyone else."

She clucks her tongue. "Do you like him?"

"That's not why I asked him." I look down at my bag in my lap so I don't have to look at her face. Mine, I can feel, is kind of red.

"Then why'd you ask him?"

"So I wouldn't have to go alone."

With a sigh, she shoulder-checks and moves into the other lane. "I'm kind of surprised you're going at all."

"Mom made me buy a ticket." I scratch at a seam on the bag, feeling the stitches under my fingernail.

"Yeah, but still."

"Am I not allowed to do something unexpected?" I snap. I'm getting really tired of this. It's like nobody can believe I'd do anything other than sit in my room and . . . well, I don't really know what they think I do. "I thought everybody *wanted* me to do normal stuff."

"We do. It's just that . . . this is kind of big."

"Which is why I need your help."

She shakes her head again. We're almost at our street, and all I can think about is sequestering myself in my room and trying to forget everything that happened today. "Why do you need my help?" she asks as she turns the final corner.

"Because I don't even know where to start."

"You probably wouldn't like anything I picked out."

"Yeah, well, you're not picking out my dress. I can do that myself. I just need your opinion on it."

"Is that all?"

"No. I need help with my makeup and hair."

"So?" She casts a quick glance at me out of her perfectly shadowed eyes.

I turn to her in disbelief. "You've spent hours watching those videos, Skylar. You know what you're doing. I don't want to go wearing nothing but lip gloss and some blush, and that's probably what's going to happen if it's left up to me."

"You won't look like yourself if you wear a lot of makeup."

I roll my eyes and turn away. "Maybe that's a good thing."

There's a long silence as she pulls up to our house and parks the car. After pulling the keys out of the ignition, she takes a deep breath.

"Did you ask Eph?"

"He doesn't want to go."

"Yeah, but did you ask him?"

I shake my head. "I thought you didn't like him."

"God, Ari. You make me sound like a bigot. It's not that I don't like him. He's nice. And he's got a cute face."

"But you can't stand looking at his body," I say, gathering up my bag and reaching for the door handle. "Got it."

"No, that's not what I meant." She slaps the automatic

locks, trapping me. I turn and glare at her. "It's not Eph that I have a problem with now. I mean, yeah, he freaked me out when I was a little kid. But I'm over that."

"Are you?"

"Maybe I'm just worried about you, okay?" Her sharp words hit me so hard that I suck in a breath. She pinches her mouth into a puckered circle and rubs her lips together, as if smearing lipstick. "You're so close. Like, attached at the hip."

"Not anymore."

"Yeah, but you were. For years. And I watched your anxiety get worse during that time. Whenever I saw you, you were freaking out or worrying about something. I guess I kind of connected that to him."

I shake my head. "If anything, he helped."

"Was it really helping? Or was it an unhealthy attachment?"

"Stop listening to Grandma."

"Maybe she has a point. I mean, what are you going to do when you go your separate ways?"

"In case you haven't noticed, that's what I'm trying to work on. Why do you think I haven't been going over to his house every afternoon? Why do you think I agreed to go to grad? Why do you think I asked Jared to go with me?"

She shrugs. "I thought maybe you'd finally gone crazy."

I narrow my eyes at her. "Didn't you always think I was crazy?"

With a deep sigh, she flicks the door locks and gets out of the car. I quickly follow, slinging my bag over my shoulder. "You're not crazy," she says. "You're just . . . weak."

My shoes scuff to a stop on the driveway. I can't believe what I'm hearing. "I'm *weak*?"

"Kind of."

"Nice, Skylar."

"What do you want me to do? Lie?" She shakes her head as she climbs the couple of steps to the front door. "You depend on other people too much. You're like this little kid who can't do anything for herself. So you attach yourself to the people who'll do everything for you."

I shake my head as I follow her into the house. "What, exactly, do you think Eph does for me?"

"Keeps you calm. Whatever that trick is where you stand back-to-back, it seems to sort of work. Even if it looks weird as hell."

"We haven't done that in ages," I say. After kicking off my shoes, I pad down the hallway to my room. Skylar pauses just outside her bedroom door.

"So . . . do you still want my help?" she asks. I turn around and give her a quizzical look.

"Who else am I going to ask?" With a shake of my head, I grasp the doorknob and push the door closed. I can't figure my sister out sometimes. Just now, was she trying to give me what she saw as a much-needed reality check, or was she trying to make me mad enough that I wouldn't want her help? Even though there's only a fourteen-month age difference between us, sometimes it seems like we're as dissimilar as people from different generations.

CHAPTER SIXTEEN

I think I might have made a big mistake.

Or . . . a lot of little ones. But I didn't stop the chain and now I'm kind of stuck, unless I want to be the topic of gossip at school. I bought a dress. I made sure Jared and I were on the same page. I let Skylar have her way with my makeup and hair. Actually, I have to say, it does look pretty good. She kept everything toned down and tasteful. The makeup highlights my features more than it tries to alter them.

"You look so pretty, honey," Mom says when I step out of Skylar's bedroom, only to find Parnell and Eph in our living room, sitting on the couch. They both kind of spring up as I walk into the space, my skirt rustling.

"I just had to see your dress," Parnell says, her voice distorted a bit by her smile. "It's lovely."

I look over at Eph, who's standing there with a grin on his face. "What?" I ask.

He shrugs. "I like the colour."

"It sets off her eyes," Skylar says from behind me. I jump a little, not having realized she followed me into the living room. "Just a sec, Ari." I feel a gentle tugging as she readjusts the clip that's directing most of my hair—curled and sprayed to within an inch of its life—over one shoulder. "Okay. You're good."

I don't feel good, I think as I nervously clutch the sparkly little purse. Eph steps a bit closer, his bare feet silent on the carpet. He's wearing shorts and a t-shirt, and I'm so envious of his level of comfort that I have to stop myself from running back to my room and peeling the dress off.

"Need a hug?"

I shake my head. "You'll mess up my makeup."

His eyebrow rises. "How much have you got on?"

"Plenty." I take a deep breath, and it sounds embarrassingly loud and shaky in the crowded room.

"You'll be fine," Mom says. "It's just dinner and a bit of dancing."

"And then we're going to par-tay," Eph says, wiggling his hips in what's probably supposed to be some sort of dance move. The loops on his shorts sway wildly. Parnell shakes her head with a little laugh.

"It shouldn't be *that* wild."

He shrugs, still grinning, and keeps his eye contact going. *I wish I was going with you*, I think. *But since you're so stubborn . . .*

"Is that Jared?" Mom suddenly asks. My heart leaps into my throat.

"He's early."

"Not really," Skylar says, stepping forward to peer out the front window. A small white car is just pulling into our driveway. "Mom probably wants to get some pictures. Right?"

"Oh! Right," Mom says, and hurries off to find her phone while I shoot Skylar an annoyed look.

"What?" she asks, widening her eyes in innocence.

I have half a mind to answer the door and rush Jared out of here before there's any more fuss, but I know I'd never hear the end of that from Mom. So I let Skylar answer the door while I stand in one spot and curl my fingers into my purse. There's going to be glitter all over my hands if I'm not careful.

Jared walks into the living room looking pretty at ease. In his hand is a clear plastic carton with some sort of flowers inside. Trailing right behind him is Grandma, who appears to have pulled herself up from the depths of the basement just for the occasion. She gives Skylar a knowing smile as she sidles past Jared.

"Do you have his boutonniere?" she asks me.

"Mom picked it up from the florist this morning," Skylar says before I can even open my mouth. I look over at Jared, who seems to have just noticed Eph standing there.

"Thought you weren't going," he says.

"I'm not. But Mom wanted to see Ari's dress. And I wanted to make sure you were a perfect gentleman tonight."

Jared's eyebrows rise. "What do you think I'm going to do?"

"No idea. I'm just saying. If you do it, I'll kick your ass."

Jared snorts. "Whatever, man." He steps forward with a

smile and opens up the carton. "Want me to put this on?" he asks me. I glance over at Eph, a little surprised by his display of chivalry. It's not like he isn't protective of me. I just didn't think he'd say something like that in front of everybody.

I'm hoping he doesn't know some reason why it really needed to be said.

But there's not much I can do about that now other than worry, and if I do that all night, I'm going to be miserable. So I transfer my purse to my right hand and hold out my left. Jared slips the corsage's elastic around my wrist. It's tight, but not unbearably so, and when I raise the little bundle of flowers to my nose, I smell the comforting scent of carnations.

The next few minutes are spent posing while Mom takes so many pictures that my vision is spotty from the flashes. She gets a ton with me and Jared (which is a given), a couple with me and Skylar (which is understandable; she did do my hair and makeup, after all), and even one with Grandma.

"Eph, I want to get one with you."

He looks like Mom just suggested he pose with a spitting cobra. "I'm not exactly dressed for it," he says with a nervous chuckle. But Mom won't be deterred.

"Just one. For posterity."

Shaking his head, he takes his place beside me as Jared edges out of the way.

"Hands off my date," Jared says. I don't know if he's trying to be funny or if it popped out before he really thought about it. But it makes Eph and his mom laugh, and then the rest of us join in, a little more hesitantly.

"You look beautiful," Eph whispers in my ear as he stands

so close I can feel the warmth of his body against my bare arm. I turn my head to look at him, noticing the warm softness in his expression. *Why couldn't you have done this with me?* I think. *You're the one I really want to spend the evening with. Not Jared.*

"Look at me, Ari," Mom says. "Your hair's sitting funny when your head's turned like that."

Reluctantly, I pull my gaze away from Eph and turn toward the phone, which flashes so suddenly that I blink.

"Are we done yet?" I ask, willing my eyes not to water. I don't want to have to have Skylar fix my makeup.

"Yes," Mom says with a little laugh as she examines the photos on her phone screen. "We're done. Go have fun." She looks at Jared. "Home by eleven?"

He nods. "I'll try. Can't predict the traffic, though."

Mom nods, satisfied. Even if we're a few minutes late, I'll still have plenty of time to change into something more comfortable and make it over to Eph's so Asher can drive us to the dry grad.

"My mom's going to want copies of those pics," Jared says as he takes my elbow and steers me toward the door. I glance back at Eph, who gives me an encouraging smile.

"I'll send the best ones to Ari and she can send them to you," Mom says. "Sound good?"

Jared nods. "Yeah."

I see Grandma shake her head. She's never liked that word.

Out in the cooling afternoon, the air seems scented, but I realize as I step carefully down the path toward Jared's car that it's mostly my wrist corsage. I lift it and take in a slow breath, savouring the scent. He grunts with laughter.

"Smells good?"

"Yeah. Thanks."

He shakes his head. "Mom bought it. I have no idea about those things." He opens the passenger door so I can get in. "Might want to keep it up near your nose. Dawson said my car smells like a locker room."

A little alarmed by that thought, I carefully gather up my skirt with my free hand and climb in. It's actually not as bad as all that, though, even when Jared closes the door. The new-car smell (weird, considering the vehicle is obviously a few years old) is strong enough to cover up almost everything else.

It isn't until we've been on the road for a few minutes that Jared clears his throat. I clutch my purse and turn to him.

"Did you put him up to it?" he asks.

"What? Who?"

"D-P."

"Put him up to what? I didn't even know he was coming over."

He shakes his head. "Like he could kick my ass."

"He's been using nothing but his legs and feet for eighteen years. I bet he could."

Jared snorts, but doesn't say any more about it. I turn away and look out the window as I try to mentally prepare myself for the next few hours.

As it turns out, though, I don't really need to. The banquet is fairly subdued (at least during the meal portion), and I turn out not to be the only girl at our table. Dawson brought Chandra and Dylan is sitting next to some girl that I've never met, but who seems pretty nice. She must also have no sense of smell, because I catch a few whiffs of something pretty unpleasant coming from her date's direction. None of the guys say anything, much to my surprise. Maybe they just don't want to embarrass him (although, that's never stopped them from ribbing him before).

After we eat (well, after some of us eat; I barely touch my food since I still feel like I swallowed a whole flock of butterflies), the vice-principal gets up to the mic and starts what almost seems like a stand-up routine. On the screen behind her flash some of the most embarrassing baby pictures I've ever seen. It's not like I would've known who most of the kids in the photos were . . . until Ms. Delacroix tells us. Then there's plenty of laughter, raucous hooting, and a few red faces.

"Nice one, man!" Dylan cries as a photo of a grinning toddler sitting on a little plastic potty is splashed across the screen. I sense Jared stiffen beside me.

"At least it's proof that I know how to hold stuff in. Unlike *some* people."

Dawson and Blaine burst out laughing. Dylan's date squirms a little in her chair and refocuses her gaze on Ms. Delacroix, pretending she hasn't heard anything.

Luckily, though, the routine doesn't go on forever, and we're finally set free onto the dance floor as lights beam through the jellyfish-like decorations that are hanging from the ceiling. Jared elbows me in the arm, harder than seems necessary, given that I'm sitting right next to him.

"Want to dance?"

"Sure." I stand up, grabbing my purse out of my lap. Since Dylan's date doesn't look like she's about to go anywhere, I hold it out to her. "Do you mind watching that for me?"

246

She raises her eyebrows, obviously confused as to why I would ask a perfect stranger to watch my purse. But it's not like there's anything to steal. All that's in there is my phone (which is locked), a lipstick, and a twenty-dollar bill. She takes it, still looking uncertain, and I hurry after Jared, who's already strode out onto the dance floor to talk to one of his other friends.

It goes pretty much like that for the rest of the evening. I avoid all the slow dances, though, as I don't know if I trust Jared to not try to squeeze my ass when he's got his hands on me. I don't know if he notices, anyway. We're having fun, dancing in a big group out in the middle of the floor, flashes of brightly coloured dresses contrasting with the basic darks of the tuxes and suits.

After the fourth dance, I ask to take a break. My feet are kind of hurting in my pretty (but cheap) shoes, and I'm afraid that my deodorant isn't going to hold up if I get too sweaty. After retrieving my purse, I head for the bathroom.

There's a bit of a line, which gives me time to glance in the mirror (I look fine, surprisingly enough; I'm so hot that I was afraid the makeup might've been running down my face) and check my phone for messages. There aren't any, but that's no surprise. I do see, though, that it's getting late. It's already ten-thirty. Ms. Delacroix must've rambled for a while.

When I get back to our table, Jared and Dawson are leaning on it with their elbows, deep in conversation. Dylan and his date are out on the dance floor, while Blaine is nowhere to be seen. Resisting the urge to flop into my chair (I sit delicately, like the lady this dress says I am), I try to give Jared a pointed look. But he doesn't seem to notice I've returned. Dawson does, though, and sits back in his seat with a sigh.

"Tired?" he asks me.

"Why? Do I look tired?"

He smiles and pulls his phone out of his pocket to check the time. His expression suddenly changes. "Shit. It's getting late." He turns to me and raises his eyebrows. "You see Chandra in there?"

"Where?"

"The crapper."

Jared punches his shoulder. "Hey."

"What? Girls shit, too. Right, Ari?"

I just shake my head. Jared leans closer to Dawson so he can see the phone's screen.

"Yeah . . . I promised Ari's mom I'd have her home by eleven."

Dawson smirks. "Guess you'd better get Cinderella home, then. Before she turns into a pumpkin."

"Cinderella didn't turn into a pumpkin, dumbass," Jared says as he stands up. His bowtie is looking a little crooked. He's probably the one who should've checked himself out in the mirror. "See you later?"

"Yeah."

"Chandra coming?"

Dawson shrugs. "No idea. If she wants to."

Jared nods and puts his hand on the small of my back as he leads me out of the banquet hall. Chaperones are standing guard just outside, giving all of us a really good examination and standing so close that I want to shrink back. But Jared just steers me through the gauntlet, out into the cool summer night.

"We have last year's class to thank for that," he mutters as he finally pulls his hand away to fish his keys out of his pocket.

"What?"

"You didn't notice them trying to sniff our asses?"

"What?"

He gives me a quizzical look. "They're checking to make sure we haven't been drinking, Ari."

"How would we have been drinking? Everything was catered."

With a chuckle, he shakes his head. "That's cute. But it's pretty easy to smuggle stuff in."

"How do you know?"

He doesn't answer. We reach his car, and he unlocks the doors. Unlike before, I'm responsible for getting myself inside. For some reason, the smell seems stronger in here now. But I don't want to risk opening the window. For one thing, my hair probably couldn't take it. For another, Jared might be one of those people who hates having the windows open, relying instead on air-conditioning. So I just try not to breathe too deeply as he starts the car and pulls out of the parking lot.

See? I say to myself as I watch the lights pass outside the car window. *That wasn't so bad. And now you can just relax and enjoy the rest of the night with Eph.*

Jared drives a little faster than I'd like, but that also means that we reach our neighbourhood sooner. I clutch my purse as we approach my street, anticipating the turn . . . but it never comes. I watch the corner sail past, craning my neck to see.

"You missed the turn," I say, my voice small.

"No, I didn't." He shoots me a quick smile.

"You told my mom I'd be home by eleven."

He grips the steering wheel, and the car accelerates a little. So does my heart. I open my purse to get my phone when he reaches across and puts his hand over it. "Relax, Ari. We're just going to the park."

"The park?" I echo, not understanding for a moment. Then I blink and shake my head. "You're going to the party?"

"We're going to the party," he says, pulling his hand back and putting it on the wheel. "Trust me. It'll be way more fun than that snoozer D-P's going to."

I shake my head. "If I don't show up at his house in the next few minutes, he's going to wonder where I am. And then he'll tell my mom and everyone will get worried—"

"So call him and tell him you're coming with me."

"I don't *want* to go with you." Frowning, I stare out the window as the sign for the park sweeps into the car's head-light beams. These grad parties are well known in our neighbourhood, mostly because they keep the neighbours up all night. Grandma usually calls the cops at some point, but it doesn't seem to help. I think the parties must get a pass. I mean, they only happen once a year. But they're not something I ever wanted to go to, and I haven't changed my mind about that.

As the car's tires crunch on the gravel track that leads to the parking lot, I go for my phone again. But instead of dialling, I just hold it in my hand.

"You going to call him?" Jared asks.

"I don't want to go to your stupid party."

He snorts. "Your party's going to be a lot stupider. Look, just give it a try. You've got time."

"No, I don't," I say, glancing at the clock on my phone's screen. "I—"

"Look, Ari," he says, his voice suddenly harsh. "You need to loosen up. There's a reason everyone thinks you're an uptight bitch."

I swallow hard, my throat feeling like it's been stuffed with a sock. "What?"

"I didn't *have* to take you to grad. I did you a favour. And if you're not going to return it . . ."

"Return it how?" I ask. My voice comes out in a squeak. He turns to me with a look of disdain.

"Jesus Christ. I'm not a rapist." He pulls the car into a parking spot and lets it idle.

"No?"

"No. But the least you could do is make an appearance. I mean, how's it going to look if my date ditches me?"

I squeeze my phone tight in my hand. "I thought this was just two friends going to grad together."

"Since when are we friends?" He shakes his head. "Now, are you going to come with me, or—"

I don't let him finish. The park is two blocks from home, for crying out loud, and I can easily walk. So I lunge for the door handle, just as there's a click. And no matter how hard I tug, the door won't open.

"Unlock it."

"No."

"Jared, unlock the door!" My voice is shaking. My under-arms are so wet that they're probably ruining my dress, but

251

I don't even care. Abandoning the useless door handle, I turn to my phone. But Jared grabs it and pulls it out of reach. As one large hand pins me back against the seat, the other awkwardly slips my phone into the cupholder in his door.

"You're not getting it back until we have an understanding."

"Give it back!" I shriek. My brain seems to have disengaged completely, and those three words keep repeating in my head. But when my plea does nothing to soften the look in his eyes, I turn and peer out the window into the darkness. There are lights in the parking lot, but I can't see anything except a bunch of other cars—more than would usually be here this late at night. There are no people around. Nobody to witness what's going on in this car.

Eph. Eph. Please. Help me. Help me! I'm scared. He's got my phone. I don't know what he's going to—

"Are you going to listen?" Jared asks. His hand feels hot against my chest. I shake my head, even though I want to nod. "No?"

"Yes," I gasp. "Just give me my phone. Please."

"Not until I know you're not going to call the cops on me."

I hadn't even thought of that. Now, though, I realize that the cops are probably a better option than a boy with no arms. But it doesn't matter. My phone's on the other side of the car, and I probably wouldn't be able to reach it even if Jared weren't holding me against the seat.

"This is just a misunderstanding," he says. "I'm not trying to hurt you."

"Then give me my phone!"

"Are you going to use it?"

I press my lips together. The taste of Skylar's lipstick is bitter and waxy at the same time.

"I got into my school of choice," he says. "If you ruin that for me . . ."

"I won't," I say. But he doesn't look like he believes me. I peer over at my phone; I can just see the corner of it past the steering wheel. *God, I wish I could do what Eph does. Just lift it right out of the cupholder and . . .* The thought peters into nothingness as I try to blink away the mirage. But it's not a trick of the shadows. My phone is actually floating. As I realize what that means, I feel a giddy bubbling sensation in my chest. But I don't dare look around to try to spot my saviour. I need to get out of this car . . . and maybe Eph's just provided me with an opportunity to do it. "Jared," I whisper.

"What?"

I point at the floating phone. He turns and, for a moment, doesn't seem to notice anything strange. When he does, though, he reacts like a person who's just realized that splotch on the wall is actually a huge spider.

"Shit!" he screams, flailing his arms. His hand hits the phone, and it goes skidding onto the dashboard. "What the fuck?" He turns to me, his eyes so wide I can see the whites all the way around. "What?"

"What?"

He reaches for the keys and turns them, not seeming to realize that the car's still running. Freed from his restraint, I lunge forward and scrabble for my phone. He practically dives toward his own door, as if to get away from me.

"Let me out," I say, my voice shaking but low. He doesn't seem to hear me. Even though I'm still in the car and he obviously thinks I'm about to pull some sort of Carrie-at-the-prom trick, he pulls out of the parking spot in a frenzied crackle of gravel. "Jared, unlock the doors!"

The car skids to a stop and he plucks wildly at the lock. As soon as I hear the clunk, I tear off my seatbelt and tumble out the door. My phone falls to the ground and I stumble away from the car as it tears away in a cloud of grit and dust.

"Asshole," I say, and then the tears come. I don't know if they're tears of fear or relief or what, but they pour out of me, down my cheeks, and I'm pretty sure even the most waterproof of makeup wouldn't stand a chance. Bending down, I pick up my phone and slide it into my purse. And then I start to walk.

Jared's car is up ahead, racing through the darkness back toward the suburban street. I don't know if he can see me in his rearview mirror or not. I kind of hope he can, though, and that he's pissing himself in terror. I mean, it could've ended a lot worse than it did, but I still think he deserves a bit of humiliation.

Thank god for Eph, I think as I walk a little faster, my skirt swishing in the near silence. If it hadn't been for him . . . Frowning, I peer ahead of me. *Where is he?* I wonder. *Why don't I see him?*

But then I do. At least, I see a figure on the gravel track ahead of me. Ahead of Jared's car, too. The headlights cut across the figure, and I recognize the silhouette immediately. I also see where he is in relation to the car, a car driven by a freaked-out teenager who's running on pure adrenaline. I grab my skirt and start to run.

"Eph!" I scream. My mind is already two steps ahead,

imagining the worst. And Jared's car isn't stopping. Or swerving. Or . . .

My lungs are aching by the time I reach the spot where I last saw him. The car never stopped. I didn't hear anything, but I don't know what I would've heard if a car had hit a person. The taillights have long since disappeared, and there's not much light in this part of the track. With a sob, I drop my skirt and turn to my phone with shaking hands. I manage to get the light on.

The track is empty. There's no body. There's no blood. There's nothing but the realization that it's happened again. He's gone. And if he's been caught in that hellish world, naked and alone . . .

"Eph!" My shout comes out ragged. There's no hope left in it. Why should there be? If I'd just—

"Ari?"

I spin in the direction of the voice. For a moment, I don't see anything. But then, with a rustle of forest debris, a pair of shoe soles comes into focus. I hurry over and shine the light off the edge of the track. Eph lifts his head and grimaces, squinting against the phone's light.

"Are you all right?" he asks, and his question sparks a burst of hysterical laughter that I just barely manage to control. He's the one lying in a ditch, and he's asking *me*?

"Are you?"

"Yeah. That'll teach me to step back without looking." He struggles to sit up but can't manage it, having landed on a slope. "Give me a sec."

"Okay."

He grunts and twists as he makes another attempt, but it still doesn't work. With a sigh, he kicks with his feet and manages to sort of roll backward over one shoulder and land on his knees. Carefully, he stands up and climbs the slope back to the track. And as soon as he's standing in front of me, I have to resist the urge to throw my arms around him.

"I was afraid you'd gone . . . back," I say.

He shakes his head, dislodging a couple of dead leaves. As he looks down at himself, he sighs. "Do you mind? If I go home with half the forest in my hair, Mom's going to want to know what happened."

I hold my phone and purse in one hand as I use the other to brush the debris—mostly small twigs and dried leaves—out of his curls, and then give his t-shirt and pants a quick dusting-off. As he turns back to me with a rueful smile, I feel my throat start to tighten again.

"Ari." He leans close, catching me in one of his hugs. "I'm all right."

"But you could've gone—"

"I wasn't scared enough for that to happen. I knew I could get out of the way of that car." He pulls back and wrinkles his nose. "Just didn't count on falling down the hill."

I shake my head. "Why did you come here?"

"You called me." He tilts his head to the side with a tiny smile. "Didn't you?"

I look down at my phone. "Uh . . ."

"You know I'll always be there for you. Whenever you need me."

"I did need you."

He nods and frowns toward the parking lot. "What are you doing out here?"

"Jared tried to take me to the party."

"And you didn't want to go."

I shake my head. "He scared me. I just wanted to leave, but he took my phone. If it wasn't for you, I—"

"Me?"

"Yes, you. You freaked him out with that trick, you know. Don't worry. He didn't see you. *I* didn't even see you until—"

"Ari, what are you talking about?"

"When you floated my phone. In the car. It scared the shit out of him."

His lips are twitching. "I floated your phone?"

"Yeah." My mouth goes dry as I see the expression on his face. "Didn't you?"

"Nope." His eyebrows rise, and he looks like he's just gotten the best news in the world.

"Then who did?"

He laughs and steps closer to hug me again. "Ari. You know you're my best friend, right?"

"Yeah."

"So don't take this the wrong way. But . . . sometimes you can miss what's right in front of you."

"What?" Pulling back, I stare up into his eyes. "What did I miss?"

"You did it," he says. "You floated the phone. You scared the crap out of Jared. Not me."

"But—"

"How would I have done that? I didn't get here until he was leaving."

My eyes are wide. "But . . . I've never . . ."

"Yes, you have. Remember that day in my room? When the feather moved on my shelf?"

"That was you," I say.

"No, it was you, my telekinetic friend." He smiles and focuses his gaze on mine. "Hezekiah said it was unlikely. But not impossible. Remember?"

"Oh, my god." I look down at my hands, almost expecting them to look different. "What am I?"

"The same person you've always been, Ari." He tilts his head. "The beautiful princess rescued herself tonight."

I can't believe it. I suppose I'll have to at some point, because there's no reason Eph would lie to me about this. But . . . it's not something I thought I'd ever have to contemplate. I take a deep breath and let it out slowly.

"Did you still want to go to the dry grad?" he asks.

I shrug. "I guess. If we're not too late."

"We have to be there by midnight. I think we've got plenty of time. It only takes a few minutes to get there. Ash is waiting at home. But . . ."

"But what?"

He looks down at himself and then turns back to me with a sheepish smile. "I'm wearing my tuxedo and everything, so . . . would you like to dance?"

In spite of everything that's happened tonight, I let out a little laugh. "That's not a tuxedo. That's a tuxedo t-shirt and track pants."

"Close enough."

"You really want to dance with me?"

He nods and steps closer so I have to raise my gaze a little to keep eye contact with him. "Of course I do, Ari." With a nod down at my phone, he says, "Got music?"

I manage to find something, and when the slow song is

leaking through the sides of my purse, somewhat muffled, I turn to him once more. "I'll have to touch you."

"I know."

So I step forward and reach up, putting my arms around his neck. As he relaxes into the embrace, I move closer until our bodies are pressed against each other. We start to sway gently, our shoes scuffing on the gravel, and I close my eyes.

It's as wonderful as I imagined it would be: feeling my best friend in my arms, relaxed and happy, as we sway to the invisible strains of ghostly purse music. Even the chill of the night air can't break through the shell of warmth and relief that surrounds us both.

"I have something to tell you," he says softly, his voice rumbling through our bodies. "I was going to tell you later tonight, but I don't know if we'll get another chance to be alone, so . . ."

"What is it?"

He takes a deep breath. "I've made my decision."

I don't say anything. I don't even have to ask what decision he means, because there's only the one. *The* decision. Tightening my arms around him, I rest my chin against his shoulder.

"It was pretty easy," he says. "Once I was really honest with myself. What do I want? How do I want to spend the rest of my life?" He stops talking. I wait for him to say something else, but when he doesn't, I start to get a sinking sensation in the pit of my stomach.

"How do you want to spend it?" I ask, my voice almost strangled by my own fear. I wish I could be strong for him. The decision had to be hard, and he's going to need my support, no matter what he—

"I want to spend it in the life I have," he says. "With my parents. With Ash. With my friends." He takes a deep breath. "With you."

"Without arms."

He chuckles. "Really? I hadn't noticed."

"But you'll never—"

"There are plenty of things I'll never do. But I've had my whole life to get used to the idea." He takes another deep breath. "The choice wasn't what I thought it was. At first, I thought I was deciding whether I wanted to have a life where I could have arms and use my abilities. But then I realized that I was really deciding if I wanted to be true to myself and have the life I always wanted."

"You don't want to use your abilities?"

He grunts in amusement. "They're a pretty great perk. I'll admit that. If I get a little better, I might even be able to manage a pair of jeans all by myself." We sway a few more times in the still air before he speaks again. "I don't have to make that impossible choice, Ari. I can have what I want. What I've wanted since I was seven years old."

I pull back just enough so that I can see his face, but I keep my arms draped around his neck. "Yeah?"

"Yeah. See, there was this little girl who wasn't afraid of me, even though she was afraid of things like puffy baby clouds. What's ironic is that I was the one who was really afraid."

I frown. "What were you afraid of?"

"That I'd never find anyone who would like me the way I was."

"What's not to like?"

He smiles and leans his forehead against mine. "You

know what I told my mom that night when she tucked me into bed?"

"What?" I whisper.

"I told her that you and I were going to be friends forever."

"And we were," I said, my throat tightening once more. "Until I went and messed it up."

"You didn't mess anything up. I did. I was the one who made the stupid decision to avoid relationships. When you kissed me . . . I wasn't mad at you, Ari. I was mad at myself." He shakes his head a little against mine. "And too stubborn to admit it."

He stops moving. The song is still playing, but we're just standing in one spot. I don't know what to do. Am I supposed to let go of him now? *I don't want to,* I think. *I don't ever want to let you go again.*

"Ari," he says, his voice hesitant.

"Yeah?"

He swallows so hard I can hear it.

It's okay, I think, tilting my head so our noses touch. *It's me. And we're good. No matter what happens from now on . . . We're good, Eph.*

"No matter what happens," he says, as if he just heard my thoughts. I pull back and look into his eyes.

"Did you hear that?"

"Hear what?" His mouth twitches.

"How long have you been listening to my thoughts?"

There's something behind that smile of his that makes me think he's been hiding a secret for a while. "Do you remember the day we met? I came running across the street, and you were standing in your front window and—"

"Oh, my god. You heard that?" My cheeks feel so hot. "I'm sorry. I didn't . . . I didn't know you."

He chuckles. "I know. It's okay."

"You heard what I was thinking?"

"Not really. It's more like . . . I could feel your intention. That's usually how it is," he goes on, talking quickly like he thinks I'm going to interrupt him. "I'm not spying on you. Sometimes I hear words, but usually it's just a feeling."

"Is that why you came here tonight?"

He nods. "I could tell you were scared."

"But how did you know where I was?"

"Just a guess." He shrugs. "I knew Jared was going to the park party."

I reach forward and hug him with my arms, even though he didn't say I could. But he doesn't try to pull away, and he doesn't tell me to stop. I take a few deep breaths and notice that our inhalations are perfectly in sync.

"Like it or not," he says after a few long, blissful moments, "we're connected. I think we always will be. And . . . if you're up for it . . ."

I pull back with a frown. He looks so unsure that I immediately want to hug him again. "Up for what?"

"Me." He shrugs. "I can be a challenge."

"So can I. Just ask my family."

He smiles. "I'm up for it. If you are."

I don't think my happiness will let me speak. All I can do is nod while I try to keep a ridiculous, deranged grin off my face. He laughs.

"You're allowed to be happy about it."

"I am happy."

262

"You sure? You're not already having regrets or anything?"

"No."

"Good." He lowers his head a little and fixes me with a soft yet intense gaze. "So . . . maybe we can try that kiss again?"

I move slowly, wary after what happened last time, and wait for him to close some of the space between us. As he does, I feel my heart start to pick up its pace. But it's not a daring nervousness I'm feeling this time. It's giddy joy, an almost electric warmth that fizzes in the space between us. His breath kisses my skin in that instant before our lips touch, soft and gentle and just right.

This time, it's so much better. Because the air has been cleared. Because we're standing under the stars on a near-perfect summer night.

Because it's what we both want.

"If I ever get that confused about what I want again," he says breathlessly when he pulls away a minute later, "just do that. It should knock my sense right back into me."

I just laugh and lean in for a hug, one of his kind this time.

"Should we get going?" he asks. "Ash said he's ready to take us whenever we want to go."

"Do you want to?"

He shrugs. "I'd rather just spend the night with you."

I pull back quickly, blinking like I've got something in my eye. He starts to laugh.

"Whoa. I didn't mean it like that. Not that I *wouldn't* want to, but . . ."

"We've only kissed twice. I'm not sure if we're ready for *that* yet."

He smiles and, for the first time since the incident that almost stole him from me forever, I see the self-assured Eph that I knew for so many years. The Eph that I fell in love with. *That I am in love with*, I think.

"I love you, too, Ari," he whispers.

And I don't even care if he heard my thoughts. There are worse things in life than the person you love the most knowing how you feel.

I think he understands that now, too.

ABOUT THE AUTHOR

NISSA HARLOW wanted to be a writer from the time she was a small child, but it took a while before she finally did anything about it. In the meantime, she worked as a volunteer day-camp counsellor, a movie extra, and a digital-photo editor. She even once worked on a conveyor belt in a chocolate factory (which was as stressful—and delicious—as it sounds). These days, she lives in British Columbia, Canada and writes the types of stories she wants to read. This is her first book.

nissaharlow.com

CPSIA information can be obtained
at www.ICGtesting.com
Printed in the USA
BVHW070351121121
621379BV00005B/130